# The Indian Love Apple

Christine Reeve

For Susan

Travelling with me, she enabled creation.

There at the beginning of the story, she will be, forever, my big sister.

# The Indian Love Apple

I seek reassurance from your face

Do I see the true you?

Dark eyes and hypnotic burr

Bewitched, I am halfway there

The hint of faraway places

Lure me in with fascination

If I dedicate to you my all

Will you value and embrace?

Is your soul as pure as your form?

Or as the Indian love apple

Poisonous at the core.

Christine Reeve

# 1

## The death of a child

Sally was shocked when she saw her sister. Faye, usually displayed a vibrant personality. Her choice of clothing is colourful and of a hippy style. You may call it mismatched! And her wild red hair is normally out of control. But today she looked dull, pale and worn, her eyes puffy and pink rimmed.

'What on earth has happened?' Sally asked. She opened her arms and Faye stepped in.

. . . . .

Faye became aware of Charles shortly before he was born. His parent's relationship brought them to the attention of social services and hence they joined Faye's long list of families for whom she cared. The father, Jed Mitchell, a drinker, a thief, and generally a nasty man, made his partner Dawn's life miserable with mood swings and loose fists. She suffered regular beatings from him. Dawn's safety and the safety of the unborn baby worried the health team so Faye, as her social worker, arranged to meet them.

First impressions proved to be exactly as Faye expected. Dawn was bone thin, her skinny limbs sticking out from around the large bump of her baby belly. Nervously she glanced at Mitchell before answering Faye's questions. While Mitchell, pretending to care, held Dawn's hand. His falseness shone through, Faye wasn't fooled by his doting smile. She'd met men like him before during her ten years in the job. She left their home concerned for Dawn and the child and anticipated many visits and much support for mother and baby.

Luckily, days before the birth, the police arrested Mitchell for the attempted robbery of a post office. Dawn, relieved and happy, swore she would never have her partner back. Faye put her in touch with a women's protection group who helped to rehome her in a new area to start afresh.

Born into a calm and organised home, baby Charles was thriving and content. Dawn behaved like any other proud mother with the cause of the chaos, thankfully, locked behind bars. The new house was clean and cared for. Faye thought all Dawn's troubles were over and she had started a new chapter of her life, just her and the baby. Some of the things she told Faye about living with Jed Mitchell made Faye's toes curl up. She'd certainly had a time of it.

Faye carried on visiting her as normal whilst the baby was small, not finding anything to alarm her. Everything seemed well, so she cut down the number of visits but didn't sign her off completely.

Charles, a happy little boy, smiled at Faye showing white milk teeth, top and bottom. He would  happily hold her hand with his chubby little fingers or sit on her knee. His big round blue eyes took everything in from beneath his curly blonde fringe. A gentle child, usually content to push his cars around the floor, making driving noises and baby babble as his mum and Faye chatted. He was lovely. Faye adored him.

Then the visit before last, Dawn was different. She seemed cagey and couldn't get Faye out of the house quickly enough. Ordinarily, they would have a cup of tea and a good chat, all open and friendly. She said she had an appointment, but Faye wasn't convinced and tried to arrange a date for the following week. Dawn said she wasn't going to be in on that day or any other day Faye suggested.

Faye deeply wishes she'd got to the bottom of it there and then. Dawn had been doing so well. Charles was two years and three months old.

A week later, Faye decided to call unannounced. The last visit made her uncomfortable and she wanted to see her. Dawn answered the door and Faye saw immediately the bruises on her upper arms. Dawn crossed her arms over her chest putting her hands on the bruises to hide them. She'd seen Faye looking at them. At the corner of her left eye was a scratch with beads of dried blood on it and a little purple bruise below on her cheek. She looked unkempt and withered somehow, as if she had lost weight. A pair of men's shoes sat on the bottom step of the staircase behind her, just inside the lobby. Faye looked at them and raised her eyebrows in question. Dawn followed her gaze but said nothing. She didn't offer an explanation. Faye didn't ask but she knew then that the father of the baby was back with her. He had found her!

'Is everything alright?' Faye asked quietly. Dawn glanced over her shoulder towards the lounge door.

'Everything's fine! I'm just going out so can you come back another time?' she said.

'Is Charles OK?' Faye persevered. Sharply Dawn replied,

'Of course he is!' and tried to close the door on Faye. Through the gap in the half-closed door Faye whispered,

'Is there anything you want to talk to me about?'

'No, please go!' Dawn urged and closed the front door. Faye went back to the office and requested to speak with Ingrid, her supervisor as soon as possible. She was concerned, very concerned!

The following day Charles was rushed to hospital. He had injuries suggesting a skull fracture and other trauma to his chest. He died shortly after he was admitted.

Distraught, Faye blamed herself. She couldn't stop thinking about the child. She had walked away from their door. Just walked away! If she had insisted on seeing Charles on that day, she may have made a difference. If she'd insisted on entering the house, she may have made a difference. She should have but she walked away, and Charles died.

. . . . .

Faye squinted at her phone's screen. Her sister, Sally, was ringing. Faye blew her nose and wiped her eyes and pushed her hair back from her hot, damp face. Little dark red ringlets stuck to her forehead, she dashed her hand at them irritably and sighed,

'Hello Sally,' she said in a dull monotone.

'What's the matter with you, Faye? You're not your usual perky self,' Sally teased down the phone.

'Oh, Sally, I'm having a terrible time. One of the families I work with, their child has died and as their social worker, I'm responsible. It's all my fault! I'm so upset about it. Ingrid is trying to be kind but it's all my fault and I don't know what to do.'

'Ingrid's your boss?'

'Yes, she's really kind, but I know she's looking at my role in all this.' Sally heard a couple of sniffs and a nose blow.

'Oh no, Faye! Can I do anything?'

'No, nobody can. I saw the signs, but I didn't act quickly enough,' she gave a shuddering sigh.

'Do you want me to come over?' Sally asked.

'Oh, would you? That would be great. I just need someone to talk to. Someone who's not from work.'

'I'll be over on Saturday, after I close the salon. It'll be about seven o'clock, is that OK?'

'Yes, that'll be lovely,' Faye sniffed.

'Don't worry, Faye, we'll sort it out,' Sally said comfortingly.

'Nobody can sort this mess out. I loved that child and I'll probably get dismissed. I'm so upset, Sally.'

'I'll be there on Saturday, hold on till then. Please hold on till then. Love you.'

. . . . .

Faye lives in the house they both grew up in. Their mum died when Faye was 13 years old and Sally 16. Older than their mum by twenty years, their father suffers with dementia and now resides in a nursing home. Most of the time he doesn't know the girls, but for a few lucid moments, now and again, he recognises them and is pleased to see them. Sally mothered Faye during the tough years after losing their mother. She has continued to do so ever since, especially during the time when their father began to lose his daily living abilities. The sisters are closer than most siblings. They also adore their father; the death of their mother has formed a strong bond between them.

Personality and looks wise, Faye and Sally are totally different, but they enjoy a love for each other that only sisters with such a history can share. Time passes and with busy lives and the distance between them, they often don't see each other for several weeks but still regularly talk on the phone.

Sally bought a property in the next town and converted it into a smart hairdressing salon with a little flat above, in which she lives. The salon, The Classic Cut, serves the better part of the town. In addition to hairdressing, she provides nail care, spray tanning service, eyebrow sculpting and a bridal package, which consists of makeup, nails, hair styling, hair adornment, i.e. fresh flowers, tiaras and so on. The salon is busy, but the bridal package is booked up many months in advance. Sally puts a lot of hours into her salon. Four years on, she's very happy with her efforts.

On Saturday evening Sally arrived as promised. She was taken aback by Faye's aura of sheer unhappiness.

'Oh my lord, you look dreadful! What on earth has happened?' and opened her arms. After a lengthy hug Faye pulled back and said with a sniff,

'How long can you stay?'

'I'm on top of things at the salon. Monday is closing day as normal, so I can stay until Tuesday morning if you want me to.' Sally's eyes examined Faye's face with concern.

'Brilliant, you are just what I need,' she offered a weak smile and stepped back into Sallys arms. After another comforting cuddle Sally said,

'Let's make some supper and you can tell me all about it, Faye. I hate to think of you being upset.' She disentangled herself from Faye's hot, damp body!

'What are we having to eat? I'll help. I'll just pop my bag up to my bedroom.'

Sally's room remained unchanged since she moved to the flat. In fact, the whole house had not been touched for years. It was comfortable but a little shabby. Faye wasn't interested in decor.

As Sally went upstairs, she shouted over her shoulder,

'Your big sister's here now. Don't worry, we'll sort it.'

Faye sighed, her shoulders slouched, she slowly ambled towards the kitchen, her tatty old slippers dragging across the lino.

. . . . .

Sally at 31, was the big sister in age only, shorter than Faye by an inch. She was also about 20 pounds lighter with a slim build, a light complexion and pump-straight, light brown hair that reached down to her shoulder blades. Her hair was cut level across the bottom of the length to within a millimetre, with a blunt cut fringe completing the picture. Her style was classic. She chose smart trousers and blouses as her normal everyday wear, sometimes varying it with a pencil skirt. Invariably she had small heeled or flat, plain shoes. On her days off she usually wore jeans and t-shirts or a blouse, but always tended to look smart, even in jeans.

Faye, by comparison, had a round face, ruddy cheeks and freckles. Her hair was reddy-brown and wild! Whatever Sally did with it, it remained manically frizzy and untameable. With the length below her shoulders, she would tie it back with a bobble, but within minutes, stray wisps would be finding their way out. When she was hot, tiny ringlets surrounded her face, sticking to her hot skin, making her look quite angelic - in a flustered way! Careless with colour coordination to the point where she didn't have any coordination at all, she wore long flowing skirts or leggings and sloppy tops. Fashion wasn't important to her, she didn't give it any thought. But she was as dedicated to being a social worker as Sally was to her salon. They had that in common.

. . . . .

Faye baked two jacket potatoes with melted cheese and a side salad. Sally noticed as she finished her meal that Faye had only picked at hers. After clearing away, Sally said,

'So come on Faye, sit down and tell me all about it.'

'Oh Sal, thank you for coming, I don't know what I'd do without you. I'll start at the beginning and then you'll get the whole picture,' and she told Sally about Charles' death and her perceived hand in it.

As she finished, a long silence followed. Faye and Sally stared at each other, statue-like. Taking a deep breath Faye carried on,

'The rest of the week has been hell. I've written reports, been questioned by the police several times, and had interview after interview. Ingrid, well, she's supportive, but I know she's holding me to account and I don't blame her, I blame myself. She must think I'm useless. I don't think I can carry on in this job. It's just too much. The poor child. Poor little Charles. It's all my fault,' she ended grimly, her eyes red and wet.

Sally interrupted,

'OK, look Faye, it's not your fault, you didn't harm the child. It wasn't you who hurt him. It was the father, I presume, who did it. And the mother shouldn't have let him back in if she knew what he was like. She should have put the baby first.'

'It's not that easy. Men can be very persuasive. She's not a strong-minded woman,' Faye defended, 'I should have been strong for her.'

'Listen, you could not force yourself in through the door. You are not to blame. Get that into your head. Faye, you did what you did, and the parents of the child did what they did. It's not your fault, it's theirs. What about the others in your team? Could they have helped in any way?'

'Jayne is rushed off her feet. Brenda and Mark? They have their own caseloads. They are extremely busy too. We each have between 20 and 30 families. We are so packed right now!'

'It could have been any one of you who had this case. Would any of the others have handled it differently? I don't think so. You wouldn't lay the blame at their door, would you?'

'But I feel so guilty. Charles was so sweet! He was lovely, I loved him!' Faye wailed and broke down crying. Sally leaned forward and cuddled her.

'I've not slept, I keep going over it in my mind,' she said through her tears.

'Go on, have a good cry. Let it all out. But saying what you should have done isn't going to change anything now! You! . . . Are! . . . Not! . . . To! . . . Blame! It's not your fault. You did your best for the mother. She could have contacted you when he turned up again. Come on, blow your nose. I'll make some tea, or would you rather have something stronger? I think whiskey might do you more good right now.' Sally reached over and slid a box of tissues towards her on the coffee table.

'No, a cup of tea, Sally, thanks.' She blew her nose and wiped her eyes and wailed, 'What shall I do?'

'I don't know but I think a spell of leave will probably be best. Get away from it for a while, until you feel better. You love your job, Faye, it's your life. You'll feel better in a few weeks.'

'I doubt it.' She murmured despondently.

Gloomily, Faye stared at the fireplace. It was a beige coloured art deco tiled fireplace. Put in the house in the 1930's, it had never been replaced. The right-hand corner tile of the hearth had become unstuck and had laid in its place, on top of the thin layer of cement for years, like that, causing no trouble. Faye lifted the edge of the tile with the toe end of her slipper. She let it fall again. It landed fractionally out of line. She turned away from it, ignoring its predicament.

Sally returned from the kitchen with two mugs of tea, each with a good lacing of whiskey.

'I'll tell you what, speak to Ingrid on Monday about a bit of time off, I'm sure she'll agree to it, and we'll have a look for a little break, somewhere warm, somewhere where you can forget Charles and his mum and the rest of your caseload for a few days. Eh? What do you think of that idea?'

'Sounds just what I need, but I may not be much fun. Besides, the police may say I've not to go anywhere until after the case is closed. The court case may be ages off yet,' Faye mumbled, staring at her tea.

'Well, if you've written your reports and been interviewed, I'm sure there's no reason why you can't go away for a holiday and come back long before it all goes to court. Speak to Ingrid on Monday,' Sally repeated, big sister authority in her voice, 'Meanwhile, I'll start looking for a nice little getaway for us.'

'What about the salon?' Faye asked.

'Well,' Sally thought for a moment, 'Hazel could possibly do a few more hours, she's only part-time and Jo will put extra time in, I'm sure. They are good girls. Kylie, my new Saturday girl, may be able to come in after school to help. I'll look at what we have booked in. We'll sort something out.'

'You are the best sister anyone could ask for, Sally.' Faye brightened a little.

## 2

## The flight

Four weeks later Sally and Faye were in Gatwick airport waiting to board a flight to Goa in India. Sally saw the holiday; two weeks, bed and breakfast in Calangute, at The Royal Hotel, on an advertisement card in the travel agent's shop window, a few doors down from the salon. The price was reasonably cheap as it was a last-minute booking, so it seemed too good to miss. She phoned Faye to tell her about it straight away and then before either of them could waiver she popped in to book it.

Continuing to be in a state of despair Faye showed little interest in the forthcoming holiday. Finally Sally helped her pack and ensured the family home was secured before leaving for the airport.

. . . . .

Faye requested the holiday leave from work and wasn't totally surprised when Ingrid responded very favourably to the suggestion. Sat behind the desk, she said,

'I think it's a very sensible idea to remove yourself a few steps from the case for a little while. You'll be able to think clearer and make better decisions when you come back. Take your time and return when you feel ready. In fact, I don't think two weeks away will be enough, so take two months off. Then ring me and we'll arrange a meeting and see where you want to go from there,' she made a steeple with her fingers and rested her chin on the tips looking at Faye's miserable face.

'Do you think I'll ever be able to deal with a full caseload again, Ingrid?'

'Time will tell, you've had a terrible experience with this case, Faye. Just be patient. Enjoy your holiday and put it all out of your mind for a while. Then you'll be able to see the whole thing with detachment,' Ingrid pulled a file from a pile on the desk and opened it. She looked down, concentrating on the file.

Feeling dismissed, Faye said quietly,

'Thank you Ingrid. I'll be in touch. Bye.'

Not convinced she would put it out of her mind, let alone ever see it with detachment, she slouched out of the office. With eyes brimming, her confidence hit an all-time low. Ingrid had not lightened the feeling of despair in the least. Faye would have preferred Ingrid to have rejected the holiday request as unnecessary and begged her to return to work, therefore showing faith in her working abilities. Instead the opposite happened and the whole thing felt hopeless. Faye left the office with leaden feet and her head down. She felt incredibly demoralised.

. . . . .

Inside Gatwick airport, Sally tried to rally Faye.

'Come on, let's look around the shops whilst we're waiting. They don't charge VAT on top of the price, so we may get some bargains.' Sally ushered Faye into the first store selling holiday clothing and picked up a pair of flip flops. Faye tried to look interested and picked a pair up herself and searched for the price ticket.

Travelling in smart, cream, linen trousers, a cream and red patterned blouse and a red jacket. Sally could have jumped off a magazine cover. Flat, dark blue, suede shoes and a striped navy shoulder bag completed the picture.

In comparison, Faye sported a multi-coloured bandanna tied around her hairline, knotted at the back, leaving the ends to hang down. It was a little washed out with some fraying around the edges. She wore it in an effort to control her hair. A pale green, tie-dyed T-shirt, several strings of beads and bangles, topped off with a short, army style khaki-green jacket was her chosen outfit. A calf length, multi-coloured, cheesecloth skirt swirled around her legs and flat, brown leather sandals with ankle straps showed clean but untrimmed toenails. The gap between the bottom of her skirt and her sandals exposed white ankles and shins. One shin exhibited a shaving nick. The dark, dried blobs of blood along the scratch, emphasised the whiteness of her legs. No one would ever guess they were sisters.

'Let's look around first then we'll sit with a drink and something to eat where we can see our flight come up on the board.' Sally enthused. She glanced at Faye, who was looking down at her fingernails. She watched her for a moment and then whispered fiercely in her ear,

'Come on Faye, snap out of it now! It's a holiday of a lifetime. Let's enjoy it!' She nudged her in the ribs.

Faye's head snapped up.

'Yes! OK! You sounded just like Mum then!' she smiled, 'I know I've been a pain in the neck, sorry. OK, let's get holidaying!'

'That's better. Ooh look, perfume! Which one is your favourite?' Sally pulled Faye into another store. Faye really didn't know or care much about perfumes at all, but she grinned and allowed Sally to test the scents on her.

. . . . .

Later in the afternoon, on the plane, they settled into their seats for the nine-and-a-half-hour flight to Goa. Books, magazines, earphones, sweets, fruit and bottled water all placed and arranged within reach, they chatted until the first film began then Faye, surprisingly, fell asleep and, for the first time in days, had a trouble-free snooze.

Whilst Faye slept, Sally gently extricated herself from her seat and walked forward towards the loo. Six rows of seats in front, the same actions were occurring. Sally found herself walking down the aisle of the aeroplane behind a woman and then standing waiting for a vacancy sign with her.

'Hi, I hate standing at the front of the plane like this, don't you? Everyone knows what you are waiting for! It's embarrassing, isn't it?' the woman said to Sally.

'Yes, I know what you mean,' Sally laughed.

'I'm Gabby by the way.'

'Sally.'

'Where are you going? I'm staying in Calangute. I haven't been before, so I don't really know what to expect. I don't know what made me pick such a far-off place. I should have booked for Greece or somewhere, I'm on my own you see,' Gabby explained.

'Oh?' Sally replied, 'We're going to Calangute, my sister and me, The Royal Hotel. Which hotel are you in?'

'I'm in The Royal! What a coincidence.'

'Well, if you're on your own and want to come along with us, you're welcome. I don't want to presume, of course.'

'No,' Gabby replied quickly, 'If your sister wouldn't mind, that would be lovely. I wouldn't want to be a nuisance though.'

'She won't mind. When we book in, I'll let you have our room number and then if you want to tag along you can and if you don't, don't worry. At least you know someone now. You are not on your own any more.'

'You are really kind,' Gabby smiled.

'Do you usually holiday alone?'

'Oh no, it's just circumstances. Things don't always go according to plan, do they? I needed to get away.'

'You'll get along famously with my sister!' Sally laughed.

One of the toilet doors opened and the occupant came out. Gabby smiled and entered, turning she said, 'What number seat are you in? I'll wander down for a chat later.'

Sally told her the seat number and they parted.

# 3

## Gabby

The holiday didn't seem so scary now. Gabby cheered a little as she walked back to her seat. She'd made a friend, possibly two. It was the first time she'd contemplated holidaying alone, a 40-year-old, happily married woman and successful in her working role. At least she *was* happily married, until a month ago.

Gabby, short, slim and pretty, had short, choppy blonde hair which she spiked up with gel around her pert little face. The human resources manager of a large supermarket company wasn't a desperately exciting job every minute of every day, but it had its moments and her immediate team were brilliant. They were all conscientious workers and the best of friends.

Just over a month ago, Gabby left work early. She had never left early in the 14 years she'd worked there. Regular as clockwork with her routine - with all her routines - at work and home. Except for time off with the usual children's illnesses when they were young, she had never taken a day off sick. Daisy, the youngest, now 19, was at university studying business, and Philip (or Pip, as they called him) at 21-years-old, managed a small department within his father's firm.

But, on this particular day she had such severe abdominal pains, she just couldn't sit comfortably at her desk. The pains started at 10.15 in the morning and steadily became so bad that by early afternoon she couldn't stand it any longer. She had experienced period pains from time to time but nothing like this. Moving around didn't help. The usual painkillers didn't help. She had no option but to drive the few miles home with the hope that resting flat on the bed would ease it and if not, she would place a call to her GP.

Graham, her husband, the director of a very successful specialist flooring company put immeasurable numbers of hours into the firm each week. It was his baby and he nurtured it. He worked extremely hard building up the business. Gabby didn't phone his office to say she was unwell as she knew he would be busy. She hoped to be feeling better before it was time for his return home.

Respectful of each other's abilities and roles, they'd always enjoyed a lovely partnership. Graham was a good husband and father, he was good looking and had kept himself trim. She loved his dark curly chest hair. She loved him. He was 44 and yet to have a grey hair on his head or anywhere else for that matter. Gabby felt happy and content in her life. They had a beautiful home, tastefully decorated and spacious, two wonderful children and a loving relationship, even after 22 years of marriage.

Letting herself through the front door, she popped off her shoes and slowly, holding her tummy with one hand and the handrail with the other, climbed the stairs. All she wanted, and all she had in her mind, was stretching out on the bed and easing her poor tum.

Pushing open the bedroom door she stopped abruptly mid stride! Her mouth fell open and her eyes widened as she saw what was happening on the bed. What little colour remained in her face completely disappeared. It was the last thing she ever expected to see.

'Wha … ' escaped from her mouth.

Graham and a young girl, probably about the same age as Daisy, were both naked on the bed. Their heads turned in tandem and their happy faces changed to alarm as they saw Gabby in the doorway. The sight of them, in the position they were in, in her bed, their marital bed, tattooed itself into her brain forever. Stunned, Gabby could not make sense of the scene. Eyes wide and mouth open she stared. She couldn't move or speak. Rooted to the spot, she gripped the door knob.

Unnoticed, from between her legs, warm blood began to run down her inner thighs and calves. It pooled around her bare feet on the cream bedroom carpet. The pains in her abdomen had finally achieved ripeness. She miscarried in front of her husband and his young bit of stuff as she stood staring!

There was action in the room. Graham and his girlfriend were now trying to cover their nakedness. Graham was saying things to Gabby, words, meaningless words. He was looking at Gabby's face and then looking at her legs and feet and pointing. At the same time he was hurrying the girl. There was a lot of arm waving. The girl, wearing not much more than a horrified look on her face was ushered out by Graham. She left the bedroom in haste and, no doubt, with some relief.

On the landing they whispered but Gabby could hear.

'It looks like she's having a miscarriage, is it yours?' the girl asked, 'You told me you and her were over, that you weren't having sex with her!'

'Shhh!' Graham hissed, 'we'll talk about this later. Go home and I'll come as soon as I can.'

'But!' she cried.

'Shh!' he repeated again, 'Go home now!' he ordered and came back into the bedroom, arms outstretched, palms upwards. Gabby did not move, she couldn't make sense of it.

All the time the thick, clotting blood seeped down her legs onto the carpet. Unaware she was carrying it, the infinitely minuscule baby, really not more than a few hundred cells, was was swept down her legs within the blood. Gabby stood, her mouth still open, shocked. The pain in her abdomen stretched to include the whole of her body and mind. Still unable to speak, she replayed in her mind, the naked couple and their movements, until it became clear. As if out of her own body, she felt herself registering the implications of her husband's actions. Then, still in a state of other-worldliness, she looked down at her feet and saw the blood. She felt the pain and saw the blood and that too became clear.

It was all over!

## 4

## *George*

On boarding, when Gabby found her place on the plane, she discovered she was allocated the aisle seat, so being the first to get to her row, she perched, ready to jump up to let the other couple of passengers through towards the window and middle seats. A couple of minutes later an elderly lady came searching for the correct seat. She was allocated the window seat. She said hello to Gabby, then slid across into her place. Searching in her handbag she brought out an eye mask and a pretty silver and enamel pillbox. Opening the pillbox, she selected a tablet and swallowed it, explaining to Gabby as she sat and buckled up,

'I have travelled this route often and prefer to sleep through most of it,' she murmured, 'goodnight, dear.' Smiling at Gabby, she pulled the eye mask down and settled in her seat for a peaceful journey.

A few moments later, Gabby's hopes for sitting beside a nice female with whom to chat and enjoy the trip were dashed as a male passenger approached and asked to pass into the middle seat beside her. He was dressed in soft, pale blue fitted jeans, straight leg, not tight but still showing off a good figure and a small, tidy pair of buttocks. A button-down polo shirt in navy with a red trim fitted snugly around his upper body. His brown, almost black hair suggested a quality cut. He was clean shaven, his skin unblemished and slightly tanned. Finally she noticed his immaculately manicured fingernails. As he squeezed past her in the confined space to get to his seat, Gabby consciously took it all in. He smelled of expensive aftershave. She begrudgingly admired his overall attractiveness, even though she had now branded herself a man-hater for the rest of her life.

He fussed about for a few minutes, sorting his belongings and seat belt, and then settled back.

'George,' he said to Gabby, smiling and holding out his hand.

'Gabby,' she replied reluctantly, not smiling and held on to his outstretched hand for the tiniest moment. She picked up her book and prepared to ignore him for the rest of the journey.

George, glancing at his other neighbour, the old lady, already gently snoring, settled back in his seat ready for take-off. *Great!* he thought to himself: *it could prove to be a long flight, a sleeper on one side and a reader on the other. Oh well, at least I have Sunny to look forward to.*

. . . . .

George owned and worked in his shop selling jewellery and exquisite decorative and ornamental items. He had two, long term, trusted staff members and they ran the shop whilst he travelled. He sought out *objets d'art*, precious metals and stones to sell in his little emporium. His preferred purchases were Chinese sculptures and art work and beautiful Indian silverware. He loved the search and discovery of different pieces and gained great satisfaction when he had a crate of exciting new acquisitions ready to send back to the shop to adorn his windows and bring in his discerning customers.

India was his favourite destination because of Sunny, whom he first met five years ago at a hotel in Mumbai and who quickly became the love of his life. Sunny was short for Sundar, which means *beautiful* in Hindi, and he is, in George's eyes, simply beautiful. Unfortunately, Sunny had responsibilities in Delhi in the form of a wife and six children.

However, George didn't mind having a part-time relationship. It suited him, and he laughed to himself at his own little joke that Sunny gave spice to his visits to India.

George came to India far more often than was strictly necessary and Sunny always managed to get away to be with him, if only for a few days. The relationship was contained in the private world of India, away from George's alternative life in England, and they usually got together in Goa, away from Sunny's family life in Delhi. George had no explanations or answers to provide to anyone. It was a perfect, mutual set up.

Sunny was coming to Goa to share George's two weeks working holiday and they were sharing a room at The Royal Hotel. They would search out sumptuous pieces together for George to transport home. In between buying expeditions, they would spend time enjoying each other's company. George found purchasing and shipping substantial amounts of goods for his shop much easier if Sunny was with him as his Indian advocate, and he appreciated that, but it wouldn't have made any difference to his visits to India if Sunny was unable to help. George simply wanted to be with him.

Sunny wore traditional Indian clothing, which George found incredibly sensuous. He always requested Sunny to wear his dhoti kurta, especially when they were alone together. With a smooth, hair-free, beautifully sculptured, chest, George could not resist him. Sunny was tactile, physical and loving and on top of that, he was outrageously funny and entertaining. George felt true love for Sunny and it was reciprocated.

Sunny had his reasons for keeping George a secret, which George knew and accepted. He and Sunny would never share family festivals together, such as Christmas, or occasions when normal families got together. He could never buy him a personal present as Sunny would be unable to take it home without having to lie about its origin. He could never demand his presence, it always had to be carefully arranged. He knew and accepted the relationship's limitations. It was the way it was. It was enough for him - well, at present, anyway.

As the film started, George peered out of the corner of his eye at Gabby. She blinked, and he knew she had seen him look. Deciding nine hours was a long time to sit without speaking he took a breath and said,

'Where are you travelling to?' She had no option but to talk to him. She'd been brought up to be polite but allowed herself a mental sigh.

'Calangute. What about you?'

'Yes, I'm going to Calangute too! Which hotel?' *That wasn't too bad*, he thought.

'The Royal.'

'No! I don't believe it. So am I! We are going to be neighbours. Are you having two weeks?'

'Yes. Will you excuse me please?' Not wanting to encourage the conversation, Gabby stood and moved towards the front of the plane, making her way to the loo, thereby meeting Sally.

## 5

# The airport

Pandemonium is the only word for it! Pandemonium, inside the airport building in Goa. It seemed the entire population of Goa arrived at the same time. Queues, that's another word. Every passenger had to queue to get this stamped, to get that stamped, to finally allow admittance into the country. Then to cap it all, some bright spark decided it would be helpful if he removed all the suitcases from the carousel and littered the floor surrounding it with them. No one could see their cases, and if they could, couldn't get to them. Pandemonium!

Gabby stepped in between the cases. She found her feet squeezed together between two large bags. One sported a polished silver clasp with the initials GPW. Bending she tried to move it to one side so she could move her feet. She was in danger of losing her balance but unable to move the bag more than a few millimetres, she cursed gently to herself. Looking up she saw George had arrived beside her and lifted the case, the one initialled GPW.

'Oh, it's yours!' Gabby said, frowning, whilst thinking *'I might have known!'* and let him take it from her.

'Yes, where's yours? Can I help you find it?'

'Thanks, yes it's that bluey-green one right over the other side of the carousel.'

'Got it.' With that, he stretched his long legs over the empty carousel in two great strides and within seconds, returned with Gabby's case. She had to admit, albeit begrudgingly, George did seem a kind and considerate man.

'Come, let me help you to the bus.'

Reluctantly, Gabby admitted to herself that she was pleased to have someone take charge in this scary, busy, bustling, foreign land. She stepped in close behind George who carried both his and Gabby's cases. With that Gabby and George became friends.

Outside the airport it was just as mad. In the steamy heat travellers searched for relatives, taxi drivers searched for fares, and the brown shirted boys searched for customers.

Sally and Faye managed to find their transfer bus moments before George and Gabby so they stood directly in front of them in yet another queue to board the bus. The driver and his helper threw their suitcases into the metal cage on top of the old bus. Sally cringed as she saw her expensive case bouncing against the rusty metalwork. Multicoloured, the bus was lovingly decorated with garlands and idols of the gods of India. Sally thought it looked too old to even start. However, Faye admired it, it was just up her street. She loved the atmosphere of India already.

Recognising Gabby, Sally shouted at the little group behind her,

'Have you been to Goa before?' straining to be heard over the roar of humanity.

'Yes, I have. It is a little shocking, I'll admit, but once you get used to it, you'll love it here,' George said.

'Hope we've done the right thing.' Sally muttered in Faye's ear but Faye laughed and patted Sally on the back. She wasn't feeling worried at all. Gabby huddled close, not wanting to be separated from her new friends.

On the bus, Gabby sat next to George. After a furtive assessment of the inside she realised It was the only seat available, so she didn't need to make an awkward decision.

'Sorry I was rude to you on the plane,' she spoke to George but looked down at her lap. The bus was attempting to pull out into the torrent of vehicles leaving the airport. George had to raise his voice to be heard over the multitude of tooting horns.

'Oh, don't worry. Gabby, is it? I shouldn't expect people to be chatty like me. I'm just glad to be out of the airport. It never changes, it's always busy and noisy. We are on our way to the hotel now, so we can have a swim, a drink and calm down,' he smiled at her. She felt even worse, he was being so nice.

'Sounds fab!' She turned and included the sisters in the conversation.

'Sally, Faye, George suggested we have a swim, a drink and calm down when we get to the hotel.'

'Lovely! You're on. Can't wait.'

'Me too. Last one in the pool buys the first round of drinks.'

# 6

## The hotel

Two tall, ornate pillars stood at the entrance of the long drive. First impressions of The Royal Hotel were favourable and after a terrifying ride from the airport, where all drivers seemed intent on killing themselves and their passengers, the group of holiday makers felt both joy and relief at the sight of the pillars. Never had Faye, Sally and Gabby seen such driving.

'I'm sure my heart won't stand another journey like that!' Gabby said.

'You'll get used to it. It's strange to begin with, but you'll love it before you know it,' George said.

'Are you sure?' she replied doubtfully.

However, safely through the pillars, the journey was forgotten as the hotel came into sight, glorious in its surroundings. Sally had picked a good hotel, Faye silently acknowledged as they got off the bus. The grounds were green and fresh, a multitude of brightly coloured flowers splashed here and there and palm trees swayed in the gentle breeze epitomising a lushness, a garden of abundance, and a warm, humid, scented air kissed their British skins.

'Oh wow!' whispered Faye. Wide eyed she turned a full circle and breathed in the fragrant atmosphere. The worries of the last few weeks lifted from her shoulders and an aura of calm and peacefulness engulfed her.

The hotel's reception was long and low, painted white with a red tiled roof. The rest of the communal buildings were purely tree trunks with bamboo roofs. All open-air - they housed a bar, dining area, and spacious terraces filled with luxurious recliners or groups of comfortable chairs and coffee tables. Built without walls the buildings allowed the gentle, warm breeze to sweep through them. Shaded from the fierce sun, the terraces provided comfortable, well-furnished areas to sit, drink, chat, read, whatever you wanted, safe from sunburn or overheating. Beyond the terraces, the large pool, a dazzling fluidity of liquid diamonds, glinted in the sunshine. Its blue coolness invited the new guests to submerge themselves and be rid of the effects of the hot dusty journey. The pool was surrounded by an open terrace with plenty of recliners, several outside showers and then the eye was taken further across an expanse of lawn, immaculately cut with clumps of palms here and there. Huge, colourful pots provided homes to large flowering plants at every opportunity around the buildings which punctuated the wood and bamboo with flashes of interest. The warm steamy air and the backdrop of swaying palm trees completed the impression of tropical luxury. Behind the bar area, also covered by bamboo in keeping with the style of the hotel, were kitchens, tandoori ovens and barbecues.

Beyond the reception building, a wide path snaked away, bordered with shady palms and a variation of vivid blooms and interestingly alien plants. Eight blocks of six double rooms lined both sides of the path, each painted a different pastel colour giving the impression of a rainbow receding into the distance. On either side of the wide path, narrower paths lead off to the guest rooms which were cleverly built at angles so none of the rooms overlooked another. Three floors of two rooms were accessed via the back through open corridors and stairs. A young man was designated to help each of the guests with their luggage and escort them to the correct room. It was lovely. The rooms were colourful and well kept.

The new-found friends split up but arranged to be at the pool within the hour.

Faye and Sally's balcony, on the second floor, faced away from the hotel. White heron type birds strode across the fields, below the balcony, following a herd of cows. In the distance sat a small hamlet and after gazing at the little shacks for a few moments, Faye realised she could see children playing outside, people working the fields, goats and pigs wandering between the shacks and even chickens. It was a little hazy due to the heat but it was a delightful picture. Faye looked forward to getting to know the inhabitants of the hamlet from her distant perch and she called Sally, who was hanging her clothes in the wardrobe to come and see.

Faye pointed to the scene of everyday life in Goa. Standing side by side on the balcony, arms resting on the balustrade, Faye breathed,

'I think I'm going to like it here, Sal. Already I feel so much happier and calmer. It's beautiful.'

'Yes, it's beautiful,' agreed Sally. 'I'm so glad you feel that way. This is what this holiday is all about. Come on Faye, let's go and try the pool.'

The sisters quickly changed, collected their sun lotion and towels and headed off for a swim.

. . . . .

The pool delivered exactly what it had promised when they first arrived. Sally, Faye and Gabby squealed and giggled letting the cool water creep up their hot skin as they slowly submerged. Everyone shed another layer of home, be it work, husband, or any other stresses and they relaxed a few more notches as the water washed away the strain of the journey. A couple of cold drinks later, though, the time difference started to take its toll and first one and then another began to yawn and feel the journey catching up with them.

'I don't think I'm up to going into Calangute tonight,' Sally said to Faye. 'I think we need to take it easy tonight until we adjust to the time difference. What do you say?'

'Yes, I agree, I'm feeling worn out too. Tonight, shall we just eat in the hotel?' Faye suggested. 'Gabby, do you want to join us?'

'Thanks, girls, I'll see how I feel, later. What time were you thinking of eating?'

'Not sure, what if we give you a knock on our way? Or just see you here in the bar?'

'Yes, either will be fine.' Gabby agreed.

'What about you George? Do you have any plans?' Faye turned to George.

'I'm not meeting my friend for a couple of days yet,' George said. 'I'll be pottering around, down here tonight so I'll look out for you. Thanks for asking. Now if you'll excuse me, I'm also going for a snooze. See you later.' He disappeared up the path to the rooms.

The staff at the hotel bar, all young men in colourful flowery shirts, chatted between themselves as the three ladies followed George up the path. One man, however, stared after the new visitors, studying the retreating figures in depth until they disappeared. Then he carried on with his task of wiping down the bar top.

## 7

### First impressions

That evening, Faye and Sally, after a rest and a shower, collected Gabby on the way and selected a table at the edge of the dining area, closest to the pool. After dark, the hotel displayed a different atmosphere. The palm trees surrounding the pool were lit by fairy lights wound around and up the length of the trunks. Up lighters and downlighters were placed all around to enhance the grounds and the moon reflected on the pool. Beyond the lights, the night was pitch black, but the ambience was inclusive, safe and secure. Remaining warm it held the same damp humidity with scents of plants, spices and Asian secrets. The hotel staff were busy behind the bar and in the kitchens. Over the authentic background music of the sitar, cheerful chatter and clatter of crockery, pans and glasses could be heard. Smiling Indian faces welcomed the new arrivals. They sat, gazing around, taking it all in, happily chatting and perusing the menu which looked deliciously tasty and different.

Leaning against a tree trunk support at the back of the bar, an insolent look on his face, Joseph was motionless and expressionless. His eyes, however, surveyed the whole of the bar and dining area searching every face at every table. Content when he knew who sat where and with whom, he allowed himself a little nod. A sneer played around his lips.

Faye turned to Sally, a happy smile on her face,
'Oh, this is lovely. What a gorgeous setting. I love it.'

'You are right, it's wonderful!' The girls enthused over their surroundings.

'Good evening, beautiful ladies, what can I get you to drink? We have cocktails, spirits, wines, beers and soft drinks. Anything I can do for you, I will, you only need to ask. My name is Joseph, I am looking after you tonight.' Joseph smiled at the girls, his sneer gone, replaced with friendliness.

'Mmm. Can we have a few minutes to look at the menu, please?' Sally replied to Joseph, without looking up from her menu.

'Of course. I am here at your command,' Joseph performed a bow and stood back whilst they chose their drinks. He spent a moment studying each of the girls in turn. Then he swept forward again to take their order as soon as they put the drinks menu down.

'May I say, I really admire your necklace,' Joseph smiled as he spoke to Sally, pointing at her chest. She had a string of fine beads holding a large flat turquoise stone sitting comfortably at the top of her faint cleavage. 'I haven't seen one like that before. It suits you, I think it matches the colour of your eyes.'

'Excuse me?' Sally quickly raised her hands to cover the bare skin at her neckline.

'Oh, I'm sorry, I apologise, I didn't mean to be forward,' His smile vanished and he disappeared towards the bar for their drinks.

Sally thought, *What a cheek, I wouldn't trust him! How smarmy and insincere.*

Gabby thought, *Men! Typical, a one-track mind!*

Faye thought, *What a handsome man, so charming and what a fit backside!*

However they thought no more about him and began to get to know each other better. They chatted happily away. Joseph was back within minutes, his head cocked to one side as he furtively took interest in their discussion whilst he placed the drinks on the table. He stood beside their table, tray in hand, making himself almost invisible by being totally immobile as he listened to their conversation.

George appeared from the direction of the guest rooms.

'Hey George, we're over here,' Faye stood and waved at George, he waved back in acknowledgement. Joseph turned and walked away.

George visited Goa many times over the last few years on business and to meet Sunny, so he was pleased to share his knowledge with the girls for whom it was the first time in the country. He advised them of the best beaches, sightseeing tours and best restaurants in the holiday resort. Faye, Sally and Gabby soaked up the information, anxious to get as much out of the holiday as possible.

An interesting nugget of information from George was about telling the time.

'Goa is five and a half hours ahead of the UK. However, to stop the need of addition or subtraction, you only have to turn your watch upside down to see the time at home!' he laughed watching the girls enjoy a few moments taking off their watches and trying it out, wondering at the absurdity of the fact.

As the evening progressed he told them about the Grand Evening Bazaar which was held every Saturday - the following evening.

Joseph came to deliver the main courses. He gently and slowly placed the dishes on their table.

'That sounds like one not to miss,' Sally said to the other girls. 'Will you be going, George?' she asked.

'I don't think so, I've been many times and Sunny will be arriving tomorrow. We'll probably go for a meal, but I must say, you will have a great night. It's a fabulous evening. A tuk tuk will take you directly there from the hotel gate and then there are plenty of them available to bring you back, so it's perfectly safe. I can certainly recommend it.'

Joseph, hovering on the side lines, offered,

'I can escort you all if you wish.' They all turned and looked at him. Faye smiled at him but before she could reply, Sally said,

'We'll be fine, thank you, as George says, we can tuk tuk there and back, we don't need an escort.' Joseph bowed his head and walked away. His pleasant servitude smile was replaced with a scowl.

．　．　．　．　．

The evening progressed, and with the consumption of alcohol, adjusting to the time difference and the relaxing atmosphere, the new-found friends loosened up and Gabby felt comfortable enough to confide in her  companions the events leading up to booking the holiday.

Heads together over the table, Faye, Sally and George were amazed and horrified at Gabby's tale. Telling them how her beloved husband betrayed her was bad enough but when she went on saying how she lost the baby at the same time in front of him and the girl, well, it was too much for Gabby and she teared up. Several tissues, hugs and exclamations later, Sally raised her head to order some more drinks, a little stronger than the wine they had had with their meal, to find Joseph leaning in over their heads, listening intently. He jumped back stammering,

'Sorry madam, I'm reaching for your empty glasses.' Sally glared at him. *What is it about this guy?* She thought to herself but instead said acidly to Joseph,

'We'll have four brandies please.'

'Yes of course,' Joseph smiled and bowed. He moved towards the bar. *Did he have a satisfied smirk on his face?* Sally thought to herself. She was going to tell the others but when she turned her attention back to the table, Gabby was laughing through tears at something George was saying. The mood lifted back into holiday mode and her suspicion of Joseph listening in to Gabby's tale was forgotten.

## 8

## *Gabby's decision*

The following morning Gabby went to exchange a travellers cheque in the reception and decided to sit with a coffee in the warm sunshine before going back to her room. It was quiet, not many of the holidaymakers were about yet and no sign of Faye, Sally or George. Staff were busy preparing the bar and dining area for the day ahead. Gabby enjoyed the peace. The last few days had been a bit of a whirlwind so  she welcomed the opportunity to sit alone in the sun and gather her thoughts.

. . . . .

The children, Pip and Daisy, were heartbroken when she was forced to tell them what happened on the day of the miscarriage. She had to tell them, as Graham left the family home and moved in with the young girl. He moved the same day. It felt to Gabby that he left without a backward glance. With the miscarriage exacerbating the issue of his betrayal at that time, Gabby felt doubly hurt. One, he had another woman, a girl actually, as if it wasn't enough; and two, he could leave her at a time when she was losing their baby. She realised she didn't know him at all. Not knowing which was worse - him having an affair or him not caring about the miscarriage, she was devastated, confused and in amongst those feelings, she also felt angry. One thing she was certain of though - their marriage had been a facade.

They should have grieved together for the baby. Instead, alone, her heart was broken on both accounts. One, for the loss of a long standing love which she thought was forever and two, the loss of a new life, a surprise, a little gift she would have welcomed and shared with Graham.

Sipping her coffee, sadness swept through her again. She sighed, knowing there was no going back. Life in the future would be different, a challenge, but it would be honest, open and without any person who could inflict pain. She would enjoy watching her lovely children grow and mature and they would be the only people with whom she would share her heart.

Pip and Daisy needed her strength after they learned what their father had done. Gabby comforted them and then they comforted her, their shock was as strong as her own. It would take a long time for the children to forgive Graham sufficiently to continue with any form of relationship. Pip had not returned to work at his father's business and had not yet decided what he wanted to do. They all needed time to recover.

He didn't expand on the reason for leaving his job, the fact that the 'other woman' worked there was enough. Looking back over the last few weeks, Pip realised he should have seen the signs. In total ignorance of his father's shenanigans, he now recalled certain moments when, knowing what he knew now, the affair could be seen with the naked eye. He had observed his father and Cheryl, the other woman, acting silly and giddy together. One day, for example, he innocently watched them, gently pushing each other on the shoulder and laughing as they swayed back and forth. Cheryl was always appearing in his father's office, entering with any lame excuse, smiling hopelessly at his dad. Pip had thought she was sweet, if a little dipsy, and supposed his dad had a soft spot for her as he would for Daisy. Hah! What a fool he had been! One clue he should have picked up on was Mrs Ashford's attitude to Cheryl. Mrs Ashford, his dad's secretary, had been with the company for donkey's years. She obviously didn't like her. A look of disdain showed on her face whenever Cheryl came into view. Pip had assumed Mrs Ashford worried that Cheryl would replace her. A younger woman, better looking, hot on the internet etc., understandable, but he clearly assumed wrong. Mrs Ashford knew more than she let on, obviously. All this he kept to himself, his mum didn't need further anguish right now.

. . . . .

When Gabby told them she had booked a holiday to Goa, on her own, they were astounded and horrified. Pip was concerned for her safety. Travelling alone, in her raw emotional state, he didn't think it was a clever idea. Daisy thought she was quite mad and tried to persuade her to cancel the trip and book something a little tamer.

'I'm not booking an old person's holiday in some old-fashioned sea-side town on the south coast, just to put your minds at rest. I need something to take my mind off things, to push my limits and stretch myself. I really need to get away. Don't make it more difficult for me, please. I'll be fine, I'll be careful, and I'll phone you regularly.'

Gabby decided to phone Daisy now. She groped around in her bag and pulled out her mobile. The time difference meant it would be . . . she calculated the time by twisting her arm upside down and noted it would be 3.30 in the morning at home. Chuckling to herself she set her phone on the table and gazed up at the swaying palm trees. The only sound was the breeze in the trees and faint kitchen noises and gentle voices. She closed her eyes to enjoy the quiet and solitude.

A shadow across her face darkened the deep red of her eyelids to black.

'I like your phone, what type is it?'

Gabby was startled out of her reclusive state. Her eyes flew open. Joseph was standing beside her, bending over her, a smile on his face.

'What?' she stuttered, taken aback.

'Your phone, I said I liked it. Sorry, did I startle you?'

'Yes, you did, I had my eyes closed.'

'Oh, I'm sorry, madam. Listen, I am going to the Grand Evening Bazaar tonight. I would like to take you as my guest.'

'Your guest?' she queried, confused.

Smiling widely and nodding, Joseph bent over, close to her face,

'Yes, my guest, my date, if you like. I think you are a beautiful lady. I hear of your troubles with your husband, I could give you some comfort,' his smile widened even more, showing two rows of even white teeth.

Gabby's eyebrows shot up in surprise.

'*Comfort?* Where did you hear about 'my troubles' Joseph, tell me?'

'I heard you talking with the ladies, and Mr George. I would like to help you and . . .'

'No! No thank you, Joseph!' Gabby retorted, 'And I would appreciate it if you minded your own business, in future. I am not looking for 'a date' now or ever!' she glared at him. Joseph, his smile gone, took two quick steps back.

Hastily Gabby collected her bag and phone and left him standing there. Flabbergasted, she returned to her room. *The cheek of the man! How dare he listen in on my most personal and private conversations and then have the audacity to offer to take me on a date! Comfort! Indeed!* Red faced and thunderstruck she paced up and down her bedroom, and then unable to keep it to herself any longer, she ran around to Faye and Sally's room to tell them about it.

She knocked but no one answered. Gabby, frustrated, turned and scanned the surrounding areas, seeking out the girls. She knocked again and called their names. Still no answer. Chewing on her lip, she considered going up to George's room but thought against it. She didn't want to give him the wrong impression. *The cheek of that man, Joseph,* Gabby fumed. She turned and went to find George anyway, regardless. She needed to tell someone and couldn't stop herself from running up the stairs to his room two at a time.

'Ah, George, I'm so sorry to barge up here, disturbing you at this hour of the morning!' The words exploded from her mouth with exasperation, her eyebrows drawn and eyes wild. George, alarmed, stood back to let her in.

'Come in Gabby, you're not disturbing me,' his eyes wide with surprise. 'I was about to go and have some coffee, but what can I do for you?'

'Oh, you'll think I'm being silly, George, but you know that barman called Joseph?' George nodded. 'Well, he's just asked me to go to the Evening Bazaar with him. He had heard about my husband's dalliance, for want of a better word, by listening in to our conversation and thought he would try it on with me whilst I am wounded!'

'Oh, my word! The cheek of the fellow! What a prat! I would keep clear of him, Gabby. Do you want me to have a word with him?'

'No thanks, I gave him short shrift, George,' she chuckled. 'I don't think he was expecting that! Have you seen Sally and Faye, by the way?'

'Yes, they went into town to buy some anti-malaria tablets. Faye said she would buy enough for you too. They shouldn't be long. Come on, let's put a united front on and we'll get some coffee. I'll stare angrily at Joseph. That should do it.' Laughing, they went down to the bar.

## 9

## On the beach

After their trip to town the girls found Gabby and the threesome spent the day at the beach. The sun was hot and the sea inviting. Beach bars supplied comfortable sunbeds as well as a constant stream of offers of cold drinks and spicy, interesting snacks. The beach was busy but pleasantly so. All the holidaymakers were intent on relaxing and developing a tan to take home.

The hubbub from the other sunseekers around the three girls made them feel safe to lay and chat, read or snooze in their bikinis. Sally ensured they all had sufficient coverage of sun protection cream, especially Faye. Her combination of red hair and fair skin meant she was likely to burn easily.

Busy doing nothing more strenuous than choosing small treats from the menu, chatting, turning a page of their books or wading thigh deep in the warm sea, the girls enjoyed the day, it was paradise - or so it appeared.

Outwardly, Gabby was calm, enjoying the holiday and the company of Sally and Faye. Inwardly, though, she struggled. At times like these, laying on the beach, each person reading or snoozing, she may as well have been alone, she was in turmoil. What did she do wrong to make her husband, Graham, want another woman, well, a girl? That's what she was, just a girl. Gabby thought she was in a loving relationship. They enjoyed each other's bodies two or three times a week. They were tactile and kissed at other times. They shared a sense of humour. They supported each other and talked in depth about problems, rarely quarrelling. They both adored their children. What had gone wrong? She didn't know. She thought it was all perfect. How wrong could she be? A lump rose in her throat. She swallowed hard and reached for her drink. *Am I to blame?* Then in the next second, she shook off the self-recrimination and saw the situation as it really was! *No, it wasn't my fault, that bastard has broken my heart. It was all his fault!*

Faye, less than a metre away from Gabby, was going through similar mental torture. Her self-esteem had reached rock bottom prior to arriving in Goa. She silently studied each second of the last two encounters with Dawn, Charles' mother, critically reviewing her actions and reactions. It was all to no avail. It didn't change the actual outcome. Nothing ever would. At this moment Faye could not envisage herself going back to work. Not in two months, not ever. She felt so sad, guilty and miserable.

Sighing, she sat up and looked around the beach at the holidaymakers. Everyone looked happy and content. Sally was smiling with her eyes closed. Obviously blissfully unaware of any kind of angst. Faye looked over at Gabby, she too had her eyes closed but she was frowning. Poor Gabby, Faye thought, she knows heartbreak. She picked up her book and tried hard to concentrate on the story.

. . . . .

Later in the afternoon, Sally was alarmed to see the skin on Faye's face, upper chest and shoulders an angry hot pink colour. Her eyes, where her sunglasses had offered protection, stood out white against the redness of her cheeks and forehead.

'Oh, Faye! I think you've had enough sun for today, you look like a pickled beetroot,' she laughed at her.

'No! I knew I should have bought a hat. I've put on lashings of sun cream too. Is it bad?' she asked.

'Well, you look very angry in the face. I think we should pack up and head back to the hotel. It's the Grand Evening Bazaar tonight anyway. Shall we go have a nice cool dip in the pool and an ice cream before we get ready?'

Gabby laughed at Faye's colour,

'You're winning the competition for the best tan, that's for sure. Come on, we'll walk up past that little market and see if there are any large brimmed hats for sale.'

'The larger the better,' Sally laughed.

'Oh you! It's not funny. I'm going to be sore.' Pouting, Faye gathered her things.

'Put on plenty of after-sun lotion, you'll be alright. And keep off the alcohol, just drink water tonight.'

Back at the hotel, Faye thought a few lengths of the pool with her face under the cool water would help calm her reddened skin. So, Sally and Gabby left her to do a couple more lengths and set off to the rooms to get ready for the evening.

From the darkness of the bar, Joseph watched Sally and Gabby depart leaving Faye alone. His eyes glittered as he saw the opportunity to seize his prey. The fat, unfit English girl with the pallid skin and awful frizzy hair was alone. He noticed that the fierce sun had not been kind to her delicate pale skin. White discs around her eyes where her sunglasses sat made her look ridiculous. Joseph wore an expression of contempt as he strolled to the end of the pool. He calmly changed to show his most charming side replacing the disdain.

'Hey, Faye. Would you like to go to the Evening Bazaar with me tonight?' a deep voice asked as Faye surfaced at the end of the pool.

'Oh! Hello Joseph,' she spluttered through her surprise and wiped the water from her eyes. 'Thanks, but we are all going together tonight.'

Undeterred he continued,

'You have caught the sun, you look very pretty. A little colour suits you.'

'Really? Thank you, Joseph, you are kind.'

Joseph squatted down at the side of the pool, to get closer to Faye. He ensured his tight black trousers did not touch the water on the tiles. His face was about a metre above Faye's. He looked down on her.

'I liked you the minute you arrived here, but the Indian sun has made you even more beautiful.'

She squinted up at him, an incredulous look on her face.

'Well,' she laughed, 'I don't know about that, but thank you anyway,' and wished for a moment she could go with him to the bazaar.

'After the bazaar, we may have a drink back here. You could join us then, maybe?' she suggested.

'I don't know, I think your sister doesn't like me? I don't know why, I am just being pleasant to her.' He conjured a hurt look onto his face.

'Oh, I'm sure she likes you, don't worry.' Faye felt a little sorry for him. Reluctantly, she said, 'I must go and get ready. I'll see you later.'

'Actually, I wanted to talk to you. But I was nervous, and I made a mistake by trying to talk to her first. I just wanted to start talking to you, Faye.'

*Wow!* Faye was stunned into silence. *Is he flirting with me?* Astonished, her body submerged in the pool, her elbows bent with her arms resting on the side, she was motionless.

They stared at each other. Faye looked into his perfect dark eyes. Her eyes swept around his face admiring his perfect eyebrows over his perfect nose on perfect skin. *He's beautiful!* Bemused, she continued to stare at him.

'I saw you and your sister and the other lady and immediately I felt I should get to know you. You have drawn me to you. I don't know why, but it is so. I have never known it to happen before. I'll look for you at the bazaar tonight, maybe we could have a drink together there?'

'Yes maybe,' she whispered without taking her eyes from his. She felt she could listen to his Indian accent and sing-song tone all day. Finally realising she was staring into his eyes and he into hers, she mentally shook herself, dragged her eyes from his and turned. She swam to the pool steps and climbed out. Suddenly conscious of her more than adequate shape in her bikini she turned her back to Joseph and hastily wrapped her towel around her body.

'Bye, Joseph, see you later,' she called over her shoulder. Dazed, smiling in disbelief at what had just occurred she walked towards the guest rooms.

40

'Faye! Faye, come quick and look at this!' Sally shouted as she entered their room. 'I think they are macaques!' Sally was pointing up at the tree tops outside their room.

Faye, still digesting what had happened at the pool, simply obeyed Sally and looked upwards, open mouthed, not really taking in the antics of the small monkeys in the branches opposite their balcony. Sally continued,

'I think they are, but I could be wrong. I'll ask at the bar when we go down. I didn't know they lived around here, did you?' There was no reply.

'Faye, I said, I didn't know they lived around here.' She turned and looked at her. 'Are you alright? Do you think you have sunstroke? What's the matter with you?'

'No, I'm fine, just surprised by the monkeys.' She smiled at Sally. In that instance, Faye decided not to mention the conversation with Joseph. She never kept things from Sally, but somehow, this time, she decided to do just that. No reasoning, no justification, just an instant decision.

'Put on some after sun lotion then go and lay down for half an hour. I'll make you a cup of tea.' Sally turned and looked again at the monkeys then headed for the little kitchen area of the guest room. She gazed at Faye as she passed, concern on her face.

Later, whilst waiting for Gabby in the bar, Sally and Faye ordered a drink. Joseph was behind the bar. He smiled at Faye, she smiled back and gave him a little furtive wave.

'That man is always here,' Sally scowled at him. She had caught the little wave out of the corner of her eye. 'He gives me the creeps, I think there's something weird about him.'

'No, you're wrong, Sally, he's nice. I like him.' Sally turned and gaped at Faye as if she had spoken in a foreign language. However, before any more could be said, Gabby appeared. Another drink was ordered, and Joseph was forgotten, at least by Sally. Then before too long the girls were on their way in a tuk tuk to the Grand Evening Bazaar.

## 10

# The Grand Evening Bazaar

Outside the grounds of The Royal Hotel, just beyond the tall pillars, stood a line of tuk tuks. Probably twenty or more. The drivers lovingly polished the shiny coloured paintwork whilst waiting for their customers to emerge from the hotel. Canary yellow and royal blue, bright green and black, deep scarlet and tangerine, the tuk tuks were a colourful feast for the eyes. Garlands of yellow and orange flowers adorned each one and idols of the Indian Gods hung like air fresheners from the mirrors. Tasselled and embroidered gold fabrics draped the insides of the little cars and the old leather seats hinted at the age and usage.The proud drivers stood beside their little vehicles, happily calling to each other. It was expected to be a fruitful evening's work

Faye, Sally and Gabby waved goodbye to George and excitedly climbed aboard the first tuk tuk in the line. Two seats faced each other, carrying up to four people. Comfortable is not the word, but a bouncy, jolting ride carried the excited girls off to the Grand Evening Bazaar.

They were almost there when the tuk tuk joined a long crocodile of vehicles. All types of transport, including many tuk tuks, queued to enter the bazaar car park. They snaked along a road edged with bars and cafes radiating laughter and high spirits. It suggested the evening was popular with holidaymakers and locals alike. Aromas floating down the road from the bazaar and out of the cafes suggested spicy foods and treats were in store. Above the savoury smells came an over-whiff of cannabis. It added to the atmosphere of enchantment. The girls were eager to arrive and explore.

Faye's redness from the sun had faded slightly. Deciding to leave her hair loose tonight, it fanned wildly about her shoulders. She had applied shimmery green eyeshadow and black mascara. Her round cheeks were shiny with aftersun lotion. More freckles had emerged on her nose and cheeks, drawn out by the sun. She hoped to look attractive. The chance of bumping into Joseph had inspired her to make more of an effort. She felt energised. Sally was impressed assuming it was purely the holiday feeling and smiled at Faye, a loving sisterly smile. Faye smiled back, then with Joseph on her mind, she looked ahead to see if they were any nearer dismounting from the tuk tuk. Sally thought, *this is not the same person who was so distraught a short time ago* and innocently wondered if Faye had thought about the dead child during the last couple of days. She decided not to mention him and spoil Faye's new happy mood. Little did she know Charles was the last person on Faye's mind.

Finally, the driver pulled up in an enormous car park, told them they had arrived and pointed in the direction of lights, noise, smells and throngs of folks. They didn't need his help but in their shared enthusiasm, thanked him and paid him with a large tip. The driver was very happy and bowed to the girls with his hands together, prayer-like, beaming widely.

In the distance, they could hear a band playing. It sounded like a mixture of British pop and bhangra. The crowd moved in one direction and the girls joined in with the mass of people and snaked their way uphill, through the market stalls. Food stands and the stage for the music were on the plateau at the top of the hill and the masses appeared to be heading in that direction. It was difficult to see the wares on offer from all the stalls, as the crowds were so thick, however, with a little determination, when something caught their eye, they found they could struggle out of the wave of bodies and, appearing to be forcefully expelled, they fell laughing into a tradesman's compact zone.

However, the girls were mostly content to let the crowds take them along, casting brief peeks at the stalls and exiting the train of bodies into a stall from time to time.

. . . . .

The exquisite odours coming from the food stands wafted constantly towards them so, with unspoken agreement, it was time to dine when they arrived at the eating area.

Positioned in a wide circle, the stands were easy to wander round. There was food from all quarters of the world. Finally, they chose the menu from one stand for the simple reason that they saw another customer's tray being served and liked the look of it. Not knowing the names of anything, Sally ordered three of the same. The young men behind the stand were incredibly busy stirring, scooping, keeping the fires going, taking orders and serving. Rice and sauces bubbled away in enormous, double handled, gleaming, stainless steel pans.

It was a bit of a free for all around the food stands, all humanity appeared to have gathered there. So whilst Gabby was looking for an empty table, Faye was holding all the bags. She looked around her, hoping to catch sight of Joseph, but the crowds of people prevented her from seeing any further than a metre or so in any direction. Her head moved from side to side, searching faces.

Gabby managed to grab a wooden picnic table the minute it became vacant and shouted Faye. Realising she wasn't going to see Joseph she quickly joined Gabby. Sally dodged her way through the mob with three trays balanced in her hands. Each one held four small paper mache bowls, containing four different vegetarian dishes in spicy sauces, a mound of boiled rice, Roti bread and a tiny helping of very hot chilli sauce. The cutlery consisted of a plastic teaspoon. All three girls looked down at their tray, taking in the plastic teaspoon, then looked at each other. At the same time three opened bottles of Kingfisher beer were delivered by a young man to the table, making the meal complete. The girls laughed and simply enjoyed the peculiarity. It didn't take long for them to eat and they were happily fulfilled. The heat of the curry sauce added to the warmth of the evening. The strength of the chilli sauce made them gasp! Faye's little kiss curls stuck to the moist skin around her face which had reddened again from the food and alcohol.

Looking in their bags, they realised they had managed, despite the push and shove of the crowds, to do some shopping in the stalls. Gabby had bought three pairs of leather sandals and a colourful handbag. Sally had bought, for each of her staff in the hair salon, a silver filigree pendant on a silver chain and for herself, a pair of delicately decorated, wooden Nepalese massage balls. Faye had bought a sarong and a wooden elephant. She also had a little leather purse, decorated with plastic beads, some large silver earrings with green jewels and a pot of Indian Ayurveda healing cream for her tender sun kissed skin. They admired their purchases and each others. Faye decided to wear her earrings so put them on. They swung below her jawline, the green jewels shining through her hair as she moved her head from side to side. Sally and Gabby nodded their approval. It was a happy evening. Then, acquisitions packed away, they headed over to where the band played.

.  .  .  .  .

Not surprisingly, given the number of visitors to the bazaar, all the seats were taken in front of the stage. The three girls stood in the crowd assembled behind the seated area watching and listening to the band. A few single men were dancing on the small dance floor in front of the stage. The music was loud, the atmosphere electric, the heady scent of cannabis seemed stronger here. The people in the standing area were dancing on the spot in time with the music and Sally, Faye and Gabby felt themselves joining in, smiling, laughing and singing out loud to the words of the song. The beat was too good to ignore.

A hand touched Faye's elbow, she turned, smiling and found Joseph standing at her side. Her smile widened and she continued to jig up and down. He motioned for her to follow him towards a bar a short distance from the spectators. She was torn. She was pleased to see him and glad he had found her, but on the other hand she didn't want to leave Sally and Gabby just at that moment when they were enjoying themselves so much. However, flattery won out. She tapped her sister on the shoulder. Sally turned to her, also smiling and bobbing up and down. Her face fell when she saw Joseph beside Faye.

'I'm going to the bar with Joseph. Do you want a drink? Ask Gabby,' Faye shouted above the din to Sally.

'Don't go with him, Faye,' Sally shouted back. 'Stay with us. We'll never find each other again in these crowds!'

Faye felt Joseph touching her elbow again. A sharper squeeze.

'We'll just be over there. I won't go anywhere else.' Faye mouthed at Sally, she pointed to the bar. Before Sally could reply, Faye had turned towards Joseph and they both disappeared into the crowd. Sally tried to follow their progress with her eyes but lost them within seconds.

The circular bar beside the stage made the most of the serving areas for the evening's alcohol sales. It was huge yet the people waiting to be served stood four or five deep in places.

'Gabby, Joseph has taken Faye for a drink at that bar! I don't want her going off on her own with him. I don't like Joseph! I don't trust him!'

'Pardon, I can't hear you,' she shouted over the loud music.

Sally grabbed Gabby's hand and led her off in the direction of the bar. Alarmed for Faye's safety, Sally had an inexplicable underlying feeling of doom. She searched the heads of the people, seeking out the reddish frizz of her sister. Her jolly, party mood dropped from her like a stone, she couldn't see Faye anywhere.

Weaving through the crowds, they managed somehow to find themselves standing in a small gap at the bar. Sally scrutinised every face within her sights. The large circular bar was so busy, the staff were desperately trying to keep up with demand. The shape of it meant Sally could see all the people's faces standing at the bar around the other side. They all held similar expressions of hope. Hope that they will be the next one to be served. Rupees were waved in the air trying to catch the attention of the bar staff.

Now they could hear each other speak, she repeated to Gabby what Faye had said before she disappeared with Joseph. Then it dawned on her.

'That's why she put on makeup and looked so happy! She was expecting him! She never said! Wait until I see her! The little minx! If he upsets Faye, I'll swing for him. She's so fragile right now. She hasn't got over that child dying yet, whatever she says. She's a solid, sensible person as a rule but the sad affair of the child has knocked her sideways and she doesn't realise it,' Sally finished.

'I'm in much the same condition as Faye, mentally, you know. It takes a long time to recover from such a nasty shock, but I share your feelings of mistrust about Joseph. He asked me to go out with him.'

'What?' Sally exclaimed, 'Where? When?'

# 11

## The call

Gabby told her what had occurred with Joseph over her morning coffee.

'I came to your room to tell you, but you'd gone into town for the malaria tablets. Then, when I saw you again, it was busy and it just slipped my mind. Of course, I didn't know he was also trying it on with Faye or I would have made sure you both knew about it. Well, the rat! I don't know what else to call him. At least, now we know.'

'Yes, a big rat! We need to find Faye, before she gets tangled up with him,' Sally's eyes darted from person to person.

'Tell you what, I'll go this way, you go that way and we'll look around the whole of the bar. It's circular so we can go all the way round, and meet back here in ten minutes.'

'Good idea, Sally, see you shortly.' They parted and started the search. Sally took to the left of where they were. She kept as close to the bar as she could, and made her way around. The crowds continued to hug the counter of the bar, waiting to be served. Sally examined each person's hair, looking for the familiar frizz.

Gabby did the same, but set off to the right, she had to detour around large groups of people several times to stick to the circumference of the bar. The search wasn't made easy either, by the vast number of dark haired men. She made her way slowly and diligently round. All too soon she was back from where she started. Sally joined her after a few minutes.

'No luck!' Gabby declared, shaking her head.

'Me neither,' Chewing her lip, her eyes moved round the crowds in a large, slow circle.

'I don't believe it! They're there!' Sally cried, pointing to her left. 'I must have walked right past them.'

Faye and Joseph, their bottoms resting on the end of a packed wooden picnic table, were about 25 metres away, heads together, deep in conversation. They each held a half empty bottle of beer. He held her other hand up against his chest lovingly or it could be in controlling victory.

'Quick, let's get over there before they disappear again,' Gabby set off, dodging between the groups of drinkers. Sally was quick on her heels.

Joseph happened to look up, his eyes widened as he saw the ladies rapidly closing on them. Faye looked to see what had alarmed him. He hastily turned to Faye and whispered something in her ear. She nodded and smiled at him, then stood and walked towards Sally and Gabby. Joseph also stood but moved off in the opposite direction and disappeared into the crowds.

'Faye! I was worried about you! I don't want you to go off again with that man. You don't know him. He could be anything!' Sally went at Faye.

'He's not 'anything'! He's very nice and kind and I like him. You don't have to worry about me, Sal, I'm not a child!' she retorted.

'Why did he run off then, when he saw us coming?' Sally asked. Faye shrugged,

'He said he had people to see. It wasn't because of you.'

'Tell her what he said to you this morning, Gabby!' She nudged Gabby and nodded at her, 'Go on, tell her!'

Sighing before taking a breath Gabby said,

'He asked me to be his date tonight, Faye. Earlier, while you two were in town,' Gabby looked down knowing her words would hurt and humiliate Faye. Taken aback by this information, Faye stood open mouthed for a couple of seconds,

'You must have misunderstood him, Gabby, he asked me.' Chin held high, her eyes stared into Gabby's, challenging her to argue. Gabby saw at once that Faye was convinced of Joseph's integrity. She felt Faye's pride rise and knew it would be pointless to disagree. Turning to Sally, Gabby shook her head admitting defeat. She felt a rush of pity for Faye, Sally was right, she was fragile and vulnerable.

The jolly, party atmosphere, the girls enjoyed before Joseph appeared, dissolved. They decided to go back to the hotel. Faye was quiet and felt more than a little hostile towards Gabby. She had a sulky attitude with Sally and did not speak to either of them all the way back, keeping her face averted, looking out of the tuk tuk into the night.

Back in their own room at the hotel, Sally tried again,

'I'm sorry if you think I'm over protective of you, Faye. I just have a bad feeling about Joseph. I don't think it's a clever idea for you to get involved with him. He tried it on with Gabby too, you heard her.'

'We had a chat at the pool today. He's nice, Sally, he really is. I don't know what he said to Gabby, but she must have got it wrong. It's me he likes.'

Sally sighed,

'You didn't tell me. Why didn't you tell me? Did you think I wouldn't approve? Whatever he said to you, he also said it to Gabby. Why would she say that if he hadn't? He seems like a bit of a womaniser to me. I don't trust him.'

'Sally, I only had a drink with him tonight. This afternoon he said he wanted to take me to the Bazaar. I said we could have a drink afterwards, but he turned up and found me. He likes me, Sal, what's wrong with that? Anyway, we were only talking.'

'What about? What were you talking about?' Sally noticed that Faye was avoiding looking at her.

'Well, if you must know, he asked me about my job, my house at home, that kind of thing. He's really interested. He also told me about his house. He has a house a bit of a distance from here. It's a train ride away. He comes to work at the hotel during the season then goes home at the end of it, when the monsoon starts.'

'Is he married?'

'I don't think so, he didn't mention it and I didn't ask him. Anyway, it was only a drink. I can look after myself, you know.' Her chin went up again. Joseph had given her a warm exciting feeling which, although partly sullied by Gabby, she didn't want to spoil completely. Besides, for Faye, the night wasn't over yet! She ended the conversation by saying,

'I want to go to bed, Sally. I'm tired.'

Sally went in for a shower. Faye opened the balcony doors a little and when Sally came out of the bathroom, Faye was in bed with her eyes closed. Feeling unsettled but not overly concerned, Sally turned down the sheet on her bed,

'Good night, Faye. Sorry if I go on a bit.'

'It's alright, night Sally, see you in the morning.'

Sally turned off the light, got into bed and soon Faye could hear her breathing slow and regular indicating she was asleep. Faye laid with her eyes open, waiting.

.   .   .   .   .

After a little while, a male voice from below the balcony called quietly,

'Faye! Faye, come down.'

Faye slid silently out of bed. She wore only knickers so wrapped the new sarong around her and tied it under her left arm pit, leaving her shoulders bare, then silently opened the room door and crept out.

At the bottom of the steps, at the back of the guest rooms, Joseph stood waiting for her. When she appeared, he came towards her and swiftly pressed her into the shadow, against the wall in the corner. He took her in his arms and kissed her long and hard.

Taken aback somewhat, she tried to resist but within seconds she was kissing him back. His hands felt at her body, he rubbed them up and down her back. Then he found the open edge of the sarong down her left side. With his mouth pressed to hers, he found his way under the sarong with one hand and fondled her ample bare left breast. His mouth suddenly left hers and she found her body exposed to the air as he pulled the sarong to one side. She looked down. Her white skin, in the places the sun didn't touch, shone like ivory, even in that dark corner. He cupped both breasts with his palms and his mouth was upon them. His breathing altered and he dropped one hand to her groin, discovering her knickers. Faye, at this point, came to her senses and pushed his hands off her and pulled the sarong closed.

'No!'

'Faye! Come on, what's the matter? I love you. I want you. You are so beautiful. Come on, let me . . .'

'No! Joseph, no!' They were whispering.

He pressed her against the wall with his body and she could feel his excitement.

'Joseph, no! I don't want this. Get off me!' *I should have known,* she was alarmed but continued to whisper.

'Oh, Faye, it's alright. It's natural between a woman and a man.' He was kissing her again, hands on her breasts.

'No!' She pushed him away. 'I don't want to do this here, it's not right. We barely know each other. I'm going back in.'

'I'm sorry, Faye, please don't go. I just want to love you. You are the one. We are meant to be together in this way, like lovers.' He leaned in towards her and started kissing her again.

Dragging her mouth from his,

'I can't do this here, outside, it's not right. What if someone comes? I must go in.'

He stood back. She felt the night air replace his hot body on her skin. In the dark, Faye felt his manner alter, a touch of sharp mockery came into his voice.

'Alright, go in then. I won't be here tomorrow. I must go somewhere. I may not come back at all, then you will be sorry. Besides, there is something I want to ask you. It is very important, and your answer will change your life, our lives. But if you go in now . . .' he paused, she could feel him staring at her in the dark as if he was mentally phrasing his next sentence, 'I will think you do not love me and I will walk away.'

Faye stared at his dark shape for a few moments, indecision flooded her mind, she didn't want him to go away. She didn't want to lose him. She could feel her heart beating within her chest. He had asked her to the bazaar, said he liked her and just now said he loved her. She said,

'One more kiss then, just a kiss, nothing else, then tell me what . . .' She was pressed triumphantly to the wall.

The whole of his body against hers, his mouth on hers. She didn't object as he whispered his plan for them in her ear. And she didn't object as he continued with the seduction.

It was some time before she crept back to her bed.

*He loves me. He thinks I'm beautiful,* she thought, smiling as she silently slid between the sheets. Her body sticky from his actions, his odour swathing her. She hugged herself reliving the night's event and what he had asked of her.

# 12

## Faye's announcement

'Sal, Sally,' Faye gently rubbed Sally's shoulder. 'Cup of tea for you,' she placed it on the bedside cabinet. 'I'm out on the balcony, it's so beautiful out here this morning.'

Sally, opening her eyes, sat up and took a sip of her tea remembering last night's argument about Joseph. With a worried frown she watched Faye out on the balcony, peering through the early morning mist at the little hamlet across the fields. She was chewing her bottom lip.

'Morning Faye, yes it's beautiful again. How are you this morning?' Sally joined her out in the morning sunlight, cup of tea in hand.

Faye hesitated for a second, she didn't want to ruin Sally's holiday, not after Sal had done so much for her. Drawing a breath she said,

'Sally, I'm sorry about last night, about Joseph following me to the bazaar and about speaking to Gabby as I did. I acted like a spoiled teenager. I'll go and apologise to Gabby when we go down for breakfast.' She cast Sally an imploring look. 'Do you think we can put it behind us and enjoy the rest of the holiday? Will Gabby forgive me? I was horrible to her.'

'She's a lovely girl, I'm sure she'll forgive you. Shall we get ready and knock at her door on our way down to the restaurant?' Smiling, she patted Faye on the arm.

'Yes, I'd prefer to get it over with sooner rather than later. I'll go and get ready.' As Faye turned away, there was a tormented look in her eyes. Sally didn't see it but, nonetheless, she continued to feel uneasy about her. She stood on the balcony for a few minutes trying to settle her thoughts. Why did she feel unnerved? The sisters had always enjoyed a trusting, open and honest relationship. Why did she think it should be any different now? Joseph?

.  .  .  .  .

'Oh, don't think about it any more,' Gabby said. 'Men! Eh? They are the cause of all our troubles, I'm sure of it. I'm just pleased you have put that slimeball Joseph out of your life!' Laughing at herself, Gabby didn't see Faye's face struggling to maintain her friendly beam.

'Tell you what, let's walk by that posh eatery in town today and book a table for tomorrow evening. I'll phone George and see if he and Sunny are free to join us. We'll have a blowout. What do you say?'

'You are an angel, Gabby. Great idea,' Faye smiled and gave Gabby a hug. 'Now what are we going to do today?'

'Shall we look in reception, they have some excursions advertised on the stand by the window?'

A young man came to take their order for breakfast and whilst it was being prepared, Sally ran to reception and collected several leaflets advertising events and wonderful exciting trips to exotic places. During the meal, they poured over the leaflets. Eventually they chose a boat trip to an uninhabited island several miles up the coast. In addition to the sailing, the leaflet said, they offered fantastic views, fishing, a barbeque, snorkelling and sunbathing. All included in the price, it sounded perfect.

Joseph did not appear that morning. Neither was he mentioned again after the apology was offered and accepted. To the other two girls Faye appeared to have put him out of her mind. She seemed calm and content. In fact, they raised eyebrows and smiled at each other as Faye became gently enthusiastic when discussing sailing away to a tropical island.

Twenty minutes after swallowing the last piece of toast, the girls were in a tuk tuk on the way to board the boat.

. . . . .

The day was a tremendous success. Sailing to the island took just over two hours, during which time the crew handed out fishing lines, each with a hook on the end. The passengers, including Faye, Sally and Gabby squealed with revulsion as they impaled live maggots onto the hooks and thereafter shrieked with horror as first one and then another of them hooked a bite. Each little fish, hauled out of the water, was small and blackish-blue with flowing fins and tail. Too pretty to catch in such a cruel way. A crew member unhooked the fish, one by one, and laughing at the line bearers discomfort, threw them back into the sea. Faye truly hoped the little fish that she caught would survive to enjoy another day. Simultaneously the girls wound the lines in and put them away, not happy with the resultant suffering they had bestowed.

Anchoring in a bay alongside several other excursion boats, the crew assisted the girls and the other nine members of the party to wade to the beach where they joined the passengers of the other boats.

Broken shells made up the substance of the beach. Cream, white, yellow and pink, which painlessly crunched under bare feet. It was stunningly beautiful. The girls and the other members of the party enjoyed being served with cool crisp salad and roti baked fresh on hot stones on the barbeque. But the major surprise was the deliciously barbecued barracuda. Who would have expected barracuda to taste so luscious? Sitting in the shade of large square pergolas, cross legged on blankets on the extremely hot beach, eating the scrumptious foods, it was truly paradise. A dangerously large bladed knife cut fresh pineapple and coconut into pieces which was then offered for dessert. Ice-cold beer, wine or water flowed in abundance. How the drinks remained chilled, they discussed at length but without an answer. After the meal, the girls languished in the humid shade of the pergola. They laid feeling blessed and looked forward to snorkelling in the warm water.

Joseph's name did not crop up and Faye appeared settled and more relaxed than she had been all the holiday.

Sally felt she had her sister back. What she didn't know was Faye had two reasons to be happy. One - she thought she was loved by Joseph, and a little bit of flattery is always lovely. Two - he had offered her a way out from returning and facing up to the recent events at work. This alone lifted a heavy weight from her shoulders enabling her to smile genuinely again.

．　．　．　．　．

The following evening George and Sunny joined them at the restaurant. The meal was lengthy, with a colossal number of courses and deliciously spicy. The staff, attentive to their every need, drinks flowed freely and once again the companions relaxed to enjoy each other's company.

Sunny turned out to be handsome, charming, funny and extremely good company, as was George. The girls all noted the endearing looks and touches that passed between the men and were happy for them. Sunny took an interest in each of the girls, listening with full attention as they spoke. In return, George and Sunny opened up and told the girls about their relationship; how they met, how the relationship is maintained in secret, their very different home lives. Guileless and honest, George and Sunny gazed at each other and held hands as they talked. It was the first time they had divulged this information to anyone else.

'It's a relief to share it with other people,' George smiled sadly and Sunny nodded.

'We obviously feel comfortable with our new-found friends. Here's to friendship!' Sunny shouted, laughing, lifting his glass and as they all raised their glasses, another round of drinks was required.

At the end of the evening, Gabby went up to Faye and Sally's room for a late coffee and they agreed what a lovely couple George and Sunny made. They were happy and sad at the same time. Happy they could be together sometimes and sad they could not be together openly all the time.

'Maybe it's best to be together only for short spells so the novelty doesn't wear off and the day to day boring humdrum stuff does not interfere in the relationship,' Sally said.

'Yes, it sounds like a fabulous way of living but to be apart for such a long time after each trip must be hard. I don't know how often they manage to talk to each other, but I'll bet it's not often,' Gabby added.

Faye put her opinion in, waving her coffee cup in the air,

'I think it's romantic and hopefully they will shock their grandchildren in the future with their tales of love, eroticism and desire.' The girls hooted and giggled.

. . . . .

The rest of the holiday continued in the same mood. The days were thrilling with stirring discoveries. The evenings full of fabulous food, drink, friendships and laughter, sometimes with George and Sunny, sometimes just the three girls. Gabby spent each day and evening with Faye and Sally, usually meeting up at breakfast and remaining with them until bedtime.

One morning, nearing the end of the holiday, Gabby found herself alone at breakfast. Faye and Sally had not come down yet. She was being served by a familiar face, one of the young men who worked in the kitchen and bar, called Ranji.

'What has happened to Joseph?' she asked, 'I haven't seen him for quite a few days'.

'Oh, madam, Joseph has gone back home, he left the hotel early. He was asked to leave by the management, but he also said he had to do something important at home. I do not know what. Why? Did he offend you? The hotel will not be having him back next season. He has caused trouble with the guests a few times over the season, did he offend you also?'

Gabby leaned forward towards Ranji, eyebrows raised,

'No, not really, what sort of trouble with the guests?'

'He was disrespectful to the young ladies. It was reported that he tried to . . .' he looked up and stopped talking..

'Hi Gabby, sorry we're late. We slept a little longer this morning in the holiday mode, we won't like it when we're back at work having to get up early!' Sally sat down at the table. Gabby's head spun round to locate Faye. She didn't want her to know she was talking about Joseph behind her back. However Faye, smiling over at the boys behind the bar as she neared, didn't appear to have heard.

'Morning Ranji, can we order breakfast also, whilst you are here?' Sally smiled at Ranji, not picking up on the serious moment Gabby was sharing with him before being interrupted.

'Of course, madam, what would you like?' Cheerfully he searched for his pencil.

'Gabby, me and Sally were talking, do you fancy taking a trip to the market to get some take home gifts.' Faye butted in, sitting down.

'I'll just have a roll, boiled egg and a pot of coffee please.'

'Yes, same for me please.'

'Toast, butter, marmalade and tea, I think, please.' Gabby concluded. She opened her eyes wide and shook her head slightly at Ranji as if to say, 'Do not mention our conversation.' Ranji nodded and went off with the order.

'We only have two more days left so, if you want, we can go to the market today, then tomorrow we can just chill out by the pool or the beach and top up our tans for the last time. What do you think?' Sally asked Gabby.

'Sounds like a good idea. What do you think, Faye?'

'Yes, I would like to stay around the pool tomorrow.' Faye spoke with certainty.

'OK, that's decided then. I'll pop and cash a Traveller's Cheque in reception after breakfast, then we'll go spending. I've seen some fabulous leather bags for the girls in the salon. Are you buying anything Faye?'

'No but I'll come and watch you spend your money. I may need what's left of my rupees.'

'For what?'

'Oh, you never know.' Faye smiled gently and a little mysteriously.

The last full day of the holiday dawned, and the threesome settled on the sun beds around the pool. The plan was to tan, swim and relax as much as possible, before leaving for the airport in the morning. Their last day happened to be St Valentine's Day and the hotel had an evening party planned for the guests. All the staff were working - it was expected to be a full house. As the girls laid sunbathing, the staff dressed the dining area and the bar with red table cloths and tall red candles. Red, heart shaped, helium filled balloons were attached by lengths of red ribbon to the end of each table, creating a festive look. The atmosphere was affable as the staff happily prepared for the evening and the guests looked forward to the party, albeit for Faye, Sally and Gabby it was the final evening before returning to Great Britain and the February weather.

They didn't expect to see George and Sunny as it was their last night together.

'I feel so sad for George and Sunny, they won't know when they'll see each other again,' Gabby said.

'Yes, I know. How can they stand it?' Sally sighed. Faye remained silent, gazing over the glittering pool.

'We'll have to be nice to George tomorrow. I hope I'm sat beside him again.' Gabby said and laughed remembering her horror when he sat next to her on the journey here.

. . . . .

Dressed for the evening, the girls met in the bar for a drink prior to the evening meal. The staff had exchanged their floral shirts for red silk to complete the Valentine's Day party look. A live band created a lively mood and a merry evening was anticipated by all.

Faye joined in the merriment at the beginning of the evening but as time passed she became noticeably nervous and constantly looked over her shoulder towards the pillars at the entrance. Sally saw this and with a concerned look on her face, she stretched across the table and touched Faye's wrist.

Shouting to be heard above the loud music, 'What's the matter, Faye, you seem a little anxious. Are you worried about going back home?'

'Sally, I need to tell you . . .'

At that moment Joseph appeared around the corner of the bar, quickly scanned the bar area, and smiling, he sauntered over to the girls table. They all saw him, Sally and Gabby gazed open mouthed as he approached. Faye, looking up at him from her sitting position, gave him a brief smile and then her head spun back to face Sally, wearing a look of defiance.

'Faye,' Joseph spoke loud enough for all to hear, 'I have returned for you, as I said. Are you ready to go?'

'Give me a moment, will you Joseph?' Nodding at Faye, his eyes narrowed as he looked insolently into the faces of Sally and Gabby, and with an arrogant air strolled to the bar and asked for a beer. Sally watched him strut away for a second then turned and stared at Faye, her eyes wide and mouth pursed, ready to speak but without words.

The jolly Valentine ambiance plummeted faster than an icy waterfall. Gabby gawked from Faye to Joseph and back again. The staff in their lovely red silk shirts, stopped in mid-serve as if playing musical statues, gaped at Joseph and looked questioningly at each other, across at the situation unfolding and back. Meanwhile the band spluttered to a halt and silence filled the space. Sitting in the sudden quiet, the other holidaymakers, not knowing exactly why, held their breath, like an audience awaiting the climax of the final scene.

Then Faye, causing Sally to become even more aghast, announced,

'Sally, I'm not going back to the UK. I'm staying here with Joseph.'

'WHAT?'

## 13

## *The parting*

'Joseph, I'm just popping to the room to get my things.' He nodded, raised his hand in response and turned back to the bar. Faye started towards the guest rooms. Sally was hot on her heels, her brow knitted together, her eyes frantically searching the back of Faye's head in incomprehension, as she sped after her.

'What do you mean? You're staying here with Joseph? You are just popping to get your things? What do you mean? We're going home tomorrow!' Sally was directly behind her, matching step for step, her voice pitched high with alarm.

Faye spun round to face Sally and then after a slight pause, she breathed in and calmly informed her,

'We are going to live in Joseph's house, down in south Goa. He asked me to stay and I said yes. We are in love and want to be together. He has come back for me.'

'I don't understand . . . '

'I don't want to go home, back to work, I don't feel as if I can. I can't go back to my job. I'm no good at it any longer. I can't do it. But here . . . Joseph loves me, he wants me, so I'm going to move in with him for a while.'

'Faye! FAYE! You don't even know him. You only met him last week and then only for a couple of days. No, Faye!' as they climbed the stairs to their room, 'No, you're not going to live with him. I won't allow it! There's something not right about him. Both me and Gabby felt it.'

The sisters faced each other,

'Sally, he loves me. He's told me, he wants us to be together. I feel happy and alive with him. He doesn't judge me as a failure.'

'Nobody judges you as a failure. The boy died because of his nasty father and his spineless mother, not you. What about the court case? What about Dad? Faye, please come home with me. You'll regret this, I know you will. He tried it on with me on our first night here. He tried it on with Gabby . . .'

Faye's chin rose and her eyes flashed,

'She was mistaken, it's me he wants. He told me he loves me, he wants me to be with him properly, like a couple.'

'When? When did he tell you all this? When? You've hardly seen him, and he certainly hasn't been around for the last few days.'

'Err . . . at the bazaar and other times. You haven't been with me every hour of every day!' Faye avoided mentioning the late night meeting on the stairs.

'Well I have, as near as dammit!' Their voices were rising. 'You are not staying with that man! He is not right for you! I don't know what he's up to, but it won't do you any good, believe me!'

'You just don't want me to be happy! You'd rather I went home and be miserable, wouldn't you?' Faye could hear herself sounding childlike but couldn't help herself.

'Oh, don't talk daft. I love you and have your interests at heart, which is more than he has, I'll bet!'

Faye rapidly stuffed her belongings in her suitcase, gathered her bag and hat and returned to the bar with Sally in her wake. All eyes were on the sisters as they returned, the staff and other holidaymakers silently agog. Sally remained steps behind her, pleading, arguing, ordering and at last shouting at Faye to try to make her stay. But to no avail!

Faye said no more to Sally but shouted to Joseph,

'I'm ready, Joseph.'

He appeared to relish the attention and stretched out the moment. As if in slow motion he drained his glass and placed it on the bar.  Sneering at the staff he crossed the floor and took Faye's suitcase. His head held high, an air of triumph haloed around him. Smugly he grinned in Sally's direction, gave the same self-satisfied smirk to Gabby and then to the boys behind the bar. Gabby could only stare, open mouthed, helpless to do anything.

Taking Faye by the elbow, he said,

'We need to be on our way if we're going to catch the last train.'

With that they set off, side by side, towards the tall pillars and the row of waiting tuk tuks.

'Faye, please, *FAYE!*' Sally followed them down the drive in a pathetic little trot. 'Faye, please listen to me. Don't do this. What about Dad? He's not well. What will he say? Faye, come back, let's talk about this.'

Joseph climbed into the leading tuk tuk and held out his hand to help Faye in. Faye turned to look at Sally, an apologetic look on her face.

'I'm sorry Sally, I'm going with Joseph. I've made up my mind. I'll phone when we get to his house.'

Sally's face crumpled and tears ran down her cheeks as she realised defeat. Faye, watching her strong sister distraught, felt her throat tightening. She swallowed quickly and looked away, tears starting to well up. *Was she doing the right thing?*

Utterly wretched and bereft of speech, Sally's shoulders slumped and her arms hung limply down her sides. As the tuk tuk set off, Joseph's face appeared at the little plastic rear window. A sneer played around his lips, he was mocking her.

She stood watching until the tuk tuk disappeared at the end of the road. An arm crept around Sally's waist. It was Gabby.

'Come back to the hotel Sally, come on, she's gone. You did your best. That swine has got inside her head. Come on, let's get you a strong drink.'

The band had resumed playing and the evening regained some of its jollity for the staff and other holidaymakers. Gabby led Sally back to their table. Gabby waved at one of the bar staff and ordered two large brandies. Sally, shaken to the core, cried and through her tears, she snivelled to Gabby, trying to comprehend what had just happened and what she could have done to prevent it. She blamed herself, she was after all, Faye's big sister.

# 14

## Shimoga

Masses of shouting people surged forward as one, unperturbed by the loud hooting as the train came to a halt at the platform. Hot smokey air squirted across the platform and swirled around them. Faye's sweltering body temperature increased as the heat from the engine increased the fieriness of the humid air. Joseph gripped Faye's hand and he joined the sway of people, dragging her unceremoniously towards an open carriage door. She became pinned between two men fighting to get onboard. Joseph, using her suitcase as an object of armour, was already up in the train doorway. He pulled, and she was wrenched with force between the men, falling ungraciously onto her hands and knees in the doorway of the train.

She climbed to her feet with some difficulty in the tight space. Looking up at Joseph for reassurance, did she see him rolling his eyes? Surely not!

It was almost midnight but packed with hot, tired commuters. All the seats were taken - standing room only. The sticky atmosphere on board held several flavours. Faye could definitely discern spice and also some kind of fuel, probably from the train but on top of that there was a large hint of sweat. *Mmm, don't know if I'll get used to that*, she silently contemplated.

Faye straightened herself up, looked around and caught Joseph's eye, she gave him a brave smile.

'How long does it take to get to your house?'

'About nine hours to Udupi, if the track is good. Then three hours to Shimoga. We'll be there by midday tomorrow.' He didn't smile back.

'Oh? It's a long journey. I didn't realise it was so far. Will we have to stand the whole way?'

'No, it will empty further down the line. We'll be able to sit and rest then. As I said, this is the last train of the day, it's always very busy.' He looked up and down the carriage as if seeking someone. Then he stared into space, his face set and conversation between them discouraged. Faye was dismayed. She had imagined a romantic train journey, sat together in a private carriage, making plans and holding hands. She silenced a sigh and tried to look, through the little gaps in between heads, out of the window. The train set off and left the station. Any hope of a view disappeared into the darkness. So she too stared into space, trying to think of something cheerful to say to him.

'I'm looking forward to seeing your house.' He looked down at her and nodded. He didn't smile.

'And I'm so excited about us spending time together, on our own. It'll be lovely to just be ourselves and get to know each other properly?' She ended her statement with a questioning lilt to encourage him to reply. Joseph looked down at her again, made a grunting noise and then continued to stare ahead.

Faye bowed her head, wondering what she had done to change his mood towards her. Her last exchange with Sally came into her mind including a picture of her sister's upset face. Doubt crept in about what she was doing. *He's probably tired*, she excused. *It's going to be a long journey and he's only just come back to fetch me. He's come back to fetch me,* she repeated in her mind and that cheered her a little.

Looking around she realised she was the only westerner in the carriage. All the other passengers were men in traditional Indian clothing. Packed tightly as they were, some appeared to be sleeping as they stood, most looked dirty having recently finished manual work. Those sitting nodded or stared out of the window into the night. There wasn't much conversation considering the volume of chatter that had been deafening on the platform. Uncomfortably, Faye noticed those standing nearby were looking at her, all of them! She lowered her eyes to the floor and remained that way. Holding onto a seat back, she realised Joseph had let go of her hand.

Hours and several stops later with passengers getting on and off, they managed to find a seat, where they could sit together. Faye tried to converse, but Joseph continued to be distant. Faye remained dismayed but hopeful that after a rest from the travelling Joseph would return to his former charming self. Joseph closed his eyes and appeared to sleep.

Faye looked around the train. Large fans attached to the ceiling, in pairs, at regular intervals along the length of the carriage whirred quite noisily. Most of the upper windows were slanted open, allowing the warm breeze to flow through. At the end of the carriage a couple of men stood smoking and chatting in an open doorway. Otherwise the rail users were quiet or slept.

Suddenly the train entered a tunnel. In several seconds the carriage filled with smoke and fumes, billowing in through the slanted windows and the open door. Faye coughed and flapped her hands in front of her face. The train exited and the air cleared quickly. However it left an impression - in between her teeth she could feel small particles of grit. As her tongue ran around her mouth she wished she had a bottle of cold water. Her clothes and skin felt dusty. She brushed herself down ineffectually. Desperately, she wanted to express surprise to Joseph and laugh about it with him, but he slept, oblivious to her needs. She settled again. After a while she became uncomfortable and wriggled on the hard, moulded plastic seat, trying not to disturb Joseph. She certainly didn't feel the happy anticipation she had expected.

The carriage continued to empty as it coursed its way south, making many more stops.

.   .   .   .   .

As dawn broke, Faye was able, at last, to see the countryside flash past the window. It appeared to be mostly farmland and seemed verdant and the soil red and fertile. She wanted to wake Joseph and point out different things but she didn't dare. She let him sleep. In the early morning, a man came down the carriage with a large tureen. He stopped at several seats. Then reaching Faye's seat he looked at Faye, eyebrows up, expecting her to know what he was selling. She nudged Joseph. In his own language he said something to the man who then poured two paper cups of hot, sweet tea.

Then for the first time since the train set off, Joseph spoke. 'Do you have rupees for the chai?'

'Oh? Yes I have, how much?' Joseph took a handful of coins from her purse. She noticed he pocketed the change. *Would he think I'm petty if I mentioned it?* she wondered. The tea seller moved on to his next customer.

'We'll be at Udupi in about 45 minutes, then a train to Shimoga. After that a tuk tuk to the village and then we walk the rest of the way. The house is on the outskirts of the village. I have been and made it all ready for us. I think you will like it. It may not be what you are used to in England, but I think you will get used to it very soon.' Joseph said.

'I can't wait to see it,' Faye's mood lifted. Joseph was talking to her again. *We'll be happy, I'm sure,* she thought.

'How far is it from the village? What's the village called? Can you describe it to me?'

'You will see soon enough,' and with that he fell silent again.

. . . . .

As the train slowed and drew into Udupi station, Faye saw narrow streets lined with pastel coloured small buildings, somewhat shabby looking with corrugated roofs, appearing to be businesses of sorts with open fronts. Tuk tuks, bicycles, motor bikes and cows filled the narrow streets. There was the odd car in amongst what looked like a melee. She caught a glimpse of a market heading off in another direction. Rows of stalls drifting away as far as the eye could see. It was early in the morning but already busy. In the distance high-rise buildings could be seen. It was a larger town than she had imagined.

Dismounting the train, Joseph helped her down the steps and carried her suitcase to the booking office. Again, he asked Faye for rupees, this time for the fare to Shimoga. She didn't mind paying, of course, but hadn't expected to. *Why should he pay for everything?*

Changing trains was yet again a traumatic rush, push and shove. At least on this part of the journey it was daylight, and whilst enduring long silences from Joseph she could look out at the landscape to see the unfamiliar environment. The train sped past villages and flat farmland interspersed with vast wide rivers and forests. A mountainous and rocky area flashed past but not before she saw a white cascading waterfall causing a misty effervescence to swirl at the foot. It took her breath away and she gazed out wondering at the beauty of it.

Finally, they alighted in Shimoga. Joseph appeared to have an urgency to get them into a tuk tuk and on the way to the village and finally to the house.

*Is he ashamed of me?* Faye wondered.

Firmly taking Faye by the elbow he guided her to the waiting queue of tuk tuks directly outside the station. Realising she hadn't seen any of her new town, as they left Shimoga Faye was eagerly trying to take in all she could.

After five or six miles the tuk tuk turned off the main tarmacked road and onto a rough track, flanked on either side by what Faye considered to be jungle. As they travelled the track became narrower and narrower. It seemed quite dark as the trees joined together overhead. Finally, the tuk tuk came into a clearing.

A hundred metres ahead Faye could see a wide street, lined by small properties. Painted white with red tiled roofs, each little house was surrounded by bamboo fencing. The street was packed dirt, no pavement, no tarmac, no street lights, just dirt. Red dirt as in the fields. Tall trees and palms were in profusion waving above the village.

The tuk tuk did a three-point turn in the clearing and came to a halt. Faye lifted her suitcase off the tuk tuk while a short conversation, in their native language, passed between Joseph and the driver. Joseph handed over a few coins and without acknowledgement the driver set off and disappeared the way he had come.

Pulling at the handle of Faye's suitcase, Joseph appraised the weight of the bag. *What does she carry in here? It weighs a tonne.* He silently ruminated. *She is an irritating woman. She is not the most beautiful and she has flab like pig fat. The sooner I can get my hands on her money, the better. She owns a house in England, a large house, from what she told me, so she has wealth. It will take all my strength to keep her sweet; she never shuts up and when she does, she's miserable.*

Within these few seconds, ignorant of Joseph's unpleasant thoughts, Faye gazed at the village. She didn't even know its name. It appeared to be just one deserted street. At the end stood a tall metal cylindrical tower, probably about five metres high. She didn't know what it could be. She wanted to ask but, glancing at Joseph's face, thought better of it. Beyond the cylinder it was jungle, behind the houses on both sides of the street it was jungle.

In the middle of the street, a colourful object caught Faye's eye. It seemed to be some type of worshipping place, as tall as a fully-grown man and made up of several different layers. Each layer was painted a bright primary colour and adorned with pretty, colourful items. She couldn't make out what they were so took a step towards it, but before she could investigate further Joseph lifted Faye's suitcase and said,

'Let's go,' and turned away from her towards an opening in the vegetation.

Leading the way with the suitcase, Faye fell in step behind him. There wasn't room on the path for them to walk side by side. Joseph kept up a swift pace and Faye struggled to maintain the speed of the march.

It was quiet. Not a sound came from the village or the jungle. Neither was there conversation between them until Faye noticed flat circular objects, with holes in the centres, lining each side of the path. They were the size of dinner plates and the holes in the centre as wide as tennis balls.

'What are they, Joseph?' she asked, pointing.

'They are the webs of the funnel spiders. They will not hurt you if you leave them alone, don't worry.'

*Oh no, I won't worry! Funnel spiders! Webs as big as dinner plates! No, I won't worry, and I'll leave them alone! No doubt about that!* Faye thought sarcastically. *I'm not sure about this place,* she contemplated anxiously as she trudged behind Joseph. Looking around, the funnel spider's webs were abundant on the ground, moreover they were hanging from the tree trunks and, as Faye's eyes traced up the trunks, she discovered the webs were in the overhead foliage too. *Oh no!* Cringing, her shoulders up around her ears, knowing the spider's webs hung over her head, she ran to keep up with Joseph. No, she wasn't sure about this place at all!

Then the house came into view!

# 15

## The house

At first sight, it seemed to Faye, like a cute little house from a nursery rhyme. She didn't think that way about it for long. The small, square, one storey building, appeared like the houses in the village - white walls with a red tiled roof. Well, it had been white at some time in the past. The walls had a greyish-green hue hinting of mould, with a darker green around the bottom. It stood alone in an egg-shaped clearing in the trees. The path from the village was the only way in or out. Dense jungle surrounded the small house giving her the impression that it was no place for humans. On one side of the house part of the roof extended to create an outside covered area, like a porch. Thin bamboo stood in a line to form a wall at one side of the outside area. Against this wall, chopped wood had been dumped in readiness to light a fire and a selection of dusty cooking pans and implements were haphazardly laying beside the firewood. In the centre of the porch, on the packed earth, a circle of stones encased ash and bits of burnt wood. A metal pan stand and a tripod for hanging a kettle laid in the dirt at the side of the fireplace.

Joseph, marching ahead with her suitcase, entered beneath the extended roof of the porch and pushed open the wooden door of the house. It scraped noisily across the floor. He entered and then paused to wave Faye inside behind him.

Halting in the doorway, Faye's jaw dropped. She had been named by her sister as the least house-proud person in the world and she acknowledged her housekeeping skills lacked finesse, but she wasn't prepared for this.

Whilst Joseph squatted in one corner of the one room house, fiddling with something, she squinted around, shocked. It was dismal, gloomy and grimy. Faye sniffed the damp air, tasting it. Her wide eyes travelled from one miserable aspect to another. Thousands of dust particles, a snow storm in the heat, swirled in the solo sun beam coming from a small window. She shivered even though the outside temperature was in the mid-thirties.

The room had one door, where she stood, and to the right, the small window. Bizarrely, the window sported curtains made in Fred Flintstone fabric! Beneath the window a Singer sewing machine stood. A treadle underneath made it completely independent of electricity. Faye's mind popped into her Grandma's house at the sight of the sewing machine but popped back to the here and now within a second. It passed through her mind that a female had lived here. Placed on either side of the sewing machine were two dining chairs. Dark wood, tall straight back chairs with red leather covered seats. The leather was cracked and torn, grey kapok stuffing peeped through. Her suitcase stood on end beside one of the chairs.

Rough, bare concrete made up the floor, no coverings, rugs, tiles, nothing. To the left lay a mattress directly on the concrete. It was threadbare, blue and white striped and badly stained. It must have been fifty years old, at least. Someone, she presumed Joseph, had tried to cover the stains with a thin, worn, faded sarong, without effect.

Against the back wall stood a cupboard with a mesh covered door. She guessed this was to keep food safe from insects or vermin. Through the mesh she could make out a pile of plates and other crockery on the lower shelf and some paper bags on the upper. On top sat a Victorian style ceramic jug and bowl set, green and cream with pink roses. There didn't appear to be much more. She didn't know which surprised her the most, the miserable lack of comforts or the Fred Flintstone curtains!

Joseph's outline suddenly glowed in a halo of light as the candles he lit fused the room with a yellow tint. Four tall white candles stood on the floor in mismatched saucers and plates. Light didn't improve the interior. The expensive scented candles she had been bought for Christmas came into her mind.

Faye had not moved since stepping on the threshold except to raise her hand to cover her mouth in disbelief. Joseph appeared totally oblivious to her silence and the shock her stillness signalled. He rose and came towards her; his charming smile resumed its place on his face.

'Where can I put my things?' she stammered, pointing to her suitcase.

'Come here, my love, never mind your things for now. Come and sit on the bed with me. It's been a long time since I held you.'

As much as she had wanted a romantic life with Joseph, at that moment Faye felt anything but dreamy eyed. It had been a good twenty-minute walk from the tuk tuk. She looked down and caught sight of her feet. The skin around her sandals held a dirty red colour from the dusty path. Her whole body felt sweaty and sticky. The house was, in her view, not conducive with romance either. She wanted to wash, she badly needed to use the loo and in addition she wanted a drink. A large drink of ice cold water preferably.

'I . . . er . . . need to use the bathroom Joseph, first. Where is it?'

'Of course, I'm in such a hurry to have you. I'll take you to the place. Then we'll take our time getting to know each other.' His face maintained a fixed smile.

She hadn't moved from the doorway so he pushed past her, a little roughly she thought, but she followed close on his heels and once out of the porch she lifted her face to the sun and breathed in the warm, fresh, sunny air. He disappeared around the far side of the house. Tripping behind him, Faye discovered the 'bathroom' was three walls made of bamboo with gaping gaps and the main event was a hole in the ground. A rusty bucket, empty, stood in the corner. Not very private as the fourth wall was completely missing but faced the jungle. Open to all who may wish to see. Except there wasn't anyone else close by apart from the funnel spiders. Then, high in the trees, the caw, caw, caw call of crows commenced, and they flapped their strong wings to announce her arrival at the bathroom. Faye, with her back against the bamboo, looked around her and up to the trees, her brows drawn and lips clamped tight. Joseph watched her for a moment then said,

'I'll wait in the house for you, shall I?'

'Oh, would you mind, I'd really like to wash too, Joseph, before we . . . er . . . after the journey, you know.'

'Huh! I'll bring you some water, wait here,' he barked. With that he snatched up the rusty bucket and disappeared back around the house. Faye took a step forward and peered down the hole. Her nose sensed something unsavoury. She felt very unsettled.

## 16

## Girls go home

Sally, desperately upset and unhappy about how the holiday ended, reran in her mind, over and over, the sight of Faye getting into the tuk tuk with Joseph and disappearing around the corner. Could she have done something to stop him getting his slimy hands on her? Faye was so vulnerable after the heart-breaking event at work, Sally berated herself for not being more observant and talking it all through with her.

After Gabby steered her back to the hotel bar, the staff, who had seen it all, surrounded them with comfort and sympathy. Each staff member had something to say about Joseph and none of it was good. It was generally agreed that he was a bad sort with a reputation at the hotel for taking advantage of lady visitors. In fact, one of the boys informed them that Joseph was sacked for disrespectful behaviour towards a young girl. He had heard a rumour and actually saw Joseph being summoned to the office. Then they all agreed an old lady, who was here two weeks ago, had reported him. It just became worse for Sally, she choked with tears and struggled to hold them back. When she eventually returned to her room alone, Faye's absence was even more apparent and she allowed the flood gates to open.

The following day, after a long and miserable flight home, Sally, Gabby and George parted..

'Thank you so much for your support, Gabby, I don't know what I would have done without you.'

'Don't be silly, Sal, I just hope Faye is OK.'

'So do I. The thing is . . . the signs were there. I should have taken more notice of my instincts and the fact that he'd already approached you for a date. Furthermore, I should have attached more significance to what Faye was going through and given her more time to talk through her feelings about the child's death. I knew she was vulnerable, I should have been stronger for her.'

'Well, you did your best. Try not to worry too much. She isn't a child, she's an educated woman, not likely to be taken advantage of, I would say,' George said. 'If I can help in any way, here's my mobile number, please give me a ring.'

'Thanks George, I'm sure you're right. She'll see sense and get herself home. So, listen, both of you, I'll keep in touch. Phone me when you arrive home to let me know you are safe and sound.'

'Yes we must keep in touch. Talk to you soon, Sally, take care.'

. . . . .

Returning without her sister, Sally was uncertain about what she should do. She knew she needed to visit their father to ensure he was alright. She decided to go and see him straight away, before going home. She missed having him there to guide her. In his condition he often didn't even know her. Sometimes he called her by her mother's name. As she entered his bedroom at the nursing home she was still dithering about telling him of Faye's decision to remain in India, she didn't know how he would take the news. However, on this occasion he didn't know Sally and rambled on quite pleasantly to her. She was relieved she not to worry him.

Back at work, the day after, the girls at the salon listened, horrified, as Sally described Joseph and then the events of the last evening of the holiday. They knew the closeness the sisters shared and vowed to help in any way they could. Sally thanked them gratefully but still couldn't fathom what to do about Faye.

The morning after Faye left with Joseph, before she arrived at the airport, Sally tried calling her on her mobile. Of course, the mobile voice said, 'we are unable to connect at this time'. And on every subsequent attempt thereafter the same voice uttered the same phrase until Sally felt like throwing the damn thing out of the window. She turned it off in despair, turning it back on only a few moments later, just in case. In between customers, bookings, enquiries and catching up on two weeks of paperwork, Sally held her phone, staring at it as if it could magically connect with Faye. Biting her lip, she worried a little bit of flaky skin with her top teeth and looked upwards to nowhere in particular.

'What am I going to do?' she asked the universe.

## 17

## Unwelcome truths

Wrinkling her nose at the offensive odour, Faye peered down the hole. *Is something moving down there?* She was close to tears. Hearing Joseph returning through the vegetation she swallowed and took a long step back. He appeared around the bamboo wall and thrust the rusty bucket at her. As she took it off him he uttered sharply,

'Water is precious here, don't waste it.'

Then he disappeared again. She noted the bucket held only a few centimetres of tepid water in the bottom. Nor did it look too clean. *So that's a long cold drink out of the question then,* Faye silently accepted. Placing the bucket in a corner of the 'bathroom', she removed her knickers and placed her feet either side of the hole. Keeping as far above it as possible she emptied her bladder. Looking right and left, she couldn't see any toilet paper, nor did she have a tissue. A tear formed in the corner of her right eye and then coursed down her cheek leaving a trail in the dust on her face. Wiping it away, it was followed by another on the left side. She felt wretched. It was not what she had imagined during the secret meeting outside her hotel room when Joseph asked her to come live with him in his house. Having no soap, no towel and a meagre amount of gritty water, she did the best she could to freshen herself up. The crows above her quietened for a few seconds then resumed their cacophony each time she moved more than a foot either

80

way. Feeling extremely exposed, her eyes constantly searched the jungle as she took off her top half. Using her knickers as a flannel, she dipped them in the water and washed herself down. Redressing her top half, her clothes sticking to her wet skin, she did the same with her bottom half, feeling only slightly cleaner. Finally, she dipped first one foot in the bucket, gave it as good a scrub as possible, placed it back in her sandal and then dipped the other one.

The remaining dirty water, she poured down the hole and hoped she was doing the right thing. However precious it was, she could not imagine using that water for anything else.

Carefully, her eyes travelling from one spider's web to the next, she made her way back to the house. Doubts filled her head as she anticipated what was ahead of her. Bravely she adopted a smile and entered the house.

'You've been a long time.' Joseph was sitting on the mattress, a frown on his face as he stared at her.

'Sorry, I feel fresher now.'

His face changed as he raised his hand to her,

'Come to me Faye, I've waited long enough for you, come here and sit beside me.'

Leaving the door open of the musty, damp house, in the half light of the candles she joined him on the mattress. A little late, but now as his hands undressed her and began to roam around her body, she knew, deep inside, it wasn't really what she wanted.

They must have both slept as the candles had burnt down and gone out. It had been a long and tiring journey. When Faye woke the light was very dim in the house. The afternoon had slid into evening. Joseph left the mattress, without a word, and went outside. Faye heard him urinate not far from the house. He coughed a phlegmy cough, spat and farted. Grimacing at the sound she sat up and reached for her clothes. They were in a heap on the floor at the side of the mattress and were damp and creased. Dressing quickly, she heard him begin to rake the ashes in the cold fireplace outside the door.

He called to her,

'In the cupboard, on the top shelf, there are a couple of bags with some food in. Bring them here. I'll light the fire and we can make some chai.'

'Great, I'm starving.' Faye did as she was bid and came out with the paper bags.

Joseph was naked, kneeling in front of the fireplace. Faye watched him pile up dried grass and sticks of wood. He carefully touched the grass with a lit match. The wood, pyramided above it, began to crackle.

The bit of sky visible between the forest and the house caught Faye's attention. It was a deep pink, driven through with streaks of pale pink and purple. The sign of another lovely day tomorrow, Faye reasoned. The crowning glory of the colourful sky was the army of swifts or maybe swallows, she didn't know which, screeching through the air, catching their supper on the wing. They were unconsciously re-enacting the film version of the battle of Britain. Faye was awestruck. She stood watching, gently laughing at the birds. Joseph glanced over to her, obviously not impressed with the aerial show.

'It won't do you any harm to starve for a little while. You could do with losing a few pounds!'

Faye, taken aback, spun round. She stared at him but did not reply. *Ouch!* She knew she had a fuller figure and never had she denied this but to be told so bluntly! It hurt! She hung her head. Joseph, apparently immune to her feelings, disappeared around the side of the house and returned a few seconds later with a kettle. Squatting back at the fire he stood the tripod over the struggling flames. Hanging the kettle from the tripod he sat back and reached for the paper bags.

Under the darkening evening sky, the only light came from the fire. In the porch, beside the door there lay two dusty rectangular cushions. Faye thought they may have once belonged to a settee. Joseph sat himself down on one and motioned Faye to sit on the other. The cushions were hard and not much cleaner than the ground. At one time they would have been pretty in cream silk with pink roses.

Unceremoniously he passed Faye a bread bun,
'Here.'

'Thanks.' She responded, and they ate in silence. Feeling uncomfortable with the atmosphere Faye tried again.

'Mmm, this is nice, light and tasty. What is it?'

Joseph slowly turned his head and looked at her, giving her the look that said, 'don't you know anything? Are you stupid?'

'It's a Goan sanna. It's made from rice.'

After that they sat in silence. The flames flickering yellow streaks against their faces. Joseph did not offer any more conversation and Faye felt cowed by his attitude and alarmed at his changeable nature.

When the water boiled, Joseph made the chai. Faye watched him carefully so she knew how to make it next time. He passed her an apple doughnut from the second paper bag. The chai and the doughnut did not lift the mood of the evening. Faye, convinced she'd made a big mistake coming here with him, was very troubled. And then he said,

'I'm going to the village. I won't be long.'

'What? Why? You're leaving me here? On my own?' Faye stared at him in disbelief, her eyebrows high on her forehead.

'I said I won't be long. Oh, and the water is in the butt round the other side of the house.'

'How long will you be?' There was a hint of desperation in her voice. She hadn't expected to be left on her own, on the first day. He replied, terse and loud,

'I have said I won't be long! Don't ask so many questions! And don't let the fire go out!.'

He brushed roughly past her into the house. Two minutes later, fully clothed, he set off down the path.

Faye, stunned, stared into the blackness of the jungle.

*Oh my God! I'm alone in the middle of this dark, spider filled jungle! What have I done? I don't understand!*

She glanced at the sickly fire, it wouldn't take much to lose it. She looked in the direction of the path, Joseph's retreating figure had already disappeared. Horrified at being alone in this unfamiliar place, she stared into the jungle. Confused and close to tears, Faye wasn't prepared for this and was totally befuddled by his changed attitude towards her.

With no idea of the time, she went inside the house. It was pitch black. She felt around in the corner where Joseph had lit the candles earlier when they had arrived. Finding a stub of a candle, about an inch-long, she went outside and lit it off the fire. Faye opened her suitcase and found her shower gel and shampoo. She discovered that by accident she had packed both hers and Sally's beach towels, for which she was very grateful. Taking the bowl from the top of the cupboard she placed it on a chair which she moved to the open door. Feeling the weight of the kettle, there was sufficient for a warm wash. She needed to feel clean. It was the only thing she had control over at this moment. Goodness knows what time Joseph would be back and why he had to go on their first evening? Faye soaped herself all over in the gloom of the candle and washed her hair. Rinsing it was a little awkward but she managed. Then, after checking the fire and loading on some more wood, she dressed herself and, unhappy and confused, sat by the fire to wait for Joseph.

. . . . .

Sometime later the night noises of the jungle woke Faye with a start, the fire was out and her neck stiff. The screeching, howling and rustling, so close to her, sent her into the house on her hands and knees. She manhandled the door closed and, in total darkness, found the mattress with her hands and clambered onto it. Laying flat, tears welled and spilled sideways down her face into the temples of her hair.

She didn't know the screeching came from the sweet little macaque monkeys she had seen with Sally from their balcony. She didn't know the howling came from a miniscule but colourful frog who was looking for his mate. The rustling, she didn't know, was a combination of bats, mongooses and wild pigs. It was just as well she didn't know about the leopards.

'I'm leaving in the morning.' She declared out loud to the darkness and closed her eyes. How she went back to

84

sleep she'll never know but when something touched her bare leg she screamed, long and loud!

'Faye, shhh, it's me.' Joseph breathed at her. The scent of alcohol touched her nostrils as she felt Joseph's body along the length of hers.

'Did I scare you?'

'What time is it? Where have you been all this time? There were noises out there. I had to come in. I was afraid. You left me alone. What time is it?'

'Shh, my little one, I am here now. Come here, let me kiss it all better. That's it, come into my arms, my darling.' His hands were feeling for the hem of her skirt and it appeared, in the darkness, he was very adept at working blind. 'I'll take your mind off it all, come on Faye.'

'Joseph, no!' Faye, wide awake, tried to sit up, 'We need to talk. I'm not happy about all that's happening in this place.'

'I'm sorry, Faye, I'm not always considerate. But we will get used to each other. You are the only one for me. I love you Faye. You are so beautiful. Come on now, show me you love me.' His hands found the spot they were searching for.

'But Joseph wait . . .' His mouth silenced her protests. She succumbed to him but all the while, deeply, she felt sad and furthermore she felt spineless.

The following morning, Joseph got up and relit the fire. He didn't mention the night before. He made chai and managed to produce another couple of sannas from somewhere.

Faye, dressing hastily and tying her hair back, joined him on the cushions by the fire.

'Today, I have to go out, I am seeing a man about some work. You can go to the shop in the village and buy some food for the next few days. You also will need to refill the water butt. I'll show you where the containers are kept. This house could do with a clean. The lazy slut who was here before you didn't do a thing?'

'The lazy slut? Who was that?'

Ignoring her he carried on,

'The villagers do not like westerners, so do not talk to them. Just get what you need and come straight back. The mahouts will probably be at the sanctuary but the women will be around. Do not talk to them, do you hear me?'

'What's a mahout and what sanctuary?'

'The elephant sanctuary, of course.' There was that look again, the - are you stupid? - look,

'The mahouts are the elephant keepers. Stay on the path and you will be safe. The shop is at the end of the village just in front of the water pump.

'What time will you return?'

'When I arrive. Don't ask so many questions, woman. Come here I'll show you where the water containers are.' He headed off around the side of the house.

On the opposite side of the house to the 'bathroom' was a lean-to with a roof made of blue plastic sheeting. Underneath lived an old rusty push-bike with flat tyres, a pair of plastic containers which would hold 10 litres each and several odds and ends of gardening implements. Next to the lean-to stood the water butt. It was a blue plastic barrel, which once contained something totally different but unknown. A tap protruded from it, two thirds of the way down. The lid was a home-made disc of wood which was none too clean but worse, it was none too level, it didn't seal the top, suggesting to Faye that things could get inside the water barrel if they desired. Things like funnel spiders, earwigs, centipedes, that kind of thing.

Joseph lifted the plastic containers and passed them to Faye.

'Fill these and pour the water in the butt. You will need to go twice to ensure we have sufficient water for the next couple of days. Like I said, water is precious, so make sure you fill the butt up to the top.'

Nodding, she took the containers from him and followed him back around to the porch where he then ordered,

'Get me some water so I can wash. I have to go soon.'

No please or thank you, Faye noted, but she did as she was told, feeling like a doormat. She scurried back around the house and brought him a kettle of water from the butt.

As he rinsed his face outside in the sunshine, Faye started to clear away the cups. She bent over to collect all the cooking implements. She had decided to wash them before she attempted to cook anything. From behind, Joseph, without warning, lifted her skirt and started fondling her buttocks. She rapidly stood and spun round ready to object. But his mouth covered hers. Then commencing his smiling, crooning act, his arms around her, he manoeuvred her into the house and onto the mattress, her protests ineffectual.

After he had left to see the man about some work, Faye washed herself all over again. Sighing she thought, *Does he love me or am I just a piece of flesh to him? Will we make a life together?*

# 18

## The Village

Faye tried to look as tidy as possible to walk to the village. She didn't want the local people to find fault with her on her first visit. It sounded, from Joseph, that foreigners weren't welcome. She didn't want to make it worse by looking like a tramp!

Her face gleaming and her hair fastened back, for the moment, she left the house. A racket overhead made Faye look up sharply as the crows proclaimed her departure. Caw! Caw! Caw!

She felt very insecure about going on her own, but she had no choice, Joseph wasn't here. Setting off, with grim determination, down the path, she worried about the reception she may receive from the villagers. But more, she worried about getting past the funnel spiders webs unharmed. It took her almost half an hour of traumatic spider web watching to reach the outskirts of the village. The heat was intense. She no longer felt fresh and clean. She ran her hands over her hair. Dismayed, she realised it had taken on a life of its own due to the humidity and ineffectually tried to tidy it, securing it in the bobble again.

Arriving at the clearing where the tuk tuk put them down, she could see a mountain in the distance, through the trees. It was long and low. She looked at it twice because of its beauty. Sunshine and shadows accentuated its ridges, it was stunning. *I'll see that every time I visit the village,* she thought cheerfully.

The two water containers were in the large fabric bag she had bought especially for the beach. She planned to look in the shop to see what they sold, purchase what she needed, then fill up the water containers and make her way back.

The village looked deserted as she walked down the sole street towards the houses. The large water tower at the end of the street was in her sights. She confidently strode out and a short way down encountered the colourful object, she'd noted as they alighted from the tuk tuk. Realising it was a place of worship, a place to leave offerings to the Gods, she paused to take a closer look.

A large circular base at the bottom, painted bright blue, appeared to have been constructed from concrete, but that didn't take away its importance. Above the base, on five colourful levels, different gods depicted their faith. Impressed at the details Faye acknowledged the importance of the idol. It was beautiful in a primary-colour, tawdry way. Faye walked slowly around the statue, examining each aspect. Bereft of offerings today, Faye thought she may leave something to show the villagers she was sympathetic to their lifestyle. Staring at the colourful object she cocked her head to one side and chewed her bottom lip in thought. What she would leave, she didn't know at that instant.

After a few moments, she straightened and carried on down the village street. Faye sniffed, there was a strange smell in the village. Not a horrible smell but definitely not a flowery fragrance. It was a little bit horse, with a large hint of manure, and earthy, but that wasn't a truly realistic description. Faye couldn't just put a name to it. Puzzled, she walked on. Another thing struck Faye as odd - each of the little houses were completely surrounded by fencing made of thick, sturdy bamboo, about two metres high, sharpened to points at the tips. It made the houses look imprisoned within. Curiously Faye peered through the bamboo fence of the first house in the row. She was pleasantly surprised to see rows of vegetables growing neatly in the garden. Obviously someone tended it regularly and at the back of the yard a coop of half a dozen, skinny white chickens. She moved on.

All the gates were closed, except for one and as Faye made it halfway down the street she became aware of two women standing together at the open gate. One lady wore a beautiful blue and gold sari. The other was in peach, with a white pattern. The fabrics were glorious, rich and bright in the sunshine. The ladies were probably both in their mid-thirties, Faye guessed. Their heads were bare, and both had long black plaits down their backs.

The lady in the blue and gold sari held a baby, her left arm hooked around its tiny frame. Faye unconsciously took in all the details of the little family. The baby sat on mum's hip wearing just a nappy. Its fist was firmly in its mouth. Saliva dribbled down its forearm, dripped off its elbow and drizzled a wet shiny streak on the front of the beautiful sari. The mother did not seem to mind. Faye registered the baby's chubby leg hanging down from its nappy. Its knee and the top of the foot and little toes had a covering of red dirt as if it had been crawling. It appeared to be around eight months old. She couldn't say if it was a boy or a girl.

Six dark eyes stared at Faye as she walked towards them. Faye accepted that the baby would be curious and didn't mind but the impact of the other two pairs of eyes, taking in everything about her, whilst she came up the street, made her step falter a little. Trying to avoid their eyes she looked at the ground and felt profoundly uncomfortable as if she was being critically picked apart.

The two women continued to stare at her and as she came level with them they spoke to each other in their own language. Still they didn't take their eyes off her and she sensed their relentless attention as she walked on by. What she didn't know was the content of their conversation.

'This is the girl I saw yesterday with Joseph. They arrived in a tuk tuk and walked up the path to his mother's house.' Jolindi, the mother of the baby, informed her neighbour, Nahla.

'Oh, not another one! Joseph just does not care! He is a wicked man. He should have sold the house after his mother died and shared the money with his sister. Instead he uses it as a den of iniquity. How many females has he had there?'

'This one will be the fourth. Poor girl, she doesn't have a clue. That house is damp and ramshackle, it doesn't even have electricity. I wouldn't want to live in it.' She turned and looked at her own house, beyond the bamboo fence. A faint smile showed on her face, a snapshot of her feelings of pride and thankfulness of her home. She turned back to Nahla,

'I'll tell Rav when he gets back from the sanctuary but before when I mentioned it to him, when the last girl arrived, he told me to mind my own business. Rav doesn't like Joseph either but he won't get involved.'

'What shall we do?' Nahla asked Jolindi.

'Well, we can't do anything. We can only watch and hope she sees sense and gets away before she gets hurt. Her hair is very wild and red. We'll call her Laal Baal, Red Hair.'

'Yes, a good name!' They laughed together. 'She must be stupid to be taken in by Joseph. Where's Joseph's wife?'

'I don't know, long gone if she has any sense. I've never even seen her.'

Faye tried to act nonchalantly and walked on lifting her head high. She felt extremely self-conscious and uncomfortable. Did she hear the women say Joseph's name? She was sure they did.

She arrived at the end of the main street. They were obviously talking about her. She heard them laugh and knew they were laughing at her. Her self-esteem at a new low, she went directly to the water pump, passing by the shop. She couldn't cope with dealing with the shopkeeper, at this moment, while she felt so inadequate within herself.

Standing in the shade of the pump, she searched in the fabric bag for her mobile. Trying to act nonchalantly, she gazed up at the sky as her hand felt around the bottom for the familiar padded plastic rectangle. She didn't need to look as her fingers identified the object and brought it out into the sunshine. In front of the two ladies, Faye pretended that standing in front of a huge water pump in the depths of the Indian jungle to use a mobile phone was a normal everyday moment.

The phone cover rekindled memories of Sally. She'd brought it back as a gift for Faye after a visit to London with her staff at the salon. The sleeve depicted Londons famous sights - Big Ben, the Tower of London, a big red bus and a policeman. She saw in her mind's eye Sally laughing and saying, 'Now see how long you can go without cracking your screen!'

Faye grimaced as she recalled her recent actions causing Sally's tears as she climbed into the tuk tuk with Joseph. Feeling guilty she sighed as she opened the cover and pressed Sally's number. Nothing happened! Faye shielded the phone from the light with her hand and screwed up her eyes seeking the little motifs along the top of the screen. There wasn't a signal, she had no bars! Disappointed, but not surprised, she also noticed she was almost out of charge. With no electricity at the house, what was she to do? Biting her lip again in indecision, she turned off the phone and stashed it back in the bag.

She lifted out the water containers and eyed up the water pump. It can't be hard, she thought, but didn't know where to start.

Jolindi and Nahla continued to watch her.

'Come on, Nahla, let's give her a hand. She looks a bit lost.'

Faye watched the women walking towards her. Glancing left and right she struggled with an urge to flee.

'Do you need some help?' Jolindi said,

Faye looked at her blankly, not understanding.

'Look, I'll show you. She doesn't speak the language, Nahla. Let's fill them for her then she'll know next time.' She passed the baby to Nahla.

Taking a container from Faye, Jolindi began the pumping action with the handle enabling the water to pour out. Dexterously she held the pump handle in one hand and the large container in the other and in seconds the water overflowed from the neck of the container.

'Here, you have a go.' She indicated to Faye to fill the other one. When Faye pulled the pump handle, Jolindi nodded, showing Faye she was doing it correctly. When the container was full Faye put it down and turned to the women.

'Thank you, thank you.' Faye put her hands together as if in prayer and bowed to the women. It was all she could do to show her appreciation. She felt much better about the two ladies now, much happier. She would soon get used to the way of life.

Jolindi and Nahla walked back to their houses up the street.

Over her shoulder Jolinda called,

'Next time you are on your own. See sense and go home before you get hurt, you silly girl!'

Of course, Faye didn't understand a word, but she understood the sharpness of the lady's words. Feeling a little cowed, nonetheless, she was grateful for their help. The ladies disappeared into the house where they had stood as she came down the street. The gate slammed closed securely behind them.

Lifting the water containers, one in each hand, Faye realised she wouldn't be able to carry shopping and the containers back to the house in one go, so deciding to first just have a look to see what the shop stocked, she placed them by the entrance, then she could have an hour walking to the house and back to think about what to buy.

It seemed dark inside after being out in the sun. Faye peered around. The shop was empty apart from a man behind the counter. He looked up as she entered and surprise registered on his face. He didn't smile or welcome her in any way but said something under his breath. Faye again felt ill at ease.

Actually, the shop keeper said, 'The bus is not here yet, where has she come from?'

Each day a bus stopped at the village shop after its tourists visited the elephant sanctuary. The tourists had the opportunity to purchase souvenirs. Faye didn't know this, nor did she know that the shopkeeper was happy to take anyone's money, so she raised her hand in acknowledgement to him and looked around the shop at all his wares. The shop sold basic fresh food stuff. Bags of flour, rice and other dried goods. She couldn't see any meat but there was some fish on a slab under a glass cover.

However, by the door hanging on thin ropes were carved wooden elephants of three different sizes. Fridge magnets, also of elephants, stuck to a spinning stand at the other side of the door. On a shelf immediately inside the entrance an array of cuddly furry animals sat, from very small to approximately 25 cm high and included elephants, monkeys, crocodiles, leopards and lions. In addition there was a very good selection of hats, the type one would wear for safaris; straw, wide brimmed, beribboned and even a few fezzes. Boxed beakers with pictures of elephants with matching melamine trays stood proud on the opposite wall. Keyrings hung in abundance, again with elephants depicted, in clumps at various heights around the shop. Faye, still unaware of the nearby elephant sanctuary, gazed at the frivolous objects for sale with wonderment. *What's the fixation with elephants?* she vaguely pondered to herself.

Faye waved at the shop keeper again and left to carry the water back to the house. They were very heavy. In this heat it would be a challenge to take them back once. Did Joseph say she had to fill them twice?

From her window, Jolindi watched her struggle past towards the path to the house. She sighed. After a few minutes she walked along to the shop and said to Larso the shopkeeper,

'Did Laal Baal come in your shop?'

'Laal Baal?' he chuckled, 'That's a good name for her. She came in and went out again without buying. Where did she come from?'

'She is with Joseph at the house of his mother. He has brought another one!'

'Oh dear, will he ever see the errors of his ways? The rest of his family are good catholic people. I cannot understand him.'

'Neither can I. I hope she sees sense and leaves him before anything happens to her.'

'She doesn't deserve that Joseph, no-body does. He certainly has a gift for fooling the ladies. Goodness knows what his chat up line is. I'll have to ask him and try it myself!' he chuckled again.

'Larso, you are not in the same class!' Smiling, Jolinda returned home and forgot about Laal Baal. Her husband would be home from the elephant sanctuary shortly for his lunch.

. . . . .

An hour later Faye made her second trip down the village street. This time she brought only one water container as she knew, in this heat, she could not make three journeys.

Re-entering the shop, she chose a couple of fresh fish from the granite slab. Faye could not recognise the breed but hoped for the best. She bought a selection of vegetables and a bag of rice. Unsure about spices she passed them by, deciding to ask Joseph if he knew what to buy. Seeing an item resembling Tiramasu she impulsively purchased that also, thinking it would sweeten Josephs mood. Looking in her purse, she realised the rupees she exchanged in the hotel would not last very much longer. She would need to go into town, she suspected, to find a bank.

Thankfully the walk home with the food and water, passed uneventfully. No spiders jumping out, no strange, noisy creatures presented themselves. Then the crows welcomed her again with their screeching.

Faye lit the fire and prepared the meal in readiness for Joseph's return. Whatever time that would be, she didn't know, but would be prepared. The only thing she was worried about was the level of water in the butt and what Joseph would say about it. She didn't know what to do with the fish, so she cut off their heads, tails and removed the innards. The scales she left on, not realising they had to be scraped off. She washed the fish, vegetables and rice with the smallest amount of water possible.

After the meal was prepared she swept the floor of the house. It didn't take long, there was only one room. She wiped the cupboard top and straightened the sarong on the mattress. She washed the single window hoping it would allow more light but it didn't appear to make much difference. Rolling a stub of candle between finger and thumb Faye regretted not thinking about buying more. Maybe she could get some in town tomorrow, she pondered. After the housework she washed herself, again in a meagre amount of water and sat down to wait.

## 19

## *Card and pin*

What woke her? It was dark, the fire almost burnt away to nothing. She heard rustlings a short distance from the house. Sitting up she felt behind her for a candle stub and crawled to the fire. Throwing a few twigs on, she hoped it would quickly revive itself and wriggled the ashes with the poker, relieved to see some new life. She lit the candle from a sickly flame. Peering out into the darkness she called nervously,

'Is that you, Joseph?'

'Yes, I'm home. I'm starving, I hope there is something cooking, I can't smell anything?' He appeared in the porch, a shadowy outline poorly lit by the measly fire and candle flame.

'I'll start cooking tea now you are back. Where have you been? Did you see your friend about a job?' Innocently amiable, she smiled up at him. He turned on her,

'You should have my tea ready for me. What have you been doing all day? Lounging about the place?' Sharply he ordered,

'Get me some warm water, I want to get washed. And stop asking so many questions. It's nothing to do with you, what I do!'

'Sorry, Joseph. I'll get you some water.'

Disappointed that he had come home in a bad mood, she scurried round to the butt in the dark with the pan. Remembering she'd only half filled the butt, an overwhelming feeling of trepidation filled her in case he noticed whilst in this mood. Butterflies played havoc in her tummy. Turning the tap she let the water rise three quarters of the way up the pan and returned to the porch setting the pan on the tripod.

'The meal won't be long. I'm doing it now.' She received a grunt in return.

Not knowing much about spices she'd planned to ask Joseph to help her but in view of his mood she decided to cook the rice, vegetables and fish with simply a good seasoning of salt and pepper and hope for the best.

When his water warmed she poured it into the green flowery bowl and set it down beside the fire. Joseph squatted by the water and washed himself. She noticed he was using her body wash which had been in her suitcase. Joseph saw her looking and glared back, daring her to comment. She raised her eyebrows slightly and looked away. She couldn't remember leaving it out. *Has he been through my things?* She hadn't unpacked anything from her suitcase. It stood on its little wheels where he put it when she first arrived at the house, just inside the door a little to the right. Apart from getting out her clean clothes, towels, shampoo and body wash, nothing else had come out of it and she felt sure she put everything back in afterwards. There was nowhere to put anything anyway. Her large cloth bag sat on top of the case to save it from getting dirty. She didn't want to feel mean or petty, he could use the body wash, she didn't mind but a hint that he had been through her suitcase left her feeling a little disconcerted. She frowned.

Completing his wash-down, he wrapped a thin cloth around his hips and sat on the cushion beside the fire.

The rice was boiling and vegetables were frying at the side of the fish. Faye silently prayed the meal would satisfy him and felt very nervous. She brought him a cup of water and smiled her most amenable smile. He ignored her. Her faith in a pleasant evening spiralled downwards.

After draining the rice, she set the meal on the plates with precision. She heard once that the eyes taste the meal before the mouth. Passing him his meal, she again smiled her smile, hoping to radiate the confidence she didn't feel.

Joseph looked at the meal. Faye sat on the other cushion on tenterhooks, watching him, with her plate on her knee. He forked a mixture of vegetables and rice into his mouth and chewed for a second. He stopped chewing, swallowed and slowly turned his head to look at Faye.

'It's tasteless. Don't you know how to cook, woman?'

'I'm sorry, I need you to show me how to use the spices, Joseph.' He ignored her again.

Faye sat still, she hadn't the appetite to try her own meal. Joseph broke off a few flakes of fish and put it in his mouth. He chewed again for a few seconds. Suddenly his mouth gaped open and complete distaste showed on his face, he spat his mouthful into the fire.

'What have you done to the fish?' he shouted.

Startled, Faye lifted her chin and pushed back against the house wall, just in time! He threw his plate over the fire to the other side of the porch, narrowly missing Faye's head. Fish, vegetables and rice splayed in all directions. Enraged he continued,

'You haven't taken off the scales! Are you trying to poison me? You are the worst cook I have ever met. What sort of a woman are you? I come home expecting a tasty meal and this is what I get. What is the matter with you? I should have stayed in town with my friends.'

'I'm sorry, Joseph. I really tried. I'll do better, I promise.' Distraught, Faye put her plate down on the floor with haste, her face crumpling under his harshness. Pleadingly she begged,

'Will you show me how to use the spices, please? I'll buy some tomorrow and we can make a meal together?'

Joseph grunted and refused to look at Faye.

Sniffing, she went to refill the pan to make chai. Again, she felt her stomach flip as she thought about the half empty butt. *Is it me?* she asked herself silently. *I make him so angry, I must try harder.* The pan filled half-way with water and wiping her nose and eyes on the hem of her skirt, she unhappily found her way back to the porch, to Joseph and his overwhelming mood.

After making the chai and subserviently offering Joseph a cup, she brought out what she hoped would make things a little easier between them – the Tiramisu like sweet.

'Joseph, I don't know what this is, and I can't ask in the shop because of the language difference, but I hope it's something you like.'

'It's like a cheesecake. I like it.' No thank you was forthcoming.

They ate in silence, the minutes stretching out. Faye was miserable but at least he ate one of the items she provided.

The candle burnt itself out, so Faye went indoors and rummaged around for another stub. Dreading mentioning the need for more candles, she returned to the cushion by the fire and taking a deep breath let the words flow fast,

'Joseph, the candles have almost gone. I'll buy some more tomorrow but, within a day or two, I'll need to get some money out of the bank. My rupees have nearly all gone. Can we go into Shamoga in the morning so I can visit a bank?'

Joseph sat mute for some minutes, staring, expressionless at the fire. Faye didn't know whether to repeat herself or not. She sat static with indecision, her face glum and eyes downcast expecting the next explosion of temper. Suddenly she felt the atmosphere alter. It was almost physical.

'My Darling, I'm sorry I have been angry with you tonight,' smiling, he turned towards Faye, 'I know you are not the best housekeeper a man could wish for. I must have more patience. Tomorrow I have an appointment. I cannot take you to Shamoga. However, if you need money I will get you some money. I can take your bank card and get you some. How much will the bank let you draw out?'

'That's kind, Joseph but I really wanted to go to the town myself. I haven't even seen it and I wanted to have a look around.'

His smile disappeared as slowly and loudly, he replied,

'I said I'll take your card and get you some money out. Don't make such an issue of everything.' Then in a normal tone, 'Do you have sufficient rupees for tomorrow's meal?'

'Yes, I think so.'

'Well then, I will get you some money. You can just buy the food for tomorrow.'

Faye couldn't help herself pouting. Joseph reached across the cushions and pulled her over to him. Semi reluctantly allowed herself to be drawn towards him until she was beside him on his cushion. He drew her in close, his left arm around her shoulders. His right hand was running up and down her body, lingering over her breasts and thighs.

'My little love, stop being so childish. It is just a town. Tomorrow, when I return, I will show you how to make a perfect tasting gravy. I know you can't do everything, I don't expect you to. Now are you feeling happier?'

'Well . . .'

'Go and find me your card and tell me the PIN so I can draw you some money. How much do you think?' He pushed her up from the cushion and turned her to face the direction of the house door. Uncertainly, she stood for a moment until his hand connected with her bottom, propelling her forward, and she stepped into the dim, cheerless house.

'The bank will probably only allow £100 worth of rupees per day. It may be different here but that's how it is at home.' She called back to him. She was bending over her big cloth bag, feeling around in it for her purse.

Suddenly he was in the room with her, directly behind her, his breath on her ear and the heat of his body against her back. His voice was loud and somehow excited.

'£100 worth of rupees *per day* you say?' He breathed heavily behind her. He emphasised 'per day'. Faye noticed but preferred to ignore the implications.

'Yes, but like I say, it may be different here.'

'Mmm,'

She turned, purse in hand, to return to the porch but he pressed her sideways by her shoulders. They fell together, onto the damp, lump-filled, mattress. His mouth covered hers. His hands were already searching for the hem of her skirt.

Under his kiss her mind cried, *No! Please, I*

*don't want this.* She hated herself at that moment as she allowed him to pull down her knickers.

'What is your PIN?' she heard his muffled request. 'My angel.' He crooned as he found his way. Both his missions were accomplished within minutes.

.  .  .  .  .

The following morning Joseph was up as dawn broke and the crows commenced their morning hullabaloo high in the trees. Faye heard him draw water from the butt to make chai.

*Oh! My life!* Faye thought to herself as she realised what he was doing. *The water will be so low now after last night's meal and his wash.* She waited, hardly breathing, for him to return with the kettle in a rage. Instead he raked the ashes, lit the fire and placed the kettle on the tripod.

He was singing a nameless and somewhat tune-less song. She remained beneath the thin sarong, eyes wide. The heat in the house, even at this early hour, was stifling, but she remained where she was, dreading hearing his mood switch to anger. Listening to his movements she heard him return round the side of the house. He urinated, coughed and spat, then rinsed his hands and face directly from the butt tap. *Oh my God!* Still he continued to sing.

She couldn't stand it any longer and decided to be prepared for him. Rapidly she squirmed her hot skin into her skirt and blouse and as Joseph rounded the corner of the porch, she was sitting on the cushion beside the fire, preparing the cups for the chai. Although feeling anxious, she smiled sweetly at him and waited for a response.

'Good morning my little English rose,' he almost sang to her, smiling. He stroked the top of her head then sat and charmingly took the cups and poured the chai for her.

'I'm going early this morning to enable me to be back to help you cook the meal. If you get some lamb from the shop, I'll buy the spices. I'll show you the mix my mother used, then you'll be able to make anything you want.'

Faye, virtually speechless, nodded,

'I'm looking forward to that, Joseph,' she forced out, swallowing hard.

Smiling, he downed his chai and rummaged around beside the mattress to find his clothes. He slipped them on then,

'By the way, could you wash my shirt today?'

'Yes, of course.'

'It's in that pile of clothes at the back of the room. In fact, you can wash everything.' No please or thankyou again.

Kissing Faye on her forehead he strode off down the path. It must have only been about six-thirty.

Stunned, Faye sat by the fire for some minutes wondering what had happened to make Joseph so pleasant. Then she remembered he had her bank card.

*Oh no, please don't let that be the only reason for his happiness,* Faye prayed silently. *No, surely not,* she hoped without conviction. Brows knitted together, she worried a rough edge of her thumb nail with her teeth.

．　．　．　．　．

There was just sufficient water in the butt to enable her to wash and make herself presentable to visit the village once more. As she eyed the funnel spider's webs this morning she considered that to wash clothing meant buying washing powder. Another heavy item to lug up the path. Well, at least life is more enjoyable if Joseph is happy. With hope she made her way down the path.

Almost there, she stopped dead in her tracks as an almighty roar emanated from the village! Shocked, she stood and listened. She could hear men shouting and then more roaring. Dropping the fabric bag, she crept forward fearfully, not wanting to see what was happening, but not wishing to miss anything either.

To her astonishment, three men were walking towards her, down the village street, chatting and laughing with each other. Close behind an adult elephant with a very young calf at its side. Standing approximately nine or ten feet tall, the adult elephant towered above the men and in contrast, the calf appeared tiny beside her. The mother elephant seemed content to follow the men but roared at the calf when it ran too far in front of her. Faye could see the calf wanted to explore and gallop about. It raised its short trunk and squeaked back at its mum when she disciplined it, but nonetheless, did as it was told. Astounded Faye watched silently and still. The calf was so cute and the mother so maternal. The men came level with the clearing where the tuk tuk had put Faye and Joseph down just a few days ago. They turned as if going towards Shamoga. Faye in the dappled shadow of the trees, stood spellbound, smiling widely with her hands together as if in prayer. Her heart melted and she sighed, 'Ahh,' and stared delightedly as they walked away, the men in front and the mother elephant, controlling the baby, following amiably behind. Faye stood mesmerised, she was close enough to see the calf's bristly fuzz of hair on the top of its head and down its back. She could see its tiny tail with a feathery end and its little legs confidently romping in all directions. Red dust swirled around its feet as it ran back and forth between its mother and the mahouts. A short way down the road, the men turned through an opening in the vegetation on their left. The mother and calf followed, the foliage soon swallowed them and the whole party disappeared. The roaring trumpet of the mother elephant continued to be heard for some time.

Faye grinned to herself and gave a little laugh of happiness. It dawned on her that the souvenirs in the shop had to be something to do with the elephant. She had heard the sanctuary mentioned, but being so immersed in her own trials and tribulations hadn't given it much thought. She knew, from the very first  moment in Goa, she would like it here. Seeing the mother and baby elephant validated her initial reaction to the country. If only Joseph was a little more tolerant of her shortcomings, she sighed again.

. . . . .

Having decided to make two trips, solely to fill the water butt, Faye stepped out and completed this task before midday. In all honesty, she was afraid of Joseph's temper if

104

she didn't fill it right up. Carrying two full water carriers all the way from the pump to the butt nearly broke her. Her elbows and wrists stretched to the limit and her back breaking, she didn't know if this lifestyle would suit her for long. To the calls of the crows Faye stood with hands on her lower back, stretched backwards and then shook her arms out. However, she felt she should give it a good shot. Optimistically she hoped Joseph's mood swings would come to an end if she did as he asked and they could be happy together.

Beside the water pump for the second time that day, she rinsed her face with the tepid fluid and trusted that she didn't look as red in the face as she felt.

Back at the house for the second time, Faye realised she hadn't eaten since the day before yesterday, with the exception of the Tiramisu. After Joseph threw his fish meal across the porch, her appetite died and had scraped her own meal away onto the rubbish pile as she cleared away. She found a little rice stuck to the bottom of the saucepan and hungrily stuffed it into her mouth with her fingers before picking stray grains of rice, one by one, from the sides of the pan. *I'll have to do better than this, as Joseph said, it's tasteless,* she vowed to herself. Washing it down with a cup of water, she set off again, down funnel spider avenue, to buy the food for tonight's meal, a box of candles and washing powder.

## 20

## *The Indian Love Apple*

As the sun withdrew and the night sounds commenced, Faye found herself sitting on her cushion, arms folded across her chest and face set in a scowl. She was livid! She realised that Joseph wasn't coming home to show her how to make a good gravy or curry sauce. Wretchedly, she snatched up the lamb and put it in the cupboard, hoping the heat wouldn't turn it before she could cook it.

Joseph's clean shirt hung on a coat hanger on a pole which formed the roof of the porch. In frustration, she punched at it as she passed. The soft fabric didn't offer resistance giving Faye no satisfaction.

Faye was so miserably confused and unbelievably annoyed with Joseph for abusing her trust in him to use her bank card, but mostly, furious with herself for being spineless and gullible.

Giving the mattress several vicious kicks with her toe, she screamed out loud,

'Argh! What am I doing here? That's it! First thing in the morning I'm going home!' Tears slid down her cheeks.

The only noticeable difference in her immediate surroundings was the hush following her voluble outburst. The noisy creatures of the night were quiet for a little while.

By the light of a candle Faye shoved the house door closed. It scraped across the concrete floor and shut into the wooden frame. In the small gap between the door and the mattress she dragged her suitcase and jammed it in place. No way was Joseph going to sneak in during the night, she determined. She lay on the damp, dirty mattress and cried until she fell asleep.

Sometime during the early hours, Faye heard a noise at the door. She thanked the lord she had the foresight to put the suitcase behind the door. *That'll show him,* she thought with a modicum of satisfaction, when his attempts to get in failed. Unhappily she laid, wondering what she was doing there with him. Doggedly she ignored the scrabbling and attempts to push the door open. She then ignored the drunken calls and pleas, followed by verbal abuse and thumps on the door and when it had all ceased, she turned over and tried, in vain, to go back to sleep.

As weak light permeated the room through the single window, outlining Fred and Wilma, Faye dressed, removed the suitcase and opened the door. She dragged her case out into the sunshine.

'I'm going home, Joseph.' She said, firm and loud. He was laid across the cushions by the ashes. Without moving he let out a groan.

'I've had enough! You use me like a sex slave and now, I presume, you have got yourself drunk on my money. I'm going home! I'm going to Shamoga and will get a hotel room there until I can organise a flight home. Give me back my card. I've had enough, Joseph . . . Joseph! Are you listening to me?' She nudged him with her toes. He groaned again.

'Faye,' he whispered, 'I'm sorry, I had one too many. Not on your money, but yes too much to drink. I'm sorry. Please don't go.' He still hadn't moved.

'Give me my card back Joseph. I'm going! I don't care, I can't live like this!'

Sitting up he put his hand to his head,

'Oh, my head! I won't drink ever again.'

Thrusting out her hand, palm upward, fingers beckoning, she demanded,

'My card, please!'

'Look Faye, I'm sorry, I said I'm sorry. I promise I will do better. I'll get a job and look after you properly. And I

won't drink again. Please don't go. I have a present for you!'
He reached around the back of the cushion and brought out
a cone made of newspaper and held it up for Faye to take. It
was identifiable as a cone shape but obviously had endured
much handling as it had several dents and kinks. Trying to
maintain her anger she snapped,

'What is it?' Taking it from him she peeled back the
top of the newspaper. Inside the cone were five green fruits,
looking like a cross between apples and tomatoes.

'Fruit? You've bought me fruit?' She barked.

He looked up at Faye, who was still standing
resolutely, one hand on her hip looking down at him and
applied his best sheepish manner.

'They are Indian love apples, a token of my feelings
towards you. Come sit down here beside me, my head won't
stand looking up at you,' he added with a pathetic, injured
smile.

Faye, remaining upright in her determined stance,
dithered internally. Her eyes darted from him to the love
apples to her suitcase at her side and back to the love
apples. He could see her indecision so pressed her.

'I've got you the money out of the bank as I said I
would. Here you can have it.' As he pushed his hand into his
trousers pocket, he continued,

'Do you think so little of me, to assume I have spent
your money? I have money of my own, thank you very much.
You can't feel the same about me as I do about you,
*obviously!* I should have known.' His eyes searched the
ground, his voice full of hurt,

'If you want to go, I won't stop you. Here take your
money!' He looked up at Faye and thrust his hand upwards.
His fist full of paper notes. 'I don't want any of it. Take it!' His
voice rose at the end of the torrent and his hand was flung
higher as he dramatically turned his face away from her to
look back at the ground.

Faye, in the silence, took the notes from his
outstretched hand and experienced uncertainty, her
frustration and hurt dissolved around her. *He has brought me
a present,* she guiltily pondered, *and I was ready to give up*

*on him. He's not the easiest man to get along with but he says he's sorry, that he'll take proper care of me.*

Sitting down on the cushion beside him, she felt him glance in her direction.

'I expected you back to help me do the cooking last night. I was very disappointed. I never know what time you are coming home. I feel as if I am just here for your convenience. It's not really what I imagined, and your mood swings are unbearable.'

'I'm sorry, Faye, I know I'm not a perfect man. Will you give me another chance? I'll make it up to you. I promise.' He smiled, showing his white teeth, a glint of triumph in his eyes. 'Can we start again?'

Faye gazed into the distance, saying nothing. Seconds ticked by. Joseph became impatient, fidgeting on his cushion.

'Well?'

'Alright, we'll give it another go. Are you staying at home today?'

Joseph dramatically let his shoulders sag as if in relief. Faye laughed at him.

'Yes, I'm staying home today. I have also bought you the spices as I promised. Come let's get cooking, I'm starving.'

Happily, pressing the doubt back to the edges of her mind, Faye took her suitcase back into the house and went to get the lamb.

'Oh, by the way, I'd better tell you, the Indian Love Apples. . .'

'Yes?' she came back out with the meat.

'You can eat the flesh of the apples, but do not eat the cores.'

'Why not?'

'Because they're poisonous! Very poisonous!' he informed her, watching her response.

'Oh!' Faye picked up the cone of fruit and looked inside again. Then she placed the newspaper back over the fruit and laid the cone on the floor beside her cushion. The lovely thoughtful present from Joseph was tarnished with fear. Looking back at him, was there an aspect of satisfaction on his face? She stared, her happiness sliding sideways.

*Is he joking? Does he purposely have to spoil everything? What's the matter with him? Is it me? Am I too sensitive?*

.  .  .  .  .

From the back of the cupboard in the one room house, came a pestle and mortar. Joseph ground eight different spices to a powder, most of which Faye hadn't heard of. She wrote down the list of ingredients to ensure she could reproduce the paste in the future. The spices, finely shredded flesh of a whole coconut, four garlic cloves and a chopped onion were mixed with a little coconut milk to bind the ingredients together. Two thirds of the concoction was saved in a bowl to be used over the next couple of days and the remaining third spread generously on the lamb.

Whilst the lamb cooked slowly over the fire, in a large lidded pan. Joseph instructed Faye on making chapati dough. She proudly cooked her first chapati on a blackened griddle pan over the fire and happily shared it with Joseph. It seemed all her fears were groundless.  He was charming, patient and entertaining. They had a good time together. Any lingering thoughts of going home left her. This is what she wanted, she was sure.

The lamb, cooked to perfection and spiced, hot and tasty, fed the hungry couple. Home-made chapati wiped up the juices and tepid water from the butt washed it down. A sweet rice pudding followed to complete the feast.

.  .  .  .  .

Faye laid in Joseph's arms on the mattress after an afternoon of love. They had a little sleep and when they woke up the sun was low in the sky. Joseph got up, made a pan of chai and took it back to bed for them both.

110

'I was born in this house, you know,' he said quietly to Faye, she put her cup down and Joseph laid his head on her soft naked breasts. She held him as he continued,

'It had a large vegetable garden, though much of it is reclaimed by the jungle because it hasn't been cared for. We used to have animals; chickens, goats and pigs. Oh, and there was a well. It was on the same side as the water butt. We could try to find it if you like, it would make life much easier. That's if it's still workable.' She loved listening to his rich deep voice and Indian accent.

'My father's father owned the house in the beginning. My father then owned the house. He was called Joseph too. I take after him. My mother was called Eva. I also have a sister who lives in Shamoga with her family.

'My mother used to work the vegetable plot and the animals on her own. I remember her catching a wild boar! She used to barter some of the meat for other things for me and Anika, my sister. The wild boars used to come close to the vegetables hoping for some fresh fruit and veg. My mother would set a trap and then chop up the squealing pig with her cleaver! She was fearless.' Faye heard his voice alter as he grinned at the memory.

'Sometimes she would get a piglet to raise for meat. I used to help her. As a small boy it was my job to chase away the monkeys.'

Faye laid still, enthralled by his tale, not wanting to spoil this moment when Joseph felt sufficiently comfortable to open up to her. She realised she knew nothing about him.

'We could have a look for the well, and at the same time look to see if we could replant on the land to grow our own. How would you like that?' He turned his head to look at her.

'I'd like that. What happened to your mother and father?'

'Mum died. She was here alone and died sitting by the fire, quite peacefully. It's not that long ago, actually.'

'And your father?'

'My father left us when we were young. My mother said he ran off with another woman, but I never believed her!

She didn't like him and said some dreadful things about him. I think she must have chased him away.'

What Joseph didn't say was that he felt protective towards his father. He had heard his mother saying his father was a lazy, no-good person who didn't like to work, a womaniser and a drinker. Joseph senior simply left the family home one day when Joseph was four years old and never returned. He simply disappeared and was not heard from again. Joseph didn't really know his father but somehow felt a bond with him. Maybe it was sharing his name.

In addition to keeping the animals and the crops, his mother worked as a cleaner for the unmarried mahouts at the elephant sanctuary to make ends meet, but it was her brother, Joseph's uncle who paid for him and his sister to attend school.

'When we were little we all slept in this house. When I turned thirteen, my mother sent me to live with my uncle in Shamoga. It was wonderful. It offered me many opportunities. My uncle was very kind to me.'

What he didn't say was that although he understood he was growing up and had to move out for the sake of decency, that he could no longer share one room with two females, a huge feeling of rejection attached itself to the move and remained with him for the rest of his life. Joseph pretended not to care but refused to visit his mother for several months. His uncle was strict but the headiness of the town, after the isolation of the house, drew Joseph, like a moth to the flame. He rebelled and started running around with the wrong kind.

Soon, he was in trouble with the police for petty theft and general hooliganism. Then inevitably ended up in trouble with a young girl.

The girl, Gaurav, was totally infatuated with Joseph, adored him and followed him around. She would do whatever he asked of her and she soon became with child. At this early age, Joseph recognised the power of his charm when he used it over the female species.

They were married as is the custom. Joseph aged 15 and Gaurav only 14. Joseph's uncle was not only footing the bill but yielding the shotgun, so to speak, along-side Gaurav's father and many uncles.

Gaurav moved into Joseph's uncle's house but within days, she moved back to her mother and father and never returned. The marriage, to all intents and purposes, was over. She has never married again and unfortunately, because of the beliefs and traditions of India she'll probably never be considered by another man, and sadly neither will Tarun, their daughter. Ironically Tarun takes after her father. She is tall, good looking and gracious in her movements. She is also sly, secretive and a loner.

Joseph does not support his daughter, he has only seen her once and that was when she was a few weeks old. Now at 19, she has no desire to see her father. Her mother and grandparents have nothing good to say about him.

'I used to come home regularly to help my mother, especially after Anika, my sister, left to get married. Anika is happily married with two children.'

He omitted to say that the feeling of rejection continued into manhood. He would come to visit his mother, not to be of help to her, but if he needed money, a meal or to lie low for a day or two. His mother would let him sleep on the mattress and she would sleep on the cushions by the fire under the porch.

He didn't expand on Anika and her family. His mother adored Anika and her grandchildren and spent a great deal of time with them at their home in Shamoga or whilst they visited the house. The grandchildren, Manish and Mishka, were the apple of her eye.

Joseph resented the time they spent together and even though he did not recognise it as jealousy, he hated his mother talking about Anika and the children with open adoration; how pretty, how clever, how well, how nice, how much money, how handsome, she went on and on. He couldn't stand it and would shout at her to shut up. Joseph never visited Anika, he has never seen his nephew and niece, nor does he intend doing so.

'You have a sister and a family in Shamoga? We could go visit them if you want, Joseph?'

'Yeah, we could,' he uttered without conviction.

Joseph moved directly back to the house after his mother's body had been removed. He attended her funeral, but it was Anika and her husband and of course, his uncle, who organised and financed it.

Coming and going as he pleased, he didn't take care of the house and it suffered because of his neglect. Often, he was away for months at a time after finding a lucrative way to earn money! Joseph started working in hotels as a waiter, with free accommodation and meals, plus a wage. Furthermore, the job offered the extra bonus of rich, or at least he viewed them as rich, foreign women who came for a week or two. A stream of them, ever changing, ever renewing, a line of rich foreign women available for him to exploit.

He earned enormous tips, especially from the older ladies, who mostly came in pairs, but it was the ladies travelling alone on whom he concentrated. His fine-tuned charm earned maximum money and then, of course, there was the sex.

Why his charm hadn't worked on Sally and Gabby, he could not understand.

This year, he should have worked to the end of the season, until the monsoon started, but suddenly he found himself in a situation and he had to take immediate drastic action. All because of a stupid old woman who stayed at The Royal Hotel the week prior to Faye, Sally and Gabby's arrival.

He'd been getting along famously with the old woman. On his days off he escorted her to secluded beaches, restaurants, the Grand Bazaar and several other attractions, all paid for by her, of course. She believed everything he said, or so he thought. She was travelling alone, staying at The Royal Hotel for 14 nights, on her way to meet up with her son who was living in Mauritius. Her upper arms and neck showed signs of age, dry, wrinkled and flappy skin, and she had many fine vertical lines along her upper lip. Joseph tried not to look at them. Otherwise she wasn't in bad shape for an old girl. She glowed under his flattery encouraging him to continue.

At the same time, he began his charm offensive on a beautiful, blonde teenage girl staying at the hotel with her family. The prize here, in this case, was not the money but the girl.

However, the teenager's father returned unexpectedly to the hotel one afternoon and caught them in bed. There was such an uproar. The girl was only fourteen. The whole hotel soon heard about it. Then, naturally, the old girl put her spoke in, declaring Joseph had also visited her bed and taken money from her.

So, no sooner had he chatted with Faye by the pool, on the day of the Grand Bazaar, he found himself being given the sack without notice.

The family and the old woman demanded to be moved from The Royal Hotel and had been given rooms in The Royal's sister hotel, The Majestic, at the other end of town until they were due to leave the resort. Hence, Sally, Gabby, Faye and George had not bumped into either of the troubled parties and learned of their experiences.

At his disciplinary meeting, he heard that the parents of the teenager decided not to press charges, as it may become a larger issue for their daughter, making it worse for her in the long run. The hotel manager assured the parents Joseph would be sacked without notice and gave them a free 14-night holiday voucher for the whole family. The old woman also demanded that Joseph should be dismissed without references or notice. Therefore, to be sacked without charges meant Joseph got away lightly and still had time to woo Faye to come to his house with him with the hope of getting his hands on her money.

Joseph felt it was all very unfair. The young girl shouldn't have been so easy and the old girl enjoyed every minute. It wasn't his fault and now he was struck with this lumpy mare. He sighed. Still, he had accomplished one thing - he had access to Faye's bank account.

Of course, Faye only knew what Joseph wished her to know and continued to hold him to her breast. She heard him sigh and assumed it was contentment. She felt gratitude towards him for telling her about his life and experienced a closeness with him. She analysed his story regarding the well and vegetable plot and decided it was his way of saying he wanted more permanence with her. For example, the time it would take to grow vegetables. She fantasised them working side by side, tilling the fertile red soil. She thought this was what he was getting at. She sighed too. Joseph heard this and felt her arms tighten around him. He turned his head and found a nipple with his lips. A smile curving the outer edges of his mouth.

## 21

## The Well

Joseph boiled some rice and poured the remains of the gravy over it. They sat and ate breakfast together. His mood remained happy and consequently so did Faye.

'Just in case we cannot find the well or if we find it and it's not usable, you will have to fill the butt up today as usual. It could be the last time though.'

'Yes, I suppose so, I'll go this morning. You could come with me. It would be helpful in the shop if you were there to talk me through some of the food stuff I don't know about.'

'No, you'll have to go, I have some things to do in town.' Joseph did not want to be seen in the village with Faye in case one of the villagers tried to offer him advice again. The last time someone spoke to him, it was to advise him to sell up, share the money with Anika and stop using his mother's home as a house of ill repute. It didn't end well. Joseph, taking offence, started the row but ended up badly bruised. He silently acknowledged he wasn't a fighter. Suppressing a smile he admitted to himself he was more of a lover. Faye gave him her pout.

'Don't be a baby, Faye, I'm going to buy some seeds for you to plant. When we have found the well, we'll clear some land back, so you can farm. You would like that, eh?'

'Or I could come into town with you?' She tried hopefully.

'No! Now go and get me some water to wash with.'

Faye sighed but swallowed her disappointment and held her tongue to enable Joseph to keep hold of his pleasant disposition. She was dying to visit the town and have a good look around. She also needed to charge her phone and speak to Sally. Faye opened her mouth to relay all this to Joseph then closed it again. It would wait. The crows greeted her as she rounded the house to the butt. Caw, caw.

'As soon as I return we'll start. When you get back from the village, sort out the lean-to and give it a bit of clear out. There should be a spade and other gardening tools in there for you to use. Oh, and while you are there, look for an axe. We need some more wood chopping for the fire.'

Raising her eyebrows, Faye didn't know if he meant for her to chop wood or him. She put that idea to one side to ponder on later.

The three trips down funnel spider avenue were uneventful. Faye felt more positive and happier. She gave smiles and nods to Larso in the shop and he, in return, smiled and nodded back. Fuelled with enthusiasm after her success with the lamb dish, she purchased several different vegetables to make a vegetable curry for tonight's meal. Seeing the Tiramisu sitting under glass, she again bought two for their dessert. Waving goodbye, Faye left the shop and passing Jolindi's house, she paused as she heard children laughing. The little boy, Charles, popped into her mind and guiltily, she realised she hadn't thought of him or his mum since she had arrived at Joseph's house. In fact, she hadn't thought of work at all. She wondered what Ingrid would think of her decision to remain in India. She would need to think about her working life and make a choice about her future. The money in her bank would not last forever. In addition to the money she was spending here, her monthly bills, at home, continued to be automatically debited. She turned from Jolindi's fence and ambled up the village street.

*What's more, if Joseph has his way and doesn't return my card – no, I'm not even contemplating that!* She purposely repressed that thought.

Poor Charles, she felt a touch of the old shame returning and allowed herself to feel remorse again for a few seconds. Then with an emotional shake she then stepped out briskly. *This afternoon we are going to locate the well. Together, hopefully!* Smiling, she commenced the final walk home.

Back at the house, Faye dragged everything out of the lean-to. The heat at midday was extreme. Dust, swirling from within the lean-to stuck to her perspiring face, shoulders and arms. Streaky with red dust, she resembled an orange tiger! Bits floating in the humid air made her eyes water. Wiping the wet from her eyes she transformed the tiger into an owl. She peered at the assortment of objects and made a mental itinerary.

One push bike – tyres flat.

Two plastic water containers.

One spade.

One fork – loose handle.

One rake – broken handle, half way down.

Set of three; trowel, small fork and three-pronged item, Faye didn't know its name, probably for weeding.

Four round wicker baskets and one square one, in various degrees of disintegration.

One sieve.

A wooden box approximately 12-inch x 8-inch containing 27 chunky metal hooks. Faye's mind recoiled at the thought of the previous use of these hooks. The wild boar and piglet part of Joseph's story came to mind.

One three-legged wooden stool.

One large wicker basket containing chopped wood and dried grass. That postpones the chopping wood debate! Phew! She carried it around to the porch and sat it beside the ring of fire stones.

Two coils of rope.

Three seriously dangerous looking machetes.

16 wooden oblong boxes, like banana boxes but smaller.

An array of canes of varying lengths.

She swept out the dust, coughing as it swirled with wicked intent around her, then placed everything back in tidily. Joseph had not returned from the town. Faye looked at the sun, *hmm, it's mid-afternoon,* she reasoned.

She rinsed off the red dust, with water straight from the butt. Faye prepared all the vegetables for their curry and mixed some naan dough, ready to griddle. All stowed in the cupboard safely, she opted not to wait for Joseph to return, as she didn't want him to disappoint her again. So, she donned   the only item of clothing she had in India with long leg coverings, a pair of pyjama bottoms; a long-sleeved blouse, open toed sandals but with a pair of Joseph's socks and topped it all off with her wide brimmed hat. She set off around the side of the house to try to locate the well.

Faye reasoned and hoped it would not be in the vicinity of the bathroom, loosely called, so she scanned the area by the water butt. A visual examination of the first line of bushes, long elephant grass, climbing vines and yes, the dreaded funnel spider webs, did not offer any clues as to its location. She envisioned a cute little red tiled roof above the rounded stone-built wall of the well, with a clean bucket on a chain and handle to turn as portrayed in fairy tales. That would be very helpful, but this being India, nothing is to be as expected. As the well was not visible from the house, Faye shuddered at the task ahead. She scurried back to the lean to and returned with a determined air and stood at the edge of the jungle. Then taking a deep breath, machete in hand held high, she plunged in.

Bravely striding over the first web, she slashed at the vines and pushed her way through the long, tough, elephant grass. Bushes barred her way, thorns scraped her face, insects bit her skin, but she fought on, chopping and slashing at all in her path. The high temperature was almost unbearable. After some time of pure physical hard work, she heard someone laughing behind her. She turned, Joseph was hooting at her. She was astounded. It felt to her, by her exertions, that she had covered at least 20 yards, however, Joseph was just there, standing by the butt, not more than two yards behind her.

'What on earth are you doing, woman? I can't believe you have gone in there without me. I said I would be back. Come out here and just have a look at yourself.'

Struggling back to him, giving a web a wide berth, she almost fell onto the firm earth in front of the butt. Her hat was covered in threads of disturbed webs, with leaves and twigs entwined. It had a hint of a harvest festival affair, gone wrong. Her red, curly hair stuck to her hot, damp skin around her forehead and neck. The rest of it, hanging down her back, contained quite a few bits of foliage and possibly an insect or two.

Joseph screeched with laughter at her. Then noticing her pyjama bottoms, he pointed and screamed, 'What are those?'

Faye dangerously waved the machete at him, pretending to take offence, but glad he was home, all the same. She started laughing. Joseph quickly grabbed her wrist and de-armed her. In the next instant, she was pressed against the back wall of the lean-to, with his mouth on hers and his hands searching her pyjamas for access. Her wide brimmed hat, decorated with natures finest, discarded on the ground and forgotten.

. . . . .

Later, as darkness threatened to stop them working, Joseph suddenly shouted,

'It's here, I've found it, come Faye and see.'

Faye struggled through the undergrowth to join him and indeed, there it was, a hole in the ground, approximately circular and about four feet wide. It had flat stones laid around the edge. Weeds struggled to grow in the dirt in between them. No bucket, no chain, no wall and definitely no roof or red tiles. Webs criss-crossed across the opening and as far down as one could make out, and this denied them the immediate satisfaction of seeing water. However, Joseph heroically swept them away with his arm and, on their hands and knees, they peered down into the black hole. It was too dark down there to see anything after about a depth of eight feet. A familiar but not altogether distasteful odour rose from the deep.

Faye strived to name the smell and after a few moments triumphantly declared, 'I think it's spinach water!'

'What?'

'The smell, it's like the water from boiled spinach. I don't think it's a bad smell. Maybe it will be usable?' she queried hopefully.

'Yes, let's hope. We need to find out if there's any water down there first, though. Hold on, listen . . .' Joseph picked up a stone, about the size of a small tangerine and dropped it down the hole. Together they leant forward, heads closer to the hole until they heard a wonderful 'plop!' seconds later.

. . . . .

The fire held back the darkness and the candles gave the porch a homely feeling. Faye and Joseph enjoyed a jubilant evening, sat on the cushions, eating the vegetable curry with naan bread and then the dessert. Faye still didn't know what it was called but it didn't matter. Joseph did not compliment her on her cooking but ate with relish and that told her the food was fine.

'Tomorrow I'll sink the bucket down and then we'll see if the water is clean enough to use. We may have to empty it first, we don't know what's down there. Any number of animals may have fallen in over the years. I don't know how long it will take to fill again if we need to empty it. But, if it is usable, we'll create a path from the butt to the well. That will make your life much easier, eh? Faye?'

'Yes, thank you Joseph. There is some rope in the lean-to.'

'By the way, I bought you some seeds to plant, so you can grow our own vegetables. It's the monsoon in a couple of months, so it's a perfect time to get the seeds planted. The rainfall is very heavy, it will saturate the earth when it comes so the plants need to be strong and established before it starts otherwise the crop will be destroyed.'

'Oh? Tell me about the monsoon. I've never lived through one.'

'Well, it starts in early June, usually, and rains heavily each day for about a week. Then it rains, not all day, sometimes a couple of hours, sometimes more, but every day, until September. It can be severe, pouring down and very windy, like a hurricane. So, as I said you need to get the crops established before it starts. But then, the rain will feed the plants and they will grow well.' Faye wondered at the change in Joseph. He could hardly say two words to her on the train but now he's willing to talk and explain with patience. He's like a different man. Happily, she gathered the dirty crockery whilst saying,

'Wow! It sounds a bit scary. What seeds did you buy?'

Joseph reached over to pick up his trousers. He usually discarded his clothes on the floor in the rush to make love and then afterwards he preferred to sit with only a thin cloth around his waist. Faye noticed his trousers were carefully folded. They looked new. She was sure she hadn't seen him wearing them before. A paper bag containing several smaller paper bags was handed over to Faye.

Not wanting to spoil the pleasant companionship they were sharing, she ignored the urge to comment on his new trousers. Instead she lay the envelopes on the floor beside her cushion. The unfamiliar writing on each little bag, in Hindi, baffled her, so Joseph, laughing at her inability, searched for a pencil in the sewing machine drawer and translated into English the writing on each envelope.

'Gourds, Lettuce, Watermelon, Okra, Tomato, Cabbage, Pumpkin, Beet, Coriander, Onion. Ooh,' she laughed, 'that should get me off to a good start.' *What on earth is a gourd?* She wondered. 'Ten, ten crops to start with. Maybe as we clear the land, we could put more different things in. We could be self-sufficient.' Faye enthused, forgetting she had no experience of growing her own. The bags were plain brown paper bags without instructions.

'You can have whatever you want, my beauty. Now come here to me. I need to feel you close.' This time Faye was pleased to go to him. She was sure they could make a go of it after the lovely day they had shared, finding the well, and then planning for the future. That's what it's all about. Smiling, she scooted across the cushions into his open arms.

'That's it, my little angel. Tomorrow morning, I will draw some water from the well. I'll need to take it into town to have it tested. While I am gone you can make a start on clearing some land then I'll help when I get home.'

'Oh? Can I come to town with you?' He didn't answer but covered her lips with his. She knew the answer really but again didn't want to spoil the evening so didn't press him

## 22

## Setting out the rows

Joseph left for town the next morning. He set off early as was his habit of late but, before he did he instructed Faye to bring the bucket from the toilet area and a length of rope from the lean-to. Under the ever watchful and chattering crows they knelt, side by side, at the mouth of the well. Joseph tied the rope on the bucket handle and let it sink into the hole. Letting out the rope foot by foot he told Faye to count how many feet the bucket dropped. She counted to seventeen. Almost all the rope had disappeared. They were looking at the remaining three feet of rope with concern, when he finally declared,

'The bucket is in the water!'

'How can you tell?'

'Because the rope has gone slack. I'll tip the bucket into the water then pull it out.'

'How?'

'By flicking it with the rope so it tips on its side.'

With explosive noisy grunts, heaving, sweat running from his face, arms and chest, Joseph, foot by foot, hand over hand, raised the full bucket.

'I'd forgotten how heavy it is. Go in the house, in the cupboard there's an empty glass jar. The lid should be there somewhere. Make sure it's clean. It had pickles in it so ensure it doesn't still smell or have any residue.'

The bucket came within view from the darkness. Faye watched one more moment before scrambling up and running to the house. After pouring boiling water into the jar and rinsing it out, she returned it to Joseph.

'Here,' she passed it to him. The bucket was sat on the flat stones, full to the brim.

'How does it look?'

'I've tasted it and it seems good. You have a taste.'

Faye cupped her hand and pressed it beneath the surface of the water. It was cold! She remembered how she longed for a cold drink on the day they arrived at the house. She brought it to her lips.

'It's cold,' she laughed, 'it's really cold and delicious!'

Laughing back at her he admonished, 'Steady now, don't drink any more until it has been tested. We'll know by tomorrow. Fill the jar whilst I get ready to go.'

Cheerfully he kissed Faye and waved as he set off down the path to the village, the jar of precious well water in his hand.

Cup of chai in her hand, Faye wandered outside and surveyed her new project.

*Today,* she planned to herself, *I will make a start on clearing the land from the well to that large tree. The shade of its branches, full of large oval leaves, will protect the young plants from the harsh sunlight.*

The tree was in fact a large Banyan and stood a distance, roughly, of twelve yards or metres from the well. Faye reasoned a square area of this size would be sufficient to grow all their needs and if not then she could make it larger.

Firstly though, she brought out the spade, fork, the oblong boxes and the sieve from the lean-to. She found a spot, which she thought would be on the route to the well and dug out a few feet of the undergrowth. Having made a small clearing, she scooped the soil into the sieve and from that filled one of the wooden boxes with sifted red soil. After all ten were filled she carried them back to the butt and gave them a generous watering. In each box she planted a different type of seed. Faye had an idea of how to identify the seedling as they started to grow. She cut thin twigs to about six inches long and threaded them through the envelopes on which the seeds' names were written and stood the envelope, flag-like, in the soil at the end of each box.

Rocking back on her heels, she stared at the planted boxes. A feeling of contentment rushed through her, an epiphany - *this is what I am meant to do. I've never felt so much peace and satisfaction in my life. I'd love to enjoy this feeling every day. I could get a job in a garden centre or on a farm maybe?* Suddenly comprehending, she could change her life, she smiled and out loud said,

'Come on little seeds, grow big and strong for your mummy.'

Enjoying the feeling, she sat in the red soil pondering the wonder of this new experience. At home, she contemplated, she never considered doing any gardening. She was always too busy and to be honest, not interested, she just took it for granted. Her working life, she found, consumed her completely. Sally came to mow the lawns and trim the bushes. She'd done it since their father had become unable. Every month she came. Was it every month? Maybe it was, she never really noticed. Faye imagined her back garden in England, it was a sizable space, what could she have achieved if she had applied herself? *I could buy a greenhouse!* The feeling she experienced planting the seeds and possibly starting a new life, emphasised the stress and demand of her employment as a social worker. Allowing herself to drift back to her home she thought of Sally. Again she remembered the last time they saw each other. Faye wasn't proud of herself. She must phone Sally.

She sat for a few more moments, then standing, she returned to the here and now, putting Sally to the back of her mind, she brushed the dirt off her skirt. Gazing around at the huge mission ahead of her, she smiled, re-established her new serenity. Then picking up the water containers she returned to the house and prepared herself for her walk to the village pump.

By the time Joseph returned from town Faye had made three trips to the village, twice for water and once for shopping for the evening's meal. She had created a clearing within her desired square plot of land. The clearing was perhaps a quarter of the size she wanted. Faye was exhausted and dirty but extremely pleased with herself.

'Come and see how far I have got,' she shouted to Joseph as he came up the path.

Waiting for him at the corner of the house, she pointed to the trays of seeds, laid in a line by the water butt. Joseph nodded in recognition of her achievement. Faye watched his face intently waiting for his response. He gazed at the cleared parcel of land.

After a few seconds he spoke,

'Where have you put all the scrub you have dug out?'

'It's over there, behind that large tree. I want to clear the plot right up to that tree. It will shade the plants. What do you think?'

'I think you are a clever girl. You have worked hard today. Come let's sit for a while and have a rest. I am also tired.'

'Oh? What have you been up to?' Faye asked jovially. She glanced down at his feet. Normally he would be in a pair of flip flops, today he had on a pair of brown leather, very expensive looking, lace up shoes. He watched her take in the new shoes and then search his face questioningly.

'I've told you before, don't ask so many questions.' Joseph turned on his heel and strode off round to the porch.

*Oh! He's so volatile and temperamental. I think I'll stay round here for a while and clear some more space. Let him calm down and come looking for me. Where does he get his money from for new trousers and shoes? He must be doing some work for someone. That's what all this travelling to town alone is about.* She smiled to herself. Then she remembered he had not returned her debit card. *No, he wouldn't spend my money, would he?* Troubled, she carried on with her project, regardless of her exhaustion.

An hour or so later, Joseph appeared again. This time he had two cups of chai in his hands.

'Sorry Faye, take no notice of me. I'm sorry, I shouldn't snap at you, you've done a fantastic job here, and on your own.'

She gratefully took the tea off him and had a little sip. She sank to the ground, cup in hand and sat crossed legged directly on the red soil. Joseph sat down beside her. He was wearing his flip-flops.

'I'm getting used to you,' she smiled at him. 'Can you leave my bank card on my suitcase please?'

'Of course.' He replied quietly, and his gaze scanned the area she had been working.They sat in silence for a few minutes, drinking their tea then Joseph said,

'That tree,' pointing to the tree Faye decided was her plot boundary, 'it's called a Banyan tree, a fig. It's a strange creature as it grows on the branch of another tree and eventually strangles it and kills it. The trunks you can see are actually its roots. It grows them down from the branch of the host tree in the beginning of its life.'

'Wow, I've never heard of that before. You said a fig? Can we eat them?'

'No, the fruit is not good to eat. But it's a clever idea to have some shade for your plants. The Banyan tree is sacred.' Faye looked at him, her eyebrows raised. He continued,

'It is said that the leaf of the Banyan is the resting place of Krishna, one of our Gods.'

'How lovely,' she enthused, 'how romantic, and what good fortune to have such a tree on our vegetable plot. We will grow some great food, I know it,' she smiled.

'Yes, I'm sure we will.' Laughing he got to his feet and pulled Faye up too.

'Come my little sweet potato, let's go and make our meal, then you can make me happy some more,' kissing her sunburnt, freckled nose and, slapping her on her bottom, he ushered her towards the porch.

## 23

## The council of war

Back at work, Sally tried to immerse herself in the business, but Faye's actions stayed with her all the time. She couldn't believe what happened the night before they were due to leave the hotel. She relived the moment Faye said she was going with Joseph and not coming home. She recounted time and time again, Faye getting into the tuk tuk and Joseph's nasty sneer through the back window. The only explanation she could give to Faye's behaviour was the stress and demoralisation she experienced regarding the child, Charles, and her inability to prevent his death. Sally kept thinking - *she's not herself at the moment, she's just not herself. It hit her harder than anyone knew.*

The girls in the salon were being supportive.

'What are you going to do, Sally?' Hazel asked gently, she could see how distraught she was. Her pretty English rose face was pinched and lined with worry.

'Right now, I don't know. I don't know where she is, how she is, if she's still with that creep Joseph. I don't know anything. What's more I haven't a clue how to go about finding her. She's not answered my calls or messages, in fact I don't even know if she has received any of them. Her phone says the same every time – not available at present, please try later. - It's so frustrating. I'm totally in the dark!'

'Oh dear! Listen, Sally, I hope you don't mind, but I've asked Jo to come in to cover your clients this afternoon, so you can have some time off. I don't want to sound cheeky, Sal, but you are neither use nor ornament whilst you are in this state.'

A customer opened the door and came in smiling in anticipation of her treatment. She unbuttoned her coat and hung it up.

'Hi, Mrs Dodds, take a seat,' Hazel called and gestured to the basins on the left of the salon, 'I'll be with you in a minute. Would you like a coffee?' She turned back to Sally and whispered,

'So why don't you pop off and try to work things out? You can't go on like this. Me and Jo can manage and if we have any problems, we'll call you, you're only upstairs.'

'Hazel, you are such a love, I don't know what I'd do without you. Thanks, I'll go up to the flat and phone Gabby, see what she thinks. I feel like there's a fog muddling my brain. Thanks Hazel and say thanks to Jo for me.'

'Now Mrs Dodds, what are we having done today?' Hazel sang out, smiling at Sally. She turned and swept towards the customer, scooping up a protective cape in one hand and towels in the other on her way.

Sally gratefully left the salon and climbed the stairs to her flat.

. . . . .

'Well, I'm at work right now but . . . I'll tell you what, my day ends at five, so I could hop in the car and zip up to yours straight from work. I could be there for six, you're only a few exits up the motorway. The kids are old enough to sort themselves out. I'll phone them. What do you say?'

'Gabby, that'd be great. I'll cook something. The girls in the salon are covering for me today. They can see I'm out of my head with worry over Faye.'

'If I get a minute this afternoon I'll think about the situation and when I arrive this evening we'll hold a council of war and sort something out.' Laughing she continued, 'We'll get Faye out of the clutches of that snake, Joseph.'

'Bless you, I'm so glad we met.' Sally chuckled gently.

'Not as glad as I am, I can tell you. *Oops!*' Sally could hear another phone ringing in the background. 'Got to go, Sal, see you about six,' and the line went dead. Feeling a little more optimistic, Sally tripped into the kitchen and scanned the contents of the fridge and freezer.

'Mmm, what shall I cook?'

. . . . .

Earlier when the girls left Goa for home, Sally managed to settle down to sleep for a few hours. Gabby had spent the two previous weeks pondering on her options regarding her husband's infidelity. Sat upright, her eyes on the screen, to onlookers she appeared to be watching the film but really she was putting an action plan together.

The children needed support. To do this, she had to wear a brave face to protect herself and let them think she was coping. It was the future of her children that concerned her the most. As young adults she didn't want the effects of her broken marriage, or rather, Graham's selfishness to spoil their lives. She rubbed her temples and exhaled a deep sigh. Only grim determination would see her through, she knew that, but if Pip and Daisy could come through it without mental trauma, then she would be content.

She had to start the proceedings of her divorce from Graham. Splitting everything they had worked for all their married life saddened Gabby. On the other hand, Gabby mused, the thought of taking his business from under him and leaving him with nothing but his young woman, sparked a need for revenge that she didn't know she was capable of. *And then we'll see how much she loves her older man and what he can offer her*, she muttered under her breath. How could things alter so much, so quickly and with so much devastation? Her eyebrows knitted together as she felt these dark thoughts and realised for the first time in her life she felt hatred, real passionate hatred. She felt her lips move and couldn't decide if it was a smile, a smirk or a grimace.

Her first mission, as soon as she reached home, would be to contact her solicitor and find out exactly what havoc she could wreak on him. One thing for sure, she would never allow another man into her life. She had her children, she had friends and now, especially, she needed to help Sally and Faye, it was enough.

132

. . . . .

Pip stood at the barrier, the smile on his face tinged with concern for his mum. Gabby noted the look and in that second, furthered the resolve to protect her family.

'Hey! Wow! You look well. What a sun tan! I take it, it was hot then?' He swept her up into his arms. Gabby suspected that there was nothing in the world like a hug from one's son. She enjoyed the moment then held him away and looked into his eyes.

'Oh, it was hot alright! How are you Pip? I've missed you. Where's Daisy? Is everything alright at home? Any problems?'

'Yes, it's all fine, no probs. Come, let's get you home and you can tell me and Daisy all about your trip. She's waiting for us. Cooking some lunch, I believe!'

Hooking her arm through his, she smiled up into his handsome face. *Yes, my concern now is for my lovely children,* she vowed silently. Pip smiled back, looking down at his mum, thinking, *I'm going to look after this little lady and not let any-one else hurt her.* Pip pulled her large suitcase along on its wheels whilst Gabby clutched her hand luggage, duty free and warm coat and they went out into the cold British air towards the airport car park.

Ever grateful for the friendship of Sally and Faye, and their ability to take her mind off her own problems, Gabby looked forward to seeing Sally again tonight.

. . . . .

'Come in, come in.' They embraced each other. 'Oh, it's so good to see you again.' Sally led the way up the stairs to the flat.

'Mmm,' Gabby looked around the flat, 'this is nice, Sal, and what's that aroma? It smells delicious.'

'Oh, I've just rustled up a little something for us. It's so good to see you.'

'You already said that,' Gabby laughed and gave Sally another hug. Whilst Sally finished preparing their meal,

Gabby sat at the breakfast bar in the little kitchen and they discussed the situation.

The problems being, as they saw them:

1 not knowing exactly Faye's location,

2 the distance between Great Britain and India,

3 Sally's inability to speak the language,

4 not knowing if Faye actually *wants* to come home

5 and generally, not knowing where to start.

Whilst they ate, together they hatched a plan. A basic strategy that made Sally feel better as she felt she was taking, at last, positive steps to find and rescue her sister.

Step one - phone George and ask if he would mind asking Sunny to help with any language difficulties.

Step two – visit the travel agents and book another flight to Goa. Stay primarily at The Royal Hotel and talk to the office and the staff to get Joseph's home address.

Step three – travel to Joseph's home address, hopefully finding Faye and if not take it from there.

They smiled at each other.

'That should get me past the starting gate at least!' Although feeling more positive, the enormity of the mission was daunting, and Sally's frown reflected her doubts.

Gabby watched her, examining her face earnestly.

'Would you like me to come with you?'

'Gabby, I can't ask you to do that. What about work? What about your children?'

'Sally, my children are virtually grown up. Well, Pip is for sure and Daisy is mature and sensible. Anyway, how long are you thinking of being away? It's not going to be much more than a couple of weeks, is it? It won't take months, will it?'

'I don't know, it depends if we find her, if she wants to come home, what kind of hold Joseph has over her. We may not find her, she could be anywhere now!' Sally's face crumpled.

'OK, decision made! I'm coming with you! No argument! You don't realise this, but you saved my sanity in India. Meeting you was the best thing that could have happened to me. Now it's my turn to help you. I'll sort it out with work, don't worry! Let's go and get Faye and bring her to her senses!' Gabby patted Sally's hand, smiling and nodding comfortingly. Sally gave her a wobbly smile back.

'That's that then. We'll find her. Don't worry,' Gabby stroked Sallys back reassuringly. After a few moments Gabby stood up and said,

'I'd better be getting down the road, it's getting late. I'll phone you tomorrow after I've arranged some time off at work then you can get the flights booked.'

'Thanks Gabby, you're a peach. I can't tell you how grateful I am.'

'Not necessary, really, I'm here with you totally. We're friends, aren't we?' Gabby shrugged into her coat.

'In the morning I'll phone George and tell him what we're planning to do and see if Sunny can give us any help.'

'OK, speak to you tomorrow. Night Sally.'

The following morning George answered his mobile and was delighted to hear Sally's voice.

'Hi Sally, this is a pleasant surprise, how the devil are you?'

'Hi George, yes, I'm good thanks. I'm sorry to phone you like this but I may need some help. You know Faye went off with that waiter, Joseph? Well, I haven't been able to contact her at all ever since and I'm worried sick!'

'Oh, my Lord, what a nightmare. He was trouble from our first day at The Royal Hotel.'

'He was, yes, I had a gut feeling about him from the start! I told Faye not to get mixed up with him, but she just wasn't herself, after the strain of the incident at work. It really knocked her for six. Anyway, Gabby and I are going back there to try to find her. We're starting at The Royal Hotel with the intention of tracing him from there. The thing is the language barrier may be a problem, and I wondered if you could possibly get in touch with Sunny and ask him, if we need help, could we call on him?'

'I'm sure Sunny would be pleased to offer his services should you need them. Leave it with me Sally, I'll speak to him and get back to you. Any idea where Joseph's home is?'

'All I can remember is Faye telling me that he had a house, a train ride away, further south. That's all, no place names or actual distances or anything helpful, I'm afraid.'

'Well, they should have his home address at the hotel.'

'Yes, that's what we thought.'

'OK, leave it with me and I'll phone you as soon as I've spoken to Sunny. It may be a day or two before I can speak with him though.'

'George, thank you. Speak soon.'

The next day Sally took a call from Gabby.

'Hi Gabby, you ok?'

'Yes, thanks, but the thing is, I can't get time off work until the middle of March. Melanie is going on holiday for two weeks, then Janice is away the following week. So that brings us round to March 18th, that's the earliest I can be off. Sorry Sally, I know you are itching to find Faye.'

'That's OK, Gabby, in fact, that's probably better for me, I'll have time to organise the salon and visit Dad. When we went, the first time, it was all a bit of a rush. We shouldn't need vaccinations this time, should we? Ok, we'll make it the 18th March, that'll be good. My holiday clothes are only just ironed,' she laughed, 'I'll pop down to the travel agents if I get a gap in appointments and see what they say. By the way, I'll pay for your flights Gabby.'

'No, you will not!'

'Yes, I will and there's an end to it. I'll phone you when I've been to the travel agents.'

'Did you speak to George?'

'I did, he's ringing back when he's spoken to Sunny. It may be a day or two, he said. He thinks Sunny will help us if we need him.'

'That's good, speak later.'

. . . . .

Two days later, George phoned Sally, 'Hi Sally, have you booked your flights yet?'

'Yes, we are going on 18th March. Gabby can't get time off until then so that's when we are going. I just hope

Faye is safe and well. Did you tell Sunny what we are doing?'

'Yes, and he suggested that he and I meet you there and travel south with you, just in case you need us.'

'Oh, George, I can't believe it,' she tried swallowing the lump in her throat but it was useless. She started crying, swept by considerable relief.

'You are the kindest, most thoughtful person and Sunny is an angel. Oh! What have I done to deserve friends like you, Sunny and Gabby? That will be fabulous and make it so much easier,' she wept down the phone. George struggled to understand her words through the blubbering but he got the gist.

'We can make it an adventure. Sunny suggested we drive down instead of going on a dirty smelly train, and of course, I'll get to spend more time with Sunny, an unexpected bonus for me. I didn't imagine I'd see him again until after the summer months.'

Sally sniffed, blew her nose and laughed,

'George you have made my day. I'm phoning Gabby the minute you hang up!'

'No, you have made mine by giving me an excuse to see Sunny again. So, you are going on the 18th of March. Have you booked The Royal Hotel?'

'Yes, it seemed sensible'

'OK my dear, see you there. I'm not sure what day but it'll be around that date. I'll let you know.'

'Fab! Thanks George, I feel really positive now I have an army of people with me. I can take on the world, let alone that swine, Joseph!'

'We'll find her, don't you worry. Let's keep in touch and I'll phone when I have my flight booked.'

'Bye for now.' As George pressed the disconnect key, Sally was tapping out Gabby's number to tell her the fabulous news.

## 24

## The gift

After Joseph left for town the following morning, Faye washed the breakfast things and tidied up. She swept the floor of the house, sweeping the debris straight out of the doorway onto the porch floor. To sweep the porch she dragged out the square cushions from around the fire. Pulling out the one she usually sat on, a squashed roll of newspaper came into view from down the back. Picking it up, she could smell something bad. The newspaper was wet and slick, close to becoming papier mache. Cautiously peeling back the printed covering, she rediscovered the present Joseph had brought her. Slimy, soft and sticking to the paper cone, the Indian Love Apples were rotting. The stench made her catch her breath and retch.

Faye ran, cone in hand, through her new vegetable garden as far as she could until she reached the untouched jungle and flung the cone and its contents with all her might. Caw, caw, caw came from above,

'Sod off!' she shouted back. She watched the apples spew from the newspaper and go in different directions and the newspaper floated down to disappear in the vegetation.

As if the rotting love apples were a portent, her mood summer-saulted to one of sheer fury as she remembered Joseph's new trousers and shoes. She spun on her heels and ran to the house. Starting with her suitcase, she searched every inch of the house, looking for her debit card. He said he would leave it. He hadn't. Deep inside her heart, she knew he hadn't.

'He's spending my money!' she spat out to herself. 'I'm sure of it. Well, that's what he thinks. Wait till he gets back!'

Dressed only in her knickers and bra, Faye stormed from the house, through the porch and around the back to the water butt. The crows screeched again as she raced round the corner of the house.

'Shut up, you bloody noisy articles, just shut up! I'm sick of you too!' Faye picked up a stone the size of a golf ball and threw it upwards at the crows. 'Take that!' she screamed. 'That'll shut you up!' The stone disappeared into the branches. Frustratingly it had no effect and the crows became even more excited. What goes up, must come down - the stone reappeared and landed on the lid of the water butt, bounced off and hit Faye squarely on the top of her head!

'Ouch!' she cried, rubbing her head and recognised the stone as it landed on the ground at her feet. She'd injured herself instead of the crows.

'Oh, well, that's just flaming typical of my life!' she shouted to the crows, falling to her knees and crying noisily for a few minutes. She wiped the tears and her runny nose onto the back of her right hand and then her left and started laughing. For ten minutes at least, she alternated between howling with tears and howling with laughter. She had never felt so out of control of her life. She didn't know where she was. She didn't even know the name of the village. Sitting on the ground, flabbergasted, how could she have allowed herself to get into such a predicament? Eventually, downcast, red and puffy from crying she collected the kettle and made some tea.

With a heavy heart, Faye carried on with her chores. She went shopping, filled the water butt, organised their evening meal, then carried on preparing her vegetable plot. All the time though, she seethed internally.

Whilst in the village, after visiting the shop, she saw Jolindi coming out of her gate. She waved. Jolindi waved back and shouted, 'Hello Laal Baal.'

At least, that's what it sounded like. Faye repeated it to herself over and over to try to remember the words, so she could ask Joseph what it meant. As upset as she felt over Joseph and his lies about her debit card, she smiled at Jolindi, putting on a confident and happy act, and moved along as if there was nothing wrong.

.  .  .  .  .

In the late afternoon, Faye sat on her cushion tapping her fingers, rhythmically, waiting for Joseph. She had come to a decision. She was going home, for definite.

Whilst working on the garden, Faye felt calm, more than calm, serene, peaceful and purposeful. She couldn't recall ever feeling such happiness but knew she could achieve the same satisfaction at home. Joseph wasn't going to be allowed to take advantage of her to the extent he was doing. Resolutely, she sat, listening for the crows to stir because of movement on the path. She would go first thing in the morning, asking Jolindi or the shopkeeper to find her a tuk tuk if necessary. She was sure she would make them understand. Her suitcase was repacked and ready, her bag and hat sat on the top, waiting. The skirt and top she dressed in to travel to India, just a few weeks ago, hung on the back of one of the chairs in preparation for a hasty departure if required. Her determination was solid.

Faye looked upwards as the crows began to shout. Then she heard her name being called from some distance away.

'Faye! Faye!'

Jumping up, she went to look down the path. Joseph was 200 metres away. He was carrying a sack, it looked heavy and he held it awkwardly in front of him with both hands, but he had a big smile on his face. He struggled but managed to raise one hand to wave at her.

'See what I have bought for you, Faye!' He came closer. 'Wait till you see this, you will be so happy!'

Faye frowned, her eyebrows drawn together, muttering to herself,

'Hah! I'm not falling for that again! It's probably my money that has paid for it.' However, she marched down the path to meet him.

'Where's my debit card?' She greeted him, sternly. He looked at her, taken aback but chose to ignore her, labouring with the unwieldy load. Then her curiosity pushed aside the determination to have it out with him and leave.

'What is it?'

'Wait till we get in the porch. Quick, run to the lean-to and get some rope!' he commanded, breathing heavily due to the exertion of carrying the sack. She scurried off to get the rope and met him as he entered the porch.

'Will this do?' she asked, bursting with wonder.

'Perfect. OK, listen, I have bought this for you, for your little farm that you are making here.' Placing the sack on the floor he kept hold of the neck.

She stared at him, mouth open, eyebrows raised, mentally urging him to get on with it and let her see what was in the sack. Then a movement made her look and she watched with bewilderment as the contents thrashed about forcing Joseph to hold tighter to the drawn neck.

'What is it?' she almost shouted.

'Hold the top of the sack while I make a noose. I'll have to get the rope around its neck very quickly, so you must hold it tightly, so it doesn't run away. It's only a baby so it's not dangerous!' Automatically she did as she was told and held tight to the neck of the sack.

'What is it?' she did shout this time.

'A piglet!' He knotted the rope and placed the noose on the ground beside him in readiness for rapid use. He took the sack from Faye's hands.

'Eh? A piglet? I don't know the first thing about piglets!' Her eyes widened with surprise. She was still shouting.

'It's OK, I'll tell you what to do. When I say 'Go', push both your hands into the sack and hold onto it. It will wriggle and scream like the devil, so you'll have to hold on tight. Then when I get the rope around its neck, we'll tie it to the banyan tree. It can live in the shade, it'll be fine there.'

Faye was gaping at Joseph as if he had two heads then gawked at the sack and then back at Joseph, utterly flabbergasted, speechless.

'Come on, get your hands round it and hold on tight. Ready, one, two, three, Go!'

He held the top of the sack open. Faye gulped, screwed up her eyes and thrust her hands in. She felt a hot, slightly hairy, small firm body, wriggling within the darkness of the thick woven fabric. It felt about the same size as a young Jack Russell. She clamped her hands on either side of its torso and the little pig let out an ear-splitting scream in fright. Faye screamed in response, automatically let go and withdrew her hands at speed. She didn't know who was the most scared, the piglet or her. In the trees, the crows went berserk!

'OK, stop being a baby, Faye!' Joseph shouted over the screaming. 'We cannot keep the pig in the bag all night. Now try again. This time don't let go. Ready?' She nodded, eyes wide, not convinced,

'One, two, three, go for it!' he cried.

Again, she thrust her hands in and felt them go either side of the little shaking body. It screamed, wild and loud and wriggled frantically. Faye screamed again but nodded at Joseph to say she had hold of the pig. Joseph pulled the sack down and rushed in with the noose.

Faye held the piglet head up. Black and white patches coloured the body. Its head was mostly white with sprinkles of black and pink spots around the bristly snout. The inner of its ears were pink and almost see through with thin red veins. Its little immature trotters made cycling motions in the air. All four feet were still clean and soft, an indication of its infancy. Its head thrashed from side to side trying to avoid Joseph and his noose and its little rounded bottom, with an inch long skinny, stringy tail, squirmed in time, in the same direction as its head, its body curving into a c shape, with the agility of an eel. All the while it was squealing at the top of its voice. After two or three minutes of struggling to get the piglet's head through the loop of the noose, Joseph finally shouted, over the squealing, it was safe for Faye to let go. She placed it gently on the ground. The piglet, suddenly finding itself on its feet again, backed up, away from them, wildly shaking, trying to get its head out of the noose and escape from the huge humans.

142

Faye felt nothing but sympathy for the piglet, it was very young and very scared. Watching its determined body writhe and wriggle to get free, Faye's throat constricted, and her eyes filled with tears. It was such a plucky little creature.

'Come,' Joseph motioned to Faye, 'we'll tie it up and let it calm down. I'm exhausted and hungry.' His normal, unaffected attitude suggested he has been through this type of exercise before. He dragged the resisting piglet by the rope towards the tree. It fought against him all the way. Faye jumped to her feet and ran behind them, horrified.

'You're hurting him!' she shouted. Joseph turned, stared at her, shook his head, then glared down at the piglet.

'It's a pig,' he shouted and pulled it sharply with a touch of cruelty. Faye decided to be silent for the sake of the little creature.

Tied to the base of the Banyan tree the piglet struggled and squealed for a few minutes before sitting down on its little bottom. Dejectedly it hung its head in despair. Faye's heart broke at the sight of the unhappy infant.

'Is it a boy or a girl?' she asked quietly.

'I don't know, it doesn't matter, does it?'

'How old is it?'

'About four weeks, I expect.' Vaguely he waggled his hand as if to say thereabouts.

'The poor baby, what can we give it to eat? Does it need milk?'

'Of course not. It will have our leftovers, peelings, rice, that sort of thing. We are raising it to be eaten. Do not get attached to it!' He ordered over his shoulder as he went back to the house.

Faye said nothing. She stared at the little pig. 'Do not get attached to it!' he had said. Too late - love filled her heart. *Rebel. I'm going to call you Rebel. You're the cutest little thing in the whole wide world,* she thought to herself. She made kissing noises at him. He didn't respond but lowered his head further and turned it slightly away from her.

Reluctantly Faye peeled herself away from the piglet and followed Joseph back to the house. He was lighting the fire to make chai.

'I'm going to call it Rebel.' She informed him.

'I said don't get too attached, we'll slaughter it when it grows big enough.'

*Over my dead body!* she said to herself as she walked past Joseph.

Faye went to the cupboard and looked over her stock of food. She chose a tomato and a sweet potato. Holding the food out in front of her, she approached the piglet. He watched her coming for a moment then charged at her, growling, the full length of the rope, which suddenly stopped him and swung him off his feet, turning him abruptly to face the way he had come.

Proudly she watched him. *So fierce,* she thought, *so brave for a baby.* He squealed and snorted crossly at her, stamping his cute little front trotters. She adored him. She gazed at him, smiling, but feeling a little disappointed he obviously didn't feel the same about her. She threw the tomato and potato down, within his reach, stepped back to a safe distance and watched as he sniffed and then munched on them. Squatting on her heels, she prepared herself to spend some time watching him.

'Rebel,' she whispered, totally captivated by the little scrap.

'Faye!' Joseph shouted to her, 'What are you cooking tonight?'

She sighed and turned and walked back to the house. The debit card and her mission to leave forgotten.

After she had cooked and served their evening meal, she again walked across to the Banyan tree. Rebel had found himself a hollow amongst the roots and for a second, in the half light of the evening, she couldn't see him. Her heart beat wildly in her chest! Then he moved as he sensed her approach. On a cabbage leaf she had placed most of her rice and cooked vegetables. She discovered, during the meal, that she would rather do without  enabling the little piglet to eat a good meal on his first night in his new home. Making kissing noises again, she crept closer to him. Abruptly he jumped to his feet and charged at her to the length of his rope as he did earlier. He growled, snorted and stamped. Feeling very sorry for him, Faye crouched just beyond the extent of his rope. She carefully edged his supper towards him and as he greedily gobbled at the rice and vegetables, she made, what she felt was the correct crooning sounds to him. Her intuition told her to try to connect with him. He ignored her, whilst snuffling in the food. Then he turned his back on her and returned to his hollow.

Sadly, Faye rose. She returned reluctantly to the house and Joseph.

'I have more good news for you. The water in the well is safe to drink. You may fill the butt with it in the morning. No more carrying water from the village. Good news, my little cherub, eh?'

'You want me to fill the butt? Do you think I can pull the bucket up on my own?' she asked incredulously. She thought of him struggling to pull it up and his sweating muscles.

'I think you are a strong and capable girl. You can do it. Just fill the bucket half full and you should be able to pull it up easily. Now, Faye, come on, are you going to thank me properly for your gift?' Joseph stood and leered at her. He reached for her hips with both his hands and pulled her close. She could feel he was already aroused.

As he turned her to face the house, she cast a glance over her shoulder, but now darkness shrouded the Banyan tree. She couldn't see Rebel. Experiencing an overwhelming feeling of resignation, she let herself be pushed indoors to the soiled mattress. She felt a good helping of self-loathing.

## 25

### *The doe eyed girl*

The following morning Faye rose with more enthusiasm than she had for many days. She saw Joseph off to town, or to wherever he went each day. She didn't mind his going today and didn't ask to go with him. She didn't care. The crows announced his departure as usual. Then she dashed to the house to get Rebel's breakfast and ran to the Banyan tree to see him.

Armed with toasted naan and sultanas, she gently crept towards him, crooning all the way to forewarn him of her approach.

Rebel was still curled up in his hollow. The white bits of his skin and hair had turned a dirty red from the soil. A couple of dead leaves stuck to his back. He lifted his head and sniffed, his snout searching in all directions into the air. Faye, enchanted, mouth open in a wide grin, watched with joy as he roused. Standing, he stretched. Pushing his bottom up and pointing his forelegs out in front of him, his chest touching the ground, he stretched his neck back and looked at the sky. He maintained this position for three seconds before relaxing and trotting to where Faye had placed his food the night before.

*Wow,* she thought, *he's learning! What a smart little guy.*

'Rebel,' she whispered and then said it again louder, 'Rebel! That's your name, you smart cookie. Here, enjoy your breakfast.' She put his breakfast in the same position as last night. He stood still and watched her, he didn't move away or act aggressively, just stood and watched. Making kissing noises she crept away, not wanting to alarm him whilst he ate.

'I'll come back later, Rebel,' she called over her shoulder. Suddenly she considered that Rebel did not have any water within his reach. It took some time to find a suitable container for this use, but she did. Re-entering his terrain with care, he didn't charge at her but snorted and growled for a couple of seconds until his nose smelled the fresh liquid. He drank with gusto, noisily sloshing water over the sides. His snout was in the pot but both eyes were on Faye. She left him then, content to go about her work with the little pig fed and watered and in her care.

Joseph had not mentioned raising water from the well again. Faye realised it must be another of her responsibilities. So, she decided to have a go at pulling up a bucket of water and seeing exactly how difficult it was going to be. Each day by midday, the temperature soared up towards 40 degrees. Early morning would be the best time to do anything, she supposed. The first attempt to bring up the bucket had Faye streaming with sweat, puffing and cursing. The palms of her hands were blistered and sore. However, after that, she discovered, through trial and error, how to tip the bucket, with a sharp tug of the rope, to make it only half full. That made it much easier to pull up and tip into the water container to transfer to the butt. On the first day of the working well, Faye estimated it took her longer to fill the butt than walking to the village and back. In between bucket loads, she chatted to Rebel and in return he watched her, sometimes following her movements with his eyes, sometimes curling up and appearing to doze. She did notice, nonetheless, that his little pink ears carried on working like radars, even whilst he pretended to sleep.

Faye's life had changed. Today, she had joy in her heart because of the piglet. Happily, she went around the side of the house to view her seed boxes. In two of the ten boxes, a hint of green patterned the soil, tiny bright green specks of new life.

'Oh wow! Fabulous! I'll till the earth ready for planting out and I can continue to talk to Rebel whilst I'm working.' Contentedly she prepared her day's tasks. The debit card was forgotten for the present.

Meanwhile, as Faye dragged the spade across her vegetable garden to etch out a straight line, ready for ploughing, Joseph arrived at his destination. He knocked gently on a blue coloured door. The door opened a crack for one second then was swiftly pulled open and a young, doe eyed girl, smiling widely with pleasure, stood back to allow him to enter.

'Your father has gone?'

'Yes, he went half an hour ago. He won't be home from work until seven tonight.'

'Wonderful. Come, let me hold you,' he crooned. He took one large stride into the house and with a quick glance over his shoulder to ensure no-one saw him, he kicked the door shut with his foot before taking her into his arms. He lifted her like a little doll, her legs hanging over his left arm and his right arm around her back.

'You haven't told anyone about us, have you? It has to be our little secret,' he murmured in her ear. 'You are the love of my life, my darling. Today I will buy you another present although you are beautiful enough already without any more jewels!'

'I promised I wouldn't tell any-one. Joseph, do you really love me?'

'Of course, I do, how could I not, you are so beautiful. Slim, young and eager.'

'Will we get married?'

Joseph's reply slid off his tongue effortlessly, 'Of course, now hush and let's . . . '

'What will you buy me?'

'After you have shown me how much you love me, then we will talk again about presents!' Joseph eyed the young girl, undisguised lust on his face. He kissed her eyelids, her nose and her lips.

Regardless of his kisses she continued chattering showing the difference in their priorities. Important to her young self - presents. Important to him - his bodily needs!

'Please tell me what you will buy for me. I would like a necklace and matching nose ring. Gold and rubies would be lovely.'

With the girl still in his arms he marched purposefully through the house whilst she pouted up at him. Reaching the bedroom, he almost threw her on the bed. She giggled coyly as he struggled to access her youthful, unblemished and underage skin.

## 26

## Eagles and crows

The day after, Faye went to water the seed boxes and couldn't believe how much the shoots had grown. It was only a few days since she planted the seeds and already, in one of the trays, the shoots were almost an inch tall.

'That's the magic of India,' she muttered to herself, 'the heat and humidity.' She surveyed her home made flags on the end of each seed box. The largest and strongest looking seedlings were the gourds.

'We need to find out what a gourd is and how to cook it,' she smiled to herself then turned to Rebel. 'Do you know, Rebel? No, of course you don't,' she laughed.

Rebel stood and sniffed the air with his cute little round snout. It had bits of dirt stuck to it. He didn't seem to mind. He walked as far towards Faye as his rope would allow and watched her watering the seedlings. Guess work helped Faye prepare the plot for the seedlings. She dug little holes approximately eighteen inches apart. She marked each place with a stone as she went, then at the end of the line, she turned and looked down the row and smiled with satisfaction at the straight-ish line of stones.

'How very rewarding, Rebel. Just wait until these gourds are ready for eating! We'll have a feast!' she kidded out loud to Rebel. He nonchalantly peeked at her out of the side of his eyes.

As she prepared the ground for the next few rows, she worked closer and closer to Rebel. He carried on watching her, and she continued chatting to him. They would appear to strangers to be comfortable friends, easy in each other's company, she thought and it pleased her.

Faye knew a trip to the village was necessary to buy food for their meal but after her exertions in the vegetable plot she needed a rest before setting off on the twenty-minute hike down funnel spider avenue. Carrying a cup of water, crooning and making kissing noises all the time, she sat well within the limit of Rebel's rope. He, almost imperceptibly, edged himself in her direction, taking it slowly and cautiously. Soon he sat within a yard of Faye. She had a compelling instinct to reach out and stroke him, but resisted, not wishing to spoil the moment. Rebel appeared to be showing trust and therefore she didn't want to scare him away.

His eyes, which had not left her all the time she sat with him, began to close and he sat snoozing in the shade of the large tree. Faye snoozed alongside him.

After a short nap, she tried to drum up the energy to walk to the shop. Rebel, feeling her gentle stirring, opened his eyes and stared. He didn't retreat to his hollow but sat comfortably close to her.

'Are you missing your mum? You poor little thing.' Faye cooed at him. She looked him over, taking in the whole of him, loving every tiny bit.

'I'm your mummy now.' She declared gravely. He didn't argue.

'Rebel, Rebel, your face is a mess. Rebel, Rebel, you've torn your dress! Hot tramp, I love you so!' she sang quietly to him, the same lines over and over. Feeling love and contentment, she could have sat just looking at him for the rest of the day. Rebel snoozed again, content with her near-by.

She stayed with him as long as she could then reluctantly went to wash and change for the walk down funnel spider avenue to the village shop.

It occurred to her whilst getting ready that she didn't mind Joseph going out and leaving her alone now she had Rebel. In fact, she preferred it. She could be herself and give all her attention to Rebel. Joseph would make her feel silly if he saw her showing too much love to the little piglet. Another thing, more worrying, she didn't trust him not to harm Rebel if she gave him too much attention.

Faye decided to wear the skirt and top she wore on the plane at the beginning of the holiday. The clothes were as she had left them, folded over the back of the chair, when she planned to leave yesterday, and remembered that she needed to ask Joseph for her card. Frowning, she zipped up the long flowing skirt.

However, her frown turned to a smile as she noticed that instead of it hugging her hips and cruely digging into her waist, the skirt was hanging off her waist and circled her tum just above her belly button, the material loose around her hips.

'Wow! I've lost some weight, this physical work and Indian diet is suiting me,' she muttered to herself.

She had no mirror, but if she had, she would have noticed her exposed skin was a healthy tanned colour, her freckles faint within the golden glow of her face.

Her unruly hair tied up, she set off, eager to get there and back. Back to Rebel.

After an uneventful visit to the shop, Faye strode home with happy determination. The funnel spiders no longer frightened her senseless. In fact, she had to acknowledge, she'd never seen the occupants of the huge webs. Not even when she was clearing her vegetable plot.

.  .  .  .  .

Approximately 250 yards from the house she became aware of the racket and stood still, listening carefully, trying to identify the sound and its origin. Then it dawned on her, it was the crows, they were making a proper commotion! There must be a reason, Faye told herself. Unless someone or something was about, the crows stayed quiet, so something was happening at the house!

'Rebel!' She screamed, dropped her fabric bag and ran as fast as she could, back to the house.

'Rebel!' Rounding the corner of the house, running towards the Banyan tree, she couldn't see him!

'Rebel!' Great wafts of panic rolled over Faye, 'Rebel, where are you?'

Gawping up to the crows, she caught her breath as she discovered the cause of their uproar. She stared with fright. On the upper branches of a tree, only yards from the Banyan tree, sat five large eagles. In fact, they must have been, at least, two feet tall. Their bony shoulders poking above their bodies and their necks protruding upwards like giant worms. The size of their hooked beaks terrified her. Faye could see them clearly, she was close enough. The eagles turned their heads in unison and stared back. Rooted to the spot, she took in the scene. It was mayhem. The crows, tiny in comparison, were flying around them, screaming, and taking dives at them, protecting their homes. The eagles, appearing unmoved by the frantic actions of the crows, watched their approaches and noisy attacks with disdain and contempt. One eagle rose on its feet, stood tall and extended its wings as if to fly. The wing span shocked Faye, it instantly reminded her of the Angel of the North. She had driven past the statue once, a long time ago. The eagle's wings must have spanned six feet or even more!

As if a spoken command had been issued, the eagles rose as one and took off. Their huge wings whooshing noisily through the air, they ascended above the treetops, circled once and then disappeared in the direction of the village. The brave crows continued to harass them until they were out of sight. Faye could not pull her eyes away until they were completely gone. Open mouthed she stood and stared after them. The crows calmed and settled and Faye, yanked herself away from the air display and ran, shouting, towards Rebel's abode.

'Oh my God! Rebel! Rebel! Where are you?' She was convinced the eagles had eaten Rebel!

'No! No! Please, no! Where are you baby?' It was the first time Faye had come across eagles in India and had no idea if they were looking for food, passing through, regular visitors or what. But her initial thought was for Rebel, he was young and vulnerable. Tears fell from her eyes and streaked down the dust on her cheeks. She sought out the rope. It was laying slack on the ground.

'No!'

Her eyes followed the rope and she could discern a small lump laid between the roots of the large tree. She thundered towards it.

'Rebel! Is that you?' A little head popped up out of the roots, covered in red dust. She could barely make out his open eyes.

Dropping to her knees, she cried and laughed at the same time. Her forehead in her hands, the backs of her hands touching the ground, she felt so grateful he was safe. A snort and a snuffle raised Faye's head. Rebel stood close to her, sniffing at her hands laid there in the dust. Laughing through her tears, she automatically reached out a hand to stroke him and pull him in close, but he backed away and growled a short growl. Faye accepted his attitude, he was a baby, after all and still new around here.

'Oh, you're a clever boy! Did you go and hide? Aren't you clever? Oh, you did scare Mummy!'

She sat back on her haunches and laughed with happiness that he was alive and safe and indeed that he had felt able to walk right up to her, albeit for just a moment.

'I'll make you an extra special tea tonight, Rebel. Oh, my Lord! The shopping!'

Not wanting to leave Rebel whilst the eagles reigned supreme in the trees, she stood and searched the branches of all the trees. They were empty. The crows were silent once more. Faye felt it safe to return to the path to retrieve her shopping.

'Rebel,' she said to the little piglet, he eyed her with feigned disinterest, 'I'm going back for the shopping. If anything comes near you, call me! Rebel? Do you hear? Or at least tell the crows to call me!' She laughed at her own silliness and walked away, checking the branches as she went. Feeling safe, she stepped out and quickly returned with the fabric bag.

## 27

# The elephants

That evening after the meal they sat companionably on the cushions. Faye told Joseph about the visit from the eagles.

'Oh yes, they come and perch in the trees every so often. I think they are looking for food. It is said they are a group of young males who haven't yet found their female mates. They can be a little troublesome, a bit like teenage boys!' he laughed, 'My mother always hated them! They would come down and try to snatch the chickens! She used to spend hours guarding them. You had better watch the pig, whilst he is small he could be a meal for one of them!' Joseph laughed again and added, 'I'm looking forward to it, I don't want an eagle tasting it before I do, especially after I carried it all the way up from the village!' he smirked cruelly at Faye.

'Hmm, he was hiding in the roots of the Banyan tree. He's quite smart, you know.'

'It's a pig, Faye, remember that!' Joseph's tone changed and he stared knowingly at her. The pleasant ambience they were sharing rapidly disappeared. It was palpable, Faye felt it. It was like jumping into cold water. Dismayed, she kept her head down and busied herself with the crockery. She didn't want to pursue this line of conversation knowing she couldn't trust Joseph where Rebel was concerned. She feared he would hurt him just for spite. Hiding her concern so as not to give Joseph ammunition, she made some chai and found the coconut cake she had been saving for the evening's dessert.

As the atmosphere improved, Faye decided to mention to Joseph that she hadn't yet phoned Sally. She dreaded bringing it up with him, knowing how he would respond, and had put it off and put it off, however, she needed to charge her phone and contact Sal, at least it would take his mind off Rebel. Taking a silent but deep breath, *Oh Lord, here goes,* she started,

'Joseph, the other day, whilst I was in the village, I tried to phone Sally, you know, my sister?' Joseph's head shot up and he looked at her, a frown across his face.

'Anyway,' she continued, acutely aware of another change in atmosphere, 'I couldn't get through because there wasn't any signal strength and I don't suppose it would be any better out here.' she waved her arm to encompass the house and land. As she rapidly spewed out the words she looked at him to see if he was listening – he was! Intently!

Swallowing she proceeded, 'Also, there's an additional problem of the phone losing its charge. I don't know where I can plug it in to . . .'

'Stop rattling on, woman.' He exclaimed and cut her off. Loudly, he continued, 'You always have something to complain about! Haven't I provided you with a working well, an animal for your farm, seeds for you to grow, money for you to spend in the shop on whatever you want. You always want more. You are the most ungrateful woman I know!' He turned his head from her and glared out into the night.

*Be brave,* she thought to herself.

'But she will be worried about me, and we didn't part on good terms, Joseph, if you remember.'

Faye could hear Joseph breathing heavily, he continued to stare into the darkness. Seconds ticked by. Suddenly he turned his whole body towards her and in a quieter tone said,

'Sorry, yes of course, I'll take your phone and charge it in Shamoga tomorrow, then when it's charged we'll take a walk and find a spot where there's a signal. Maybe we need to head towards the mountain. You have seen the mountain?'

156

'Yes, I've seen it.' She replied,

'Get me the phone and I'll take it.'

'Well, perhaps I can come too and try to phone her from Shamoga as soon as it's charged. There's probably a signal there, if anywhere. I'd like to see Sham . . .'

Again, he cut her off, giving a loud sigh any member of the Amatuer Dramatic Society would be proud of and looked directly in her eyes and said firmly,

'I'll take it, I said. You always want more. I cannot do enough for you, can I!' Without taking his eyes from Faye, he stood from his cushion, gave her a long fierce glare and stalked off into the night.

Faye sat on her cushion, digesting what had been said and by whom, and considered that the chat went just as she expected.

'Wait a minute!' she said loudly, to herself, the crows, Rebel, and any other creature that may be listening, '*money for you to spend in the shop!* It's my money he's giving me, he's not keeping me or doing me any favours financially. The cheeky devil! I'll tell him whose money it is when he comes back! He has the effrontery of old Nick!' Exasperated by his ability to turn her requests around she stomped around the house ineffectually venting her frustration.

'What am I doing with such a man?' she bellowed to her imagined audience of creatures.

Gathering the washing up, she placed it to one side to be washed in the morning, and marched around the house with the kettle for water.

Viciously, in anger, she kicked the butt.

'Oh bugger!' she cried, dropping the kettle. Her toe hurt like crazy.

'What a bloody fool I am!' Turning on her uninjured foot, she fell over the discarded kettle and landed on her knees in the dirt.

'What the hell else can happen?' For a few minutes, Faye sat there feeling deeply sorry for herself, rubbing her toe. Tears fell like raindrops into the dusty earth.

She had to hop to the toilet, she couldn't bear to put her foot on the floor. Gingerly, she hobbled over, checked on Rebel and took herself off to the mattress. *This is all his fault.*

*He has a big problem*, she thought, *I can't say anything, but he has to explode! What is the matter with him?*

.  .  .  .  .

He didn't return until after she had gone to sleep, and he left before she awoke. She knew he'd been in bed with her as she vaguely remembered his body against hers during the night. It was a relief that he didn't wake her for his own pleasure as he usually did. Faye suddenly wondered how she felt about that. At least whilst he desired her, she felt wanted and loved, if only for one thing. It was the first night they hadn't had sex. She decided to stow that debate and bring it out later when she was more awake.

How she slept through him getting up and dressed she didn't know, he always made a lot of noise and demanded help from her. She realised he could be sneakily silent when he wanted.

After she was up and dressed she recalled their conversation about her phone. Limping across the room, she grabbed her fabric bag from the top of her suitcase and searched its voluminous innards. Of course, she should have known - the phone was gone. That's what all the sneaking was about!

Now, she pondered, has he taken it to charge for her? Has he taken it for his own use? Or has he taken it simply so she couldn't use it?

Sitting down to watch Rebel eat his breakfast and rest her foot at the same time, she said,

'What shall I do, Rebel? I want to phone Sally, to make sure her and Dad are OK, and let her know that I am. I should phone Ingrid as well. I want control of my own money and not rely on him getting it out of the bank for me. I want my bank card back. Most of all I want to be sure I can trust him. He's probably emptying my bank, bit by bit. And another thing, I'm completely isolated here with only the women and the shopkeeper at the village to wave at. I miss having people around,' She opened her arms wide as if to enfold Rebel, but he eyed her and took a couple of steps backwards. She ignored this.

158

'I love having you here, Rebel, don't take this personally, sweetheart, but I really would like to talk to someone in English and have a good conversation and not be afraid of their fragile temper.'

She watched as Rebel nosed a slice of onion away from the rest of his breakfast. He also left the cabbage leaf that served as his plate.

'You don't like onion? Well, I won't give it to you again.' He seemed to eat everything else. He looked at her, no snort or grunt, but then turned and noisily gulped down half a pot of water.

'You're a good listener, Rebel. Can you give me advice? What shall I do?' She waited for an answer. Rebel, burped, turned a few circles and settled down for a snooze in his hollow.

'Well, thanks for your help. If I can hobble to the shop on this foot, I'll buy you some sweets. What do you fancy? Apricots?' again waiting for an answer, staring at him. The silence became overbearing, she sighed, 'OK, apricots it is.'

Looking up towards the treetops she cried,

'I'm going mad, I'm talking to a piglet and, worse still, expecting an answer!' and shouting to the crows, 'but how can I make Joseph respect me and my things?' With no reply from the crows either, despondent, she returned to the house, frustrated with Joseph and peeved with herself for being such a wimp.

Faye washed up, tidied the porch and the one room shack.

She shouted, 'Bye,' to Rebel and 'Will you watch over my little boy, please?' to the crows, placed her fabric bag over her shoulder and winced as she limped down the path.

. . . . .

Arriving at the end of the village street, she noticed, outside Jolinda's house, an elephant, two men and a boy. She stopped in her tracks. One of the men leant forward and Faye saw Jolindas figure in her gateway. The man kissed

Jolinda, turned and called to the elephant, waving some greenery at it to encourage it to follow, and they all set off towards her.

*Oh no! They're coming my way!* Faye spun around and spied a large tree trunk, she hopped to it and stood in its shelter to enable the people and the elephant to pass by without getting in their way.

The men and the boy chatted to each other as they drew nearer. The elephant appeared to be content to follow. One of the men spotted Faye and waved genially at her. She smiled and waved back. At the end of the street they turned and travelled in the opposite direction to Joseph's house and ambled comfortably away from her. In that split second she made up her mind to follow the group and discover where they went. Again, as the previous party, the mother and baby elephant, they turned left a short way down the path through an opening in the foliage. Keeping a safe distance, she walked behind them, not wanting to catch up and become a hindrance to them or spook the elephant, and get under its huge round feet. Watching the men with the elephant, she was charmed at the relationship they appeared to share. Turning and speaking gently to the animal, the men travelled comfortably down the wide path. The creature ambled on behind, the end of its trunk almost dragging on the floor.

After about half an hour, she realised they had arrived at their destination. Faye with her limited knowledge of elephants presumed it was a fully grown male. Benign and biddable, it followed where they led, until the man who kissed Jolinda, her husband, Faye guessed, stroked the elephant between its eyes and allowed it to take the foliage from his hand with its trunk and stuff it in its mouth. Unbid, the elephant, chewing its reward, nonchalantly walked off to its left. Looking around the wide beast Faye's eyes widened further as she saw where the elephant was heading. A line of the great beasts were standing quietly side by side, more than a dozen, different sizes - large and small. By the way they were standing, content and unconcerned, some chewing, some dozing, it appeared they were used to being here.

Faye stood, eyes wide, mouth open, staring in disbelief at the activity spread out in the space in front of her.

'Oh, my Lord!' she breathed.

## 28

## Sanctuary

The area, cleared of trees and bush, was approximately the size of a football field. Albeit not the same shape, the edges of the clearing undulating around the perimeter pushing into the trees as required. The site was almost level, just a slight downhill slant towards the right of where she stood and where another well worn path appeared to lead off.

In the foreground, on the right, there was a huge pen constructed of tree trunks. The logs, Faye estimated, were probably two feet in diameter, or more. Serious logs to hold serious animals. Held within the pen, an adult elephant. The pen was almost as high as the elephant's back at about nine feet high. A man could just be seen perched precariously on its back appearing to be rubbing the beast's thick, dark brown skin with some kind of oil. His knees were holding him in place as a bare-back rider would do. The elephant was evidently unhappy as it pushed aggressively forwards and backwards and side to side against the immovable log pen in an attempt to escape and dislodge its passenger. Angrily it roared a deafening roar, expressing its feelings and stamping its feet, jumping up with its front legs and crashing down, making the ground shudder, letting all and sundry know about its incarceration. Faye took a few smart steps back but felt for the poor animal and wondered what on earth the man on its back was trying to do to it. She expected him, at any moment, to be displaced and crushed beneath the huge feet.

162

Beyond the pen to the left of the clearing, stood a row of fifteen elephants in a line, chained to posts. The chain was around their ankles and then around thick wooden stakes driven into the ground. At first glance these animals seemed to be standing contentedly. However, each one lifted one foot and then another in what appeared to be a way of taking the weight off, and as the animals rocked gently, the chains made soft clanking sounds. The elephant Faye followed that morning joined the line of its own accord and stood complacently waiting. Two men were moving down the line of elephants carrying a large, evidently heavy, wicker basket. Two handles, one at each side of it enabled the load to be managed between them. At each elephant they stopped, placed the basket on the ground and took out a rugby ball shaped object. Faye watched, amazed, as one of the men offered the object to an elephant and the large beast curled up its trunk, opened its mouth wide and allowed the object to be placed gently within. She assumed it was some sort of food stuff as, thereafter, the elephant contently munched away.

With the exception of the elephant in the pen and his enraged intermittent bellowing, the overall ambiance of the place was calm, a genial, friendly, 'we know what we are doing,' type of calm.

Faye, completely mesmerised, stood gazing at the scene, eyes wide, taking it all in. Breathing in, she recognised the same smell as in the village.

'Ah,' she sighed, the smell was elephant. It was much stronger here. Again not horrible, just definitely elephant - large and awesome. She'd never seen so many elephants in one place. In fact, she'd never seen an elephant in the flesh until coming to Goa.

Unsure of the place, she didn't know whether to move forward or return the way she had come. She didn't know if the place was open to the public. If it was safe or even if she would be welcome but she was so pleased she had found it. Then the decision was made for her.

'Hello, can I help you?' A voice boomed from behind her. A loud, rich voice with the Indian singsong lilt. Faye gasped in shock and spun round,

'Oh! Sorry, you made me jump.' Then it dawned, he spoke English! 'You speak English!'

'Apologies, I didn't mean to startle you. Yes, I learnt English when I worked at a sanctuary in Africa a few years ago but I learnt the basics in school many years before. Anyway where have you come from? The tourist bus is not due for another couple of hours.' The man looked at Faye, noticed her hair and wondered if this was Laal Baal he had heard about.

'I'm living a little way from here. I followed a group with an elephant out of sheer nosiness and found this!' she motioned with a wide sweep of her arm at the clearing, 'I'm so glad I did. And so glad to speak to someone in English at last. I've been a little lonely. . . ,' Realising she was giving too much information she continued quickly, 'but this is fantastic, tell me about it.'

'I'm a mahout. I live in the village, Karnaka, about half a mile away.' He gestured toward the village, Faye guessed it was the same one.

*Karnaka, Karnaka,* she rehearsed silently so as not to forget the name.

'What's a mahout?'

'It's the job of caring for elephants. This is Sakrebyle Elephant Sanctuary. It tends to injured and wild elephants and helps them to survive alongside the human villages. Some of them are injured by poachers, some of them are shot by farmers because they have ruined their crops. The elephants sometimes become very angry and threaten human life, they can easily kill a person. We call them rogue elephants, they are extremely dangerous. They do not forget if they are attacked or hurt. Here, we bring in an angry or injured elephant, treat the wounds and treat the anger.'

He pointed towards the elephant in the log pen,

'For example, this fellow is having an oil of evening primrose massage to calm him down, then we can treat his wounds. He has nasty gashes on all four knees where poachers have tried to take him down with large knives. The poachers fix the knives to the trees, at knee level, on known elephant paths and chase the elephant. When he runs down the path the knives slash each knee. It makes him easier to

164

catch and shoot. They then take the ivory. He is lucky to be alive. His stamina is amazing. We received the message about him being injured just in time and saved him from the poachers. It will take time but he will become calm. His mahout will be patient and give him all the love and attention he needs, then he'll get antibiotics and a salve to his knees each day. He will come to trust his mahout and thereby eventually tolerate mankind again. He will never forget though,' he smiled at Faye. 'It's a very satisfying job,' he finished.

Faye was speechless, she stared at this stranger who was so willing to talk to her, and to talk in her own language, she was awestruck.

'Wow!' was all she could manage.

'Each of those elephants,' he pointed to the line of animals being given food parcels, 'are getting their medicines. Antibiotics and other medications are hidden inside the ball of hay so they will take it. Also in the hay parcel is coconut and a little honey,' he smiled at Faye and continued, 'elephants have very sweet tooths, you know. You can make an elephant do a lot if you offer it the right foods.' Laughing he then pointed to the men.

'Each elephant has his own mahout. These elephants here, some were once angry like the one in the pen or brought in very sick and infected, they are on the mend now but continue with medication and care until they no longer need it.' he pointed to the line again. 'They are free to go back into the jungle at night. The chains are for safety reasons whilst they are in the sanctuary. In the morning the mahout will go to the edge of the jungle and call his elephant and he will come back into the sanctuary for his breakfast. Sometimes the elephants come before they are called and visit the village looking for their mahout. All the mahouts live in the village.'

'I see, ah, yes, that's why it smells!'

'Pardon?'

'No sorry, I meant the elephants, their smell . . . Sorry, carry on . . .' she stumbled awkwardly. He raised his eyebrows and cocked his head but continued,

'Every house has a solidly built bamboo fence to keep the elephants out of the gardens. The women grow vegetables and, of course, there are the children to keep safe.'

'Yes I've seen the fences in the village. I thought they were a bit OTT!' she laughed and the man laughed with her, the awkward moment passed.

'They are very strong and single minded regarding food. The relationship between the elephant and its mahout continues forever, even after the elephant does not require any more treatment he will come back and visit his mahout from time to time. Some never leave. It is their choice. After they are calm they are not prisoners.'

'Wow, this is fantastic! I'm so glad I followed the guys down here.'

'Come, I'll take you a little closer. These over here, chained up, are quite safe as long as you remember they are still wild animals and don't be disrespectful. You can feed one its medication if you like.' They set off and he noticed her grimace as she strode beside him.

'What's happened to your foot, it looks bruised. Have you had an accident?'

Faye laughed, 'I was having a little temper tantrum and kicked the water butt. It was my own fault. It's only a bruise, it'll be OK in a day or two.'

'I have some special oil for bruises. We use it for the elephants' wounds but people benefit from it too. Come, I'll get it for you.' He went towards the shed at the end of the row of elephants.

'Please, no, don't worry, it will be alright. I don't want to be any trouble.'

He held up his hand and said,

'I'll be a moment. It's no trouble.' He returned with a large jar in one hand and a fold up chair in the other.

'Please sit,' he instructed.

Faye perched and slipped off her sandal, wincing at the pain and cringing at the colour of her bare skin. It was purple and blue and stained red as usual from the soil.

Kneeling on his right knee he lifted Faye's foot and rested it on his left thigh. She felt embarrassed as she didn't

166

know this man at all. Having taken off the cap of the jar he warmed the oil between his hands and gently massaged it into the skin of her foot. It felt incredibly pleasant. Faye watched him. The white oily cream turned a dirty red from the soil as he spread it on her foot. Her embarrassment was replaced by a comforting, warm feeling and it had nothing to do with her foot. She was being cared for. It was overwhelming. So unused to being treated with such kindness, Faye felt herself fill up. Quickly she swallowed and forced her brightest smile to her face.

'How does that feel?' he said.

'Fabulous, thank you so much,' she smiled but he waved her thanks away.

'My pleasure, any time,' and he laughed, 'Now are you ready to give one its medication?'

The English speaker spoke to the mahouts who guided Faye to stand in front of the large beast she had followed from the village. Her foot, she had to admit, felt better already. Mind over matter, she wondered? One of the men who brought the basket, passed a dried grass rugby ball to Faye.

'Now, just go towards her, she will open her mouth and you place the food well inside her mouth.'

Uncertainly, shaking slightly, she did as she was bid, with both hands, she offered up the parcel. The size of the elephant towering above her was overwhelming. As it opened its mouth, curling its trunk upwards, high over her head, Faye gasped, feeling very small. She could see its teeth and tongue, its pointed lower lip glossy with moisture. Nervously Faye gave a short humourless laugh and looked at the mahouts for reassurance. The man who passed her the straw parcel nodded encouragingly.

Reverently she reached up and pushed the food inside its mouth. A sizable stream of saliva streamed from the elephant's mouth and ran down Faye's arm from her wrist to her elbow as the elephant took the food from her.

'Ugh!' she giggled, 'that's not very nice, thank you very much!'

As the beast munched on the parcel of food and medication, the men laughed with Faye as she wiped the goo off her arm and flicked it onto the red earth. The elephant stretched forward and ran the end of her trunk over Faye's hair and then down her body, from shoulder to knee, sucking in her scent.

'She, this one is a female, knows you now. She has tasted your odour. She will not forget you,' he told her.

'What's her name?'

'She is called Sunahara Kaan, it means Golden Ears. Look at the edge of her ears, she has a golden strip around the edges. It is most unusual.'

'Sunahara Kaan,' Faye repeated, gazing at the elephant, 'What a lovely name. She's beautiful.'

'Yes, she is. She is very lucky to be alive. She was moments from being shot by poachers when the game wardens found her. She was extremely angry and dangerous. It has taken a long time to get her to this point.'

Faye held out her hand and Sunahara Kaan placed the end of her trunk in Faye's palm. Faye could feel the air being sucked up the elephant's trunk and laughed delightedly.

She felt blessed that she had found this place, and indeed this man. Turning to the English speaking mahout she said,

'I'm sorry, I don't even know your name. Mine's Faye.'

'Of course, I'm Viren. Pleased to meet you.' he offered his hand and she shook it, beaming at him. 'I live in Karnaka, as I said. My brother, Rav is also a mahout, he too lives in the village with his wife and child, a boy. His wife is Jolinda, you may have seen her, if you live nearby and go to the shop.'

'Yes I've met a couple of women in the village but I don't know their names. I go to the shop nearly every day. The shop has a lot of elephant souvenirs, I wondered why. It's a bit clearer now.' she smiled.

'We have a bus that comes during the day. It brings tourists from all over Goa. They pay to visit us and we use the money to run this place and buy the medications for the elephants. Laars, the shopkeeper, benefits too. After coming here, they go to the village and the shop for their souvenirs.

168

Because I can speak fairly good English, and a little French, as it happens, I am the guide for them whilst they are here.'

'It's brilliant, I love it. You are so kind to them,' she said pointing at the line of elephants, all chewing. She could see two of them were now having ointment applied to their knees.

'What time does the bus come? I've never seen it whilst I've been in the village.' It occurred to Faye that she could possibly use the bus to get to Shamoga.

'It's usually around two in the afternoon and it gets to the village, probably about three-ish.'

She stored that piece of information for the time being. She suspected it may come in useful.

Through the trees, Faye noticed a glint of sun on water. Viren saw her squint at the flash of light.

'Down here we have a lake. Come, I'll show you.'

Faye happily followed him. He led the way down the path she noticed when she arrived. On the other side of the trees forming the perimeter of the clearing and a few hundred metres down a gentle slope, Faye could discern several shapes submerged in a large lake. To the left and right, the expansive shore of the lake was fringed with a beach of red dirt out of which rose thousands of palm trees. Some of the palms had grown horizontally, others grew tall and straight. It had a tropical feel, rightly so. They swayed in the gentle warm breeze and the fronds made a swishing sound.

'Beautiful,' Faye whispered as they neared. Viren smiled.

At the edge of the lake she could make out the outlines of four elephants laying on their sides in the water, plus their men in attendance.  Further in, up to their shoulders, four more elephants, each one carrying its mahout on its back, their trunks held high above their heads, out of the water. The mahouts sat directly behind the elephant's neck, their feet trailing in the cool water.

'Oh my Lord! What's going on here?' Faye squealed with wonder.

Viren pointed to the four elephants in deep,

'Those four are going for a swim, it helps with stiffness of their joints if they have been cut or shot. You could call it physiotherapy.' he smiled at Faye and carried on, 'These guys,' Viren pointed to the four laying in the shallows, 'are having a pumice stone bath. It rids them of ticks and lice and makes them feel good.' One of the mahouts casually flipped a huge ear over exposing brown skin sprinkled with pink spots and scrubbed it with his stone. The elephant laid unmoving, content to accept the beauty therapy.

'They like a dip and a swim and then after, when they are dry, they will have a massage to keep them supple and happy. They love it. These fellows are almost healed, mentally or physically, or both. We don't recommend they come into the lake whilst having open wounds. It's not the cleanest water, as you can see,' he pointed - a huge elephant stool floated past them, wobbling on a slight wave. The mahouts ignored the dirty and muddy water and carried on, crooning to their elephants and chatting to each other.

The young calf, the one Faye saw the other day, appeared from behind his mother who was laying in the water. With his cute high pitched trumpet, he ran through the shallows and on to the shore directly towards Faye and Viren. Seeing two humans in his path, he executed a sharp right turn and ran at speed along the shore, his stocky little legs pumping purposely. His mother, who up until now had been enjoying her bath and scrub down, rose from the water, spraying her mahout, Faye and Viren with what seemed like gallons of water and took off after her mischievous son. Faye was shocked at the speed she could move. From laying in the water to full throttle down the shore in four seconds! Impressive!

Covered in dirty lake water, Faye and Viren looked at each other and laughed. It was streaming down their faces, bare arms and clothing causing the fine film of dust already on their skins to streak into filthy runs. The mahout called his elephant and the elephant called her son. With obvious reluctance the youngster obediently returned to the fold and within minutes, mother was back laid in the shallows, continuing her bathing. Her son curled himself up on the shore, instantly falling asleep as only babies can.

170

During those few seconds of madness Faye found she had been able to stroke the baby elephant on his head. She felt with wonder his bristly hair and for a second looked closely at his soft and wrinkly skin. But a connection was born when she saw the love and pride in the mother's eyes - mother and baby elephant - her and Rebel. Deep happiness flooded her being and she was so happy she chose to follow the men that morning.

'I'd better be getting back,' she said looking at the position of the sun. She still needed to shop, fill the water butt, water the plants and prepare the meal. Now she also wanted a good wash!

'Thank you so much for showing me your sanctuary, it's amazing, I love it.'

Viren smiled back at her, 'You can come anytime you like. It's my life, this place, I'm here most of the time. I'll look out for you in the village too. Be careful out in that house of Joseph's, take care of yourself.' He nodded gravely to her, losing his smile, letting her know he meant it. Then held out his hand.

*He knows who I am,* she thought, not letting surprise show on her face.

She grasped his hand and held on to it. He placed his other hand over hers. They looked each other in the eye. She stared at his face realising he was being kind and she knew, without him saying it, that he could be counted on for support if she needed it. She felt a sudden desire to confide in him and tell him everything. However, her pride surfaced so she lifted her chin, smiled her best 'I'm fine' smile and turned to leave.

'Bye Faye,' he said quietly.

'Bye for now,' she called back at him and wished she didn't have to go.

## 29

## Chapati making

Two cups of flour
Half a teaspoon of salt
One teaspoon of ghee
Cold water

Faye sat on her cushion in the porch mixing her chapati dough. A simple task, yes, but she felt she had accomplished it to a fine standard.

She called to Rebel,

'Look at this dough, Rebel, the best chapatis in India. What do you say?'

He didn't reply but stared at her for a moment then started to nose around in the earth.

'Are you peckish, baby? I'll get you something.'

Faye covered the chapati dough with part of a cheesecloth skirt she had cut up especially for that particular job. The million flies constantly buzzing around everything, every day drove her mad and she'd had to derive ways of keeping food safe from them. They even managed to get inside the meshed cupboard indoors somehow. Quickly she prepared the vegetables for the evening meal and took Rebel the peelings.

'Here you are sweetie, enjoy.' Crouching she watched him gobble down the food. When it had all gone she held out her hand. Rebel did not come towards her but she stretched forward and gently slid her fingers over his back. He didn't try to get away as he had done previously. He allowed her to stroke him.

'Oh, wow, that's nice isn't it? My precious little lad, I love you so much,' she quietly spoke to him as she continued to stroke him. He stood still for a few seconds then leaned in towards her hand, curving his body as if to say she was reaching the right spot. Faye was delighted and, not daring to move a muscle, carried on with the stroking and gentle chat.

After a few minutes Rebel moved away and did his usual circling around until he found the exact spot to lay in. Contently he lay and closed his eyes. Faye watched him filled with wonder and happiness and so as not to disturb him, crept away back to the house. *What a fabulous day,* she reflected, *first finding the elephant sanctuary and Viren and now Rebel letting me stroke him.* Happily she pulled up a bucket of water from the well and watered the gourds growing in her garden.

Shortly afterwards the crows told her someone was moving about and she peeked around the porch and saw Joseph coming up the path.

*Oh good, my phone should be charged now,* she thought to herself. And on a downward slide, *I hope he's in a good mood.* Poor expectations made her worry her bottom lip with her teeth.

'Hi Joseph, have you had a good day?' she sang out trying not to sound artificial.

'It was OK. What have you been doing all day?' he slipped out of his flip flops and lowered himself onto his cushion in the porch.

'Get me a drink, will you?' No please or thank you.

'Do you want chai or water?'

'Water from the well, it will be nice and cold.'

'Of course.'

She was walking on eggshells as usual. She wanted her phone back but knew she had to choose the right moment to ask for it.

'What have you been doing I said?' he shouted in an impatient voice as she was returning from the well.

*This obviously isn't the time to ask for the phone. Oh my Lord! Does he know I've been to the elephant sanctuary?* Her heart began to hammer in her chest! As she rounded the corner into the porch she forced herself to be calm and replaced her grimace with a smile,

'I went to the village, I filled up the butt, I watered the plants. I've also made the dough for the chapatis and prepared our meal. I fed Rebel . . . '

'I told you not to name it. We are going to eat it, it is not a pet. How many times do I have to tell you?'

'Sorry Joseph.' *No, he doesn't know about my little trip. Phew! What a relief! I really want my phone back.*

'Are you tired? Would you like a back massage? Lie on the mattress and I'll oil your back and . . .'

Joseph grunted and picked up his cup of water. He headed into the house. She heard more grunts as he lowered himself down onto the stained mattress.

*I've got to keep him sweet,* she thought and hating herself for being a two faced spineless doormat, she followed him in.

Afterwards, she made the meal and they sat in companionable silence whilst they ate. The chapatis were perfect. *Maybe now is the time to ask,* she pondered.

Joseph was doing some pondering of his own. *She is going to ask for her phone back, I know it. What can I do to keep her sweet? The money from her bank is saving my life. I can afford things I've never had before and treat Rakel occasionally.* He repressed a smile as images of the doe eyed girl passed across his mind. *My, she is one demanding girl. When I showed her Faye's phone, she thought it was for her, I couldn't take it away, but, oh, so sweet and willing. I have to manage this lump of lard to ensure she doesn't leave and take her bank card with her.* He maintained an expressionless face and felt her turn her head towards him.

'So did you get my phone charged today?' She tried a casual note, cautiously, feeling it could be a good time.

'Ah, Faye, I looked at the screen and it was only fifty per cent charged so I left it plugged in at my friend's house overnight to ensure it fully charges. It will be better and last longer. You'll have to have a little patience.'

174

Her face fell. She didn't expect anything else but hoped just the same. She should know by now that nothing of hers is returned.

Joseph observed the thought pattern showing on her face and considered quickly what he could say.

'Tomorrow I am going to see a friend . . .'

'Oh yeah?' she butted in, her tone dull, indicating disinterest. Her disappointment and frustration of being used, *again*, was bringing her close to tears. She turned away from him and stared into the jungle. Undaunted he continued,

'Yes, tomorrow I'm going to see a friend who has some chickens. He wants a new home for them. Would you like them?' Silence, Faye did not respond.

'You are doing so well with your little farm, I thought you would like some chickens. We can have fresh eggs every day. We won't eat the hens, only the eggs, don't worry. You'll have to build a run though. I'll help if you like,' he continued, his tone persuading and cajoling. She looked at him,

'How many?'

A secret smirk, he could barely keep hidden, flitted across his face with a silent, 'Gotch ya!'

'I'm not sure, about six, I think.' he paused, 'Shall I bring them home then?'

'OK,' she mumbled. 'By the way, Joseph, what does Laal Baal mean?' Joseph's eyes darkened,

'Where did you hear that?'

'Two of the women in the village said it to me? What does it mean?'

'It means Frizzy Red Hair. I told you not to speak to them in the village. They do not like europeans. Why don't you do as I say!' His voice raised, he glared at Faye.

'Well, for one thing,' she matched his raised tone with her own and glared right back! 'I don't speak to them as I don't speak their language and for another thing, I'm not going to ignore what they say to me, even if I don't understand it. And whilst we are here, you decided that I have to go to the village for food each day, so don't shout at me, Joseph, you can't have it all ways.' Silence followed her outburst and she stared at the fire, her face set.

*Frizzy Red Hair! Is that what they are calling me? Well, it could be worse. They don't know my name. Viren knows it. I wonder if he'll tell them. Anyway I'm not telling Joseph about my visit to the elephant sanctuary, he wouldn't be happy. If he finds out . . . well . . . I'll worry about that if it happens. At this moment I don't care, but right now, it's my secret, especially about the bus.*

Whilst Faye considered her nickname, Joseph, slightly taken aback at Faye's outburst, realised he had avoided another drama with Faye and she would be staying for a while longer.

Grinning at her he said,

'Come on madam, let's have a look where the chicken coop will go. My mother used to have chickens, we'll see if the same spot is suitable. Come my little peach nut, stop sulking.' He held his hand out, she took hold of it and he pulled her up and led her into the garden talking all the time until she began to show interest in the coop and making a home for her chickens.

## 30

# Wild pigs

The crows sounded their alarm. Faye, kneeling on the ground, lifted her head from her task and looked around. She couldn't see anyone.

*What's upset them*? *Eagles?* Quizzically she stood and scanned her surroundings. Glancing over at Rebel, she knew immediately something was wrong. She hurried over to him. Rebel stood, stiff legged, staring into the undergrowth growing wildly beyond his Banyan tree. Without altering his gaze, he was making little noises - snorts and a kind of mewing, like a soft grunt, his little snout trembling. He scraped the ground with his front feet, first the left then the right.

'What is it, Rebel?' she asked, puzzled by his behaviour. 'What can you see?' She followed his stare and screwed up her eyes to search the shadows of the undergrowth. After a few seconds of probing the dark, thick shrubbery, she jumped with alarm!

'What the ..!' Her first instinct was to gather up Rebel and get him to safety but she found herself rooted to the spot. Her eyes darted from Rebel's reaction, to the visitors in the undergrowth, and back again.

Faye could make out at least six pigs of differing sizes. From large a fully grown sow down to piglet size, the same as Rebel. Well camouflaged in the dark, dank vegetation, she didn't see them immediately. They were predominantly black, with lighter greyish/brown stripes on their backs. Standing in a semi-circle they stared at Rebel but all the while casting her cautious glances.

The largest pig grunted in Rebel's direction. In reply he appeared to march on the spot and mewed several times. To Faye it seemed the conversation went like this:

'Come with us, you can join our group. We are pigs like you, you should be with us.' And Rebel replied,

'I would come if I could but I'm only small and scared and I'm tied to this tree.'

Or equally the conversation could have taken a totally different line:

'What are you doing on our patch? You weren't here last time we came this way. Leave our land immediately or we will attack you!' With the reply of,

'Please don't hurt me, I'm only small and scared and tied to this tree, I can't get away.'

Jumping up and down Faye raised her arms and waved them shouting,

'Shoo! Go on, go away! Shoo! Shoo!' After a few moments of standing their ground, the largest pig grunted to the party and they turned as one and slipped away into the forest.

With relief, Faye flopped to the ground.

'What the devil? Rebel, come here to me,' she commanded. Who received the most shock, she wasn't sure.

'Come babe, come on,' she coaxed and held out her hand.

Rebel turned his back on her. His head down, he stood dejectedly for a couple of seconds before starting his circling to find his spot to lay in. He lay himself down, inching round little by little until his back was completely towards Faye.

'Oh Rebel, are you mad at me for sending them away? I didn't know, I was afraid for you. Baby, I'm sorry.' Faye reached out to him and tenderly stroked his back. He tucked his head around the far side of his body and made a sound - a cross between a sigh and a growl. Unhappily Faye crept away.

Unsure of Rebel's feelings towards the wild pigs, confused and upset, she returned to the plot to think about it. Was he at risk from them? She couldn't be sure.

*I need to observe him much more before I can even imagine what he's thinking, but he certainly didn't appear to thank me for shooing them away. Maybe he should have been untied and he could have made his own choice. How could I let him go though? He's so precious.*

Looking up to the tree tops she shouted,

'Thank you, my feathered friends for the warning. What would I do without you?' Bending, she resumed attempting to build a chicken coop.

.  .  .  .  .

The previous evening Joseph brought home some chicken wire and thin strips of wood, appearing around the porch side so pleased with himself as if he had brought her the crown jewels.

'There you are. I'm sure you'll be able to build a nice big coop with this. It nearly killed me bringing this lot up the path. I think there's a hammer and some nails in the shed.' He threw himself down on his cushion in an exhausted fashion. Not impressed, Faye answered,

'I've never built anything out of wood, Joseph. Can't you do it?'

'I'm bringing the chickens, you will have to do it. It needs to be about six foot high to enable you to get in without breaking your back. Make it in a pointed shape.' He made a shape with his fingers of a peaked roof. 'It will need nesting boxes and some shelter from the sun. And of course, it'll have to be predator proof.'

'Predator proof? What predators?'

'So you'll need to dig a trench first, about a foot deep, to bury the chicken wire beneath the surface to prevent anything digging underneath.'

'What predators?' she repeated.

'Well, tigers, wolves, foxes, you know, all the usuals.'

'Tigers? Wolves?'

'It will need to be about six or eight feet square, bigger if there's enough wire, the bigger the better.'

'Tigers?'

'That's enough Faye, India has tigers, get over it. They are more afraid of you than you are of them. So just build it as I say, and the chickens will be fine. Come let's go to bed and show me your thanks for all I do for you!'

In addition to these creatures, Joseph didn't mention leopards, asian lions or cobras. He wasn't in his usual nasty, hurtful mood. He had been with the doe eyed girl during the afternoon and she had mellowed his mood. Faye of course, didn't know this.

Sighing, she reluctantly followed him into the dingy house.

.  .  .  .  .

With fingers sore and bleeding, Faye finally hammered home the last nail. The coop looked strong but as she held onto one side piece and gave it a push, the whole thing shook. *I'll huff and I'll puff and I'll blow your house in.* However, she had achieved a covering, nest boxes and the chicken wire was buried a good nine inches below ground. It had taken all day. She was exhausted and still had to shop for the evening meal.

## 31

# Chickens and sewing

Faye fought the desire to visit the elephant sanctuary again. She was so impressed with the place and, even more, so pleased to talk to someone in her own language. She hadn't given it much thought but now as she stood, cup in hand, statuelike, gazing without seeing across the vegetable plot, she analysed her feelings. She really wanted to see Viren again. She didn't think she fancied him, as such, but still the idea of seeing him again was more than pleasing. She liked him. Simply liked him, what was wrong with that? However, she knew, without the slightest doubt, Joseph would not approve of her going there. It would lead to rows from which she would probably come off worse. It worried her that he would find out. He hadn't so far but if she insisted on visiting the sanctuary she was sure he'd get wind of it. No, she decided, it wasn't worth it. Keeping a little secret to herself was quite pleasing anyway. Nonetheless Faye continued to think about the sanctuary and despite her better judgement she contemplated when she may risk going again.

As she drank her morning chai, she wandered around the house. The vegetable plot was looking like a bona fide garden centre now with healthy plants sprouting upwards. Resolutely, instead of walking to the sanctuary, she decided to make some supports for her tender new stalks, out of the wild bamboo growing within the undergrowth. She made a mental note to purchase a ball of string from the shop later that afternoon.

In addition, she needed to keep an eye on Rebel. The visit from the wild pigs had disturbed her and unsettled their fragile relationship. Faye could not stop thinking about his reaction when the wild pigs left, turning his back on her after she shooed them off. Sadly she accepted Rebel didn't feel the same about her as she did about him. Wandering over to his home under the Banyan tree, she saw he was curled up in the usual spot in the roots. He lifted his ears and opened his eyes and stared at her but didn't get up.

*I suppose I should get a dog if I wanted true devotion. Rebel is a pig not a domestic pet. I should remember that, but he is such a cute little fellow, I love him so much. I'll get him some raisins from the shop, he'll like that.*

Faye strolled across to look at the new addition to her farm. Yesterday Joseph, true to his word, turned up with the chickens.

Pretty much the same as when he brought home Rebel, he struggled up the path loudly dictating his orders to Faye. The crows joined in the shouting!

'Faye, come and help me! Faye, can you hear, come and help!'

As soon as she heard the combined racket, she ran down the path to him. Joseph had three sacks this time. Two over one shoulder and one over the other.

'Here,' he grunted at Faye, 'they are heavier than you would think!' He thrust a sack at her and rested the other two on the ground.

'We have nine hens, all good layers, you will have plenty of eggs as I promised.'

'Wow!' she laughed happily, 'lets get them in the coop.' Gently hoisting the sack over her shoulder she led the way around the house to the coop. Within five minutes the hens stood in their new home, albeit looking a little dazed and uncertain. After the journey in the sacks their feathers were definitely ruffled.

Joseph gave her instructions,

'We have to keep them in the coop for a couple of weeks to home them, after that they can be allowed out, whilst you are here, to forage around for food. They will know where they live and will take themselves off to bed each evening.'

'Is it safe for them to be out?' she asked.

'As I said, they can be out whilst you are here. You do not listen! Here is their food, two handfuls, in the morning. They don't need anything else.' He passed her a paper bag the size of a bag of sugar.

This morning the hens appeared a little more comfortable in their surroundings. Their feathers had been tidied and smoothed. It appeared they had located the nesting boxes at the back of the sheltered part of the coop. Some of the dried grass she had arranged in there, had been kicked about but Faye was disappointed to find there were no eggs. *Maybe it will take them a day or two to feel at home.*

The bag of food had to be kept in the cupboard in the house, Joseph said, so as to keep it safe from mice and rats.

*Rats! Fabulous! What next?*

She threw a couple of handfuls through the chicken wire into the coop. She watched, open mouthed, as they raced around the coop competing to eat as much of the corn as possible. Within seconds every last morsel had been pecked up. Against Joseph's directions she threw another helping in the coop for them and as the second helping disappeared as fast as the first, realised the bag wouldn't last long.

*I'll look in the shop for some chicken feed.* She mused, *do they eat rice?* Watching her new family she decided they were quite good on the eye, plump bodies, orangy brown feathers, red combs on the top of their heads and beady black eyes. They weren't the white skinny chickens she had seen down in the village. They cocked their heads and looked back at her.

*My girls,* she cooed to them, *lay me some eggs, please.* Impressed with her brood, she stayed beside the coop for a while, amazed at their prehistoric raptor style feet scraping the earth, looking for a tasty morsel. She became aware of their dance - delighted she watched - they all did the same moves. One step forward, scrape with the left foot, scrape with the right, one step back, search the ground and repeat! Wistfully she wished she had someone with whom to share this discovery, knowing Joseph would not appreciate it. *I miss Sally, I really must get my phone back.*

As the sun hit its height, Faye had cut thirty bamboo canes of varying lengths. The temperature must have been almost 40 degrees, she estimated. Even with her hat on she was feeling a little dizzy. She went inside the house for a bit of relief. It felt a little cooler but not much, slightly less uncomfortable.

Faye wondered what to do, she couldn't sit and do nothing, she didn't have a book or a magazine to read. She gazed around the inside of the house and was faintly surprised there weren't more items belonging to his mother. Looking at the Singer sewing machine, she noticed it had two small drawers, one at each side of the table. Why hadn't she thought to look inside them before. She opened each one in turn, and discovered several different coloured cotton threads, a small box containing thirty, or so, buttons of different colours and sizes, a yard long strip of elastic, a pair of pinking shears, a pair of normal scissors, a piece of black fabric with eight needles threaded into it and a flat, square shaped, piece of tailors chalk.

It was like Christmas, Faye turned each item over in her hands and reverently placed them back tidily in the drawers. The house barely held the essentials for living and yet here, in two small drawers, there is so much treasure. She realised gratefully that small things become important when you have so little.

Faye acknowledged to herself, she never had been a homemaker, a gardener, a cook, or a seamstress. She admitted she relied on Sally too much. This attitude allowed her to be completely absorbed in her job as a social worker. *Mmm, just look where that's got me!*

Remembering how loose her skirt felt last time she put it on, Faye decided to try her hand at taking the skirt in. Putting it on, she realised it would have to be at least six inches smaller around her waist.

'Wow! Rebel, I've lost a good few pounds from my waist,' she called out to her little piglet. 'Are you impressed?

I've never been able to lose weight before.' She popped her head around the bamboo wall and looked at him. He raised his eyelids at her. She smiled back.

Thus Faye spent a pleasant, if slightly sweaty, afternoon in the house assessing the sewing machine. Finally, Faye deciphered its workings and was able to make a fair job of taking in her skirt to a level of competence acceptable to her. Pleased with her new found skills, as the sun commenced its decline, she packed away her threads and scissors and contentedly set off down the path to buy ingredients for the evening meal.

. . . . .

Faye could see chicken feed in large sacks, stacked against a wall. Larso, now used to Laal Baal coming into his store, wrote down on a piece of paper the cost of a sack in rupees. Faye thanked him with her usual bowing, hands together in prayer, but decided she couldn't carry the sack up the path on her own. She had no way of expressing this to Larso so had to leave it and hoped Joseph would purchase some more feed. Purchasing raisins for Rebel, apples and vegetables for the meal she stepped out onto the village street.

Outside Jolinda's house, stood an elephant with Rav, Jolinda's husband. Jolinda held the baby on her hip as normal, standing just inside their bamboo gate. Faye sidled slowly towards them. She wasn't afraid but simply amazed at the relationship between the elephant and the mahout. Rav and Jolinda were having a conversation and as they chatted Rav dipped his arm into a cloth bag hanging on his shoulder and passed a banana, complete with skin, to the elephant. The baby, busy chewing his fist and slavering as before, showed no interest in the elephant. Faye guessed it would be a normal occurrence to have such a visitor at the gate.

As she drew closer, Jolinda spotted her and called out. Faye didn't need another invitation and gladly joined them. Pointing to her husband, Jolinda said 'Rav' thereby introducing him to Faye. She said a few words to him and

Rav answered back. Faye couldn't understand each individual word but the gist of the conversation was;

'This is Laal Baal who lives with Joseph!'

'I have seen her at the sanctuary, she spoke with Viren.'

Faye understood and nodded to them both, pleased to be sociable with someone.

She turned and took a good look at the big animal patiently waiting for its next treat. She noticed the colouring of the ears.

'Sunahara Kaan?' she asked.

Rav responded in affirmative. He showed her the goodies in his bag, a selection of elephant delicacies. More bananas, sugar cane cut into bite size lengths, and papayas. Passing a portion of sugar cane to Faye he indicated for her to give it to the elephant.

'Sunahara Kaan,' Faye called and the big head turned, opening her large ears on hearing her name. Fearlessly Faye stepped up on her toes and popped the sugar cane daintily in her mouth.

'Sunahara Kaan,' Faye whispered as she chewed. As happened the first time they met Sunahara Kaan put her trunk tip on Faye's hair and slid it down her body, inhaling all the time.

Rav put his finger on his nose indicating that she was breathing in Faye scent, getting to know her.

Faye put out her hand, Sunahara Kaan placed the finger-like trunk end on her palm. Faye rubbed it with her other hand.

'Sunahara Kaan, what a lovely girl,' Faye crooned. Rav passed Faye a banana and Sunahara Kaan gently took it from her and pushed it between her lips. Mesmerised, *a gentle giant, placid and gracious,* Faye thought, it filled her with happiness and gratitude.

*What a delightful way to end a shopping trip. You don't get this on the high street at home!* Faye smiled her goodbyes to the little family and wandered back to the house.

.   .   .   .   .

Comfortable being on her own at the house now, she was used to Joseph not being there and coming home at all hours. She admitted to herself she preferred it when he wasn't around. Where he went each morning she didn't know, he never told her. She wouldn't give him the satisfaction of asking and she also realised she didn't care any more. She would rather he went out.

She decided to have a go at making apple doughnuts with half of the apples. She had seen Joseph make them once when they had a good cooking day. It didn't seem too difficult. The best bit though was that Rebel could have the peelings with his raisins. A treat for everyone!

In the early evening Faye took some corn to the coop thinking she would feed them before they went to bed. As she came into view of the chickens, as one, they turned their heads in her direction and ran as far towards her as the coop would allow.

*Wow! They know me already. I am The Bringer Of Their Food. They are so clever!* As in the morning, the feed didn't appear sufficient and Faye went back to get more.

'Tomorrow, girls, I'll see if the shopkeeper will sell me half a sack and then you can have more. I think I would be able to carry half a sack up the path home. I'll figure out a way to make him understand. We can't wait for Joseph to buy it, can we? We could be waiting a long time. Two handfuls is not enough for you, is it?' Faye sat back on her heels and watched the chickens devouring the food.

'Yes, tomorrow I'll buy some more for you. Maybe after I've been to the sanctuary.'

She said it out loud! Quickly she looked around making sure she was alone. It wasn't meant to be uttered aloud but it had been said and that confirmed it. She had unconsciously decided to go to the sanctuary. Meeting Rav with Sunahara Kaan on the village street gave her so much pleasure it had weakened her resolve not to go. Or could it be an underlying longing to repeat the feeling of being safe, of being cared for, to see Viren. *Tomorrow I'm going to the sanctuary.* Smiling, she returned to the house to prepare the vegetables for the evening meal.

## 32

## *Taking action*

The next morning Faye had one thing in her head and that was the visit to the elephant sanctuary. She was up before Joseph, the tea made and she was gayly chatting away to him, wishing he would hurry up and leave so she could get on with her chores and get down the path. She pretended to Joseph she had the usual day ahead of her; tending the plot, the chickens and Rebel. She even called Rebel 'the pig' in order to placate Joseph and let him get away as soon as he was ready. Feeling mean, mentally she apologised to Rebel and hoped he didn't hear her. She decided not to mention her phone, after all. She just wanted him to go.

Last night, after the meal, they talked as they lay in bed. Faye described cutting the bamboo supports for the plants, they had a discussion about the hens failure to lay eggs. Then she told Joseph about discovering the contents of the sewing machine drawers and the subsequent alteration to her skirt, the reason being a substantial loss of weight. Holding her breath, she expected a comment, a pleasant remark or congratulations, which would have been nice, considering his insult about her size on their first day here. When none came Faye sighed silently and thought, *that'll teach you to go fishing for compliments, Madam!*

'The sewing machine was my mothers. She made things for people to earn a bit of money now and again. She made those curtains,' he said proudly, waving his hand towards the Fred Flintstone fabric hanging at the window.

Laughing, Faye countered,

'I wondered about them. If there was one thing I didn't expect when I arrived here, it was Fred Flintstone curtains!' she quipped with a grin on her face.

'She was very proud of them!' came the tart reply.

'I'm sure she was.' The atmosphere suddenly cooled and Faye quickly figured that Joseph didn't appreciate her making fun of his mother's accomplishment, or indeed, see anything funny in having cartoon character curtains in this damp, joyless house. Of course Faye didn't know when the curtains were made, she silently considered, they may have been put up when Joseph and his sister were small. Knowing how very changeable he was Faye regretted her clever comment and felt chastised.

Attempting to change the subject and lighten the atmosphere, cheerfully, she said,

'You didn't tell me if you enjoyed the apple doughnuts,'

'They were OK,' he said without enthusiasm.

She had been put in her place. The apple doughnuts, in her opinion, had been a major success. For a non-cook she felt very pleased with them. They were light, non-greasy and sweet. *Stop trying to force flattery from him. You'll never get any!* she told herself, *it's a waste of time.*

Faye had planned to wait until bedtime, when Joseph tended to get into his crooning, sweet talking mode, before mentioning her phone. However, his instant change of mood over the curtains, deterred her from upsetting him further. She decided to save it for the morning.

Then this morning, as she was anxious to complete her chores allowing her time to visit the sanctuary and Viren, she changed her mind about asking him again.

Finally, he left, going to who knows where. She didn't care. Faye sang as she fed the chickens.

Since the visit from the wild pigs, Faye felt Rebel had not been the same towards her. Wanting to improve the situation, she chatted to Rebel lightheartedly. He deigned to look at Faye and allowed her to scratch his back. Relieved they were back on good terms, she experienced a return to happiness that had been absent since the wild pigs event.

He stood to allow her to scratch his other side. *We are friends again. Thank goodness.*

'I love you Rebel, and I think you have grown. You're going to be a big boy, eh?' She held her open palm out to him. It appeared he was going to nuzzle her hand and held her breath, but he changed his mind at the last minute, turning towards his little home in the roots.

'Oh, you tease!' She walked away laughing.

In record time the water butt was filled, the vegetable plot watered, the one room house swept and dusted, the fire set ready for the meal tonight and a vague shopping list mentally stored for her visit to Laars on the way home.

Opening her suitcase Faye surveyed her clothes. *Which outfit would be the best? Why am I worrying? No-one will look at me with interest. Still, I want to look tidy.*

Faye filled both the china bowl and jug with cold water straight from the well and gave herself a refreshing all-over wash including her hair. Whilst her crowning glory was still wet she brushed it all back and once tightly plaited, prayed it would behave.

Finding the Ayurveda cream, purchased at the Grand Bazaar, she gave her arms and legs a generous application. While she smoothed her skin with the creamy moisturiser she thought about that night and Sally.

*I can't believe it's been so long since I spoke to Sal. Poor Sal, she'll be so worried about me. I'm such a selfish piece. The night of the Grand bazaar was the start of it all. Joseph came looking for me and cast his spell. What a fool I was. Sally was right, he's not right for me. When he comes home tonight I'll get my phone. I won't take no for an answer. And I'll get my bank card. Then, at least, I can figure out how to get myself out of this mess. That's if there's any money left in my account! What a fool I've been. I'll bet he's fleeced me, good and proper!* She gave an ironic 'Hah'. *Well, I asked for it, nobody to blame but myself. I'll have to get myself home, one way or another.* Propping her foot up on the end of the mattress, she grimaced as she picked at a broken toe nail above the bruising while considering her predicament.

With psychological strength renewed with determination, she stood, squirted another helping of cream from the tube into her palm and walked outside and surveyed her surroundings.

Frowning, she applied the cream to her face. *What about Rebel? What about the chickens? What a stupid idiot I am.* Determination turned to sadness as she surveyed her immediate surroundings - Rebel, the chicks, the vegetables growing well and strong, *my little farm*, she sighed.

*I'll sort something out for him and the hens, I will not allow them to be eaten by Joseph or anyone else.* She felt a lump in her throat and strode five fast paces towards Rebel. Realising she didn't know what she was going to do, she pulled up short, turned and strode back to the house. Frustrated, she thought, *I'm striding about like a simpleton!* Faye hated herself for allowing this man to treat her as he had. *I've got to get away from here!*

Having come to this definite decision, one more visit to the elephant sanctuary wouldn't hurt. In fact, it should be visited if only to say goodbye to Viren.

*So what to wear?*

The sarong also bought at the bazaar that night caught her eye and she swished the luxurious fabric out of the suitcase. This is what she wore, that fateful night when Joseph called her name and she went down the stairs from their hotel room to be with him. Faye's face contorted into a wince at the memory. *However it is beautiful material . . .*

. . . . .

The walk down funnel spider avenue seemed to go on forever, but Faye felt better in herself than she had done for weeks. The sarong fitted her perfectly. It had taken a few attempts to get it on with some resemblance to how the two ladies in the village wore theirs but finally she was reasonably happy with the result. Her skin shone with the cream and her hair, for now at least, was neat. The heat was threatening to destroy her composure so she took it easy and tried to stay in the shade wherever possible.

As she came to the clearing of the elephant sanctuary she could see a group of nine men standing in a circle by the line of elephants. There could be heard some raised voices and one man was waving his hands about in what appeared to be desperation. The basket, which had held the rugby ball shaped straw bales, laid empty on the ground beside them. Faye waited at the entrance to the clearing, she didn't want to interrupt anything important. She side-stepped a few yards and sought out the shade of a tall palm tree. Searching the faces of the men, she identified Viren. He was listening and nodding to the man who was waving his hands about. After a few minutes Viren pointed to each man in turn and pointed towards a direction away from the sanctuary. As each man received his orders they broke out of the circle and set off in the direction as told.

Two men picked up the basket and disappeared to the shed. Faye presumed they had gone to make the rugby ball shaped, straw medicine nests for the elephants in the line.

In the pen, to Faye's right, the elephant who had been so angry and aggressive only a few days ago, appeared to be calm. Through gaps in the thick tree trunks Faye could see he seemed content to be chewing on thin branches and leaves, pushing them into place on the ground with a large round foot and his trunk.

'Wow! What a turn around!' Faye uttered.

When she turned back around to where the men were, she saw Viren wave to her and she trotted down the slope towards him.

'Hi Viren, how are you?'

'Faye, good to see you again. You are looking well!' She saw him look her up and down.

Highly pleased and somewhat embarrassed, she smiled but did not respond and prayed she wasn't blushing. Her skin was prone to redness at the slightest thing. Not knowing what to say, she turned to the elephants.

'How are your friends?' she said pointing to the line of chained beasts.

'Well, you may notice there is one missing.'

192

Faye looked down the line. She looked at each elephant in turn. Viren watched her face and saw it dawn.

'Sunahara Kaan! Where is she? What's happened? Is she OK?'

The men came towards them carrying the basket between them, filled with the straw medicine balls.

Viren took hold of Faye's elbow and drew her to one side, out of their way. Faye felt a jolt of pleasure dash up her arm, all her nerves tingling. She struggled to keep her face expressionless. From somewhere within her spirit, a fleeting acknowledgement was recognised - Joseph didn't, and never had, make her feel that way. She turned to Viren as he spoke and tried to concentrate on what he was saying, at the same time thinking to herself, *This is absurd, I'm leaving Goa as soon as I can. Stop it now!*

'Did I tell you when you came last time, that the elephants are free to return into the jungle each night, once they are sufficiently well?'

'Yes you did, I remember.'

'Sunahara Kaan is one of the girls who comes and goes as she wishes. She has a close relationship with Rav and is fully recovered from her physical wounds after her encounter with the poachers. She has been coming into the sanctuary and the village looking for him for quite some time. She appeared calm and stable. We thought, and obviously thought wrong, that she was mentally healed too.' He paused for a few seconds and looked around the clearing as if searching for the elephant then bringing his gaze back to Faye, continued,

'We were shocked when we received the call to say she was upsetting some farmers by destroying their crops. Only a few kilometres from here,' he gestured in the direction of Joseph's house, 'and she had shown aggression towards them.'

'Oh no! But I only saw her yesterday at Jolinda's house. I gave her some sugar cane and bananas. She was with Rav. Has she been hurt?'

'We don't know. The mahouts are searching for her. Rav has not been home since we got the call. Although he's called and called her, it seems she is out of ear shot. He is reporting back via his walkie talkie. He's been quite a distance in an attempt to find her but so far no sign of her.'

'You said you thought she was completely better? What has changed to make her aggressive?'

'We don't know that either. It could be she is having pain, she may have developed an infection, we probably will never know. If we can get her back, we may be able to settle her down again. She deserves to have a happy, contented life. If not and she causes trouble again . . . well, we'll have to hope.'

Rapidly Faye fired questions at Viren,

'You mean she may have to be destroyed? Are you allowed to do that? How many times are you able to settle and repair a traumatised elephant? What will you do? Will she come back under her own steam?' She was blathering! He smiled at her passion,

'We will do everything we can for her. The main thing is to get her back to the safety of the sanctuary so we can assess her behaviour, try to find out what has upset her and sort her out. Destroying any animal here is a complete and total last resort.'

Faye stood, mouth open, staring at him, thinking, *poor Sunahara Kaan, I wish I could help. I shouldn't even offer as I'm not going to be here.*

'Can I do anything?' The words came out anyway.

'Thank you, Faye, but there's not a lot you can do. Except . . .'

'Except what?' she asked eagerly.

'Well, I was going to say, if you hear or see her, up by Joseph's house, let me know immediately. I am always here or at home in the village. Laars will tell you where I live. On no account are you to approach her though, she is a wild animal remember, and we know her state of mind is disturbed at the moment. She could be having flashbacks from the poachers encounter, she could be very angry and not the calm amiable beast she was when you last saw her. She is very unpredictable and very dangerous!'

'I'll keep a lookout for her and don't worry, I won't go near her.'

194

'Listen, Faye, it's lovely to see you but I have things to do today so I'll have to leave you. See you soon.' Viren smiled, waved and walked away, towards the shed where the men had gone.

Feeling bereft, she turned to leave. The company, sense of refuge and sheer pleasure she found at the sanctuary suddenly came to an end. Head down, she wandered back up the path and headed towards the village to buy food for the evening meal, chicken feed and some treats for Rebel.

. . . . .

After pointing, arm flapping, gesticulating, smiling, laughing and nodding, Laars managed to supply her with half a bag of chicken feed. That was the good part, carrying the shopping up the path made her arms and shoulders ache.

When she arrived back at the house, she was so hot. The heat continued to be fierce, the air dry and dusty on the back of her throat. She dropped the bags in the porch and went directly to the water butt. Her lovely sarong was damp with sweat and dust clung around the hem. Faye drank thirstily then rinsed her face straight from the butt tap. She brought the china bowl round and filled it with water. The sun had warmed the water in the butt to tepid. Faye took off her sarong and sluiced herself all over with the water. Next she rinsed the sarong out and laid it over the bathroom fence to dry in the sun. The beautiful fabric, brighter when wet, stood out like an icon in the dullness of the house and its surroundings. It looked wonderful!

She thought about the first time she went to the toilet in the hole in the ground, horrified by the openness, feeling as though anyone could see her. Now she uncaringly walked around the place in her underwear, knowing no-one would come this way. Don't speak too soon!

## 33

## Sunahara Kaan

Sunahara Kaan moodily pushes her way through the jungle. She's heading back to the sanctuary, angry and unhappy. Trees that affect her progress are uprooted or forcibly bent out of her way. She lashes out, venting her anger. Yesterday some men from a human village, a few miles away, chased her with sticks. She didn't know why they were aggressive towards her, she was only eating sweet carrot tops. Confused and scared as the men confronted her, she shouted at the men, the men shouted back louder and threatened her with their long sticks. A deafening bang hurt her ears. Screaming, she turned tail and ran, remembering the horrendous noise from a time before when coming up against men like these. They too had long sticks that made loud cracks and booms and the outcome on that occasion for Sunahara Kaan wasn't good. She ended up hurt and seriously ill. She couldn't remember everything after that but finally came round being nursed by men at the sanctuary. These men were different, kind and comforting. Her mahout was extra kind, she loved him. He had an infected big toe nail and she could identify his own individual smell from a long way away. He brought her sweet titbits she couldn't resist. Coconut, honey and the sweet sap of the kithul palm. She would do anything for him. Even though Sunahara Kaan felt murderous towards human beings at this minute, she still had the need to return to the sanctuary and safety, to her mahout. She was experiencing a strange mixture of feelings. She didn't truly understand them and this made her feel edgy and unhappy. Another feeling inside her is saying that she needs to drink. She knows all the water holes in this area and can smell water nearby but the shock of the deafening gunshot, along with her anger, has blurred her instincts.

Sunahara Kaan becomes aware of human habitation. Her trunk is up as she takes in information on full alert. Stopping her march, standing stock still, through the trees, she eyes the dismal little house. She listens as the crows start their alarm chorus and looking up she shakes her head at them, swinging her trunk in annoyance. The aroma from the bathroom area makes her harrumph with distaste. Her inbuilt senses tell her to give it a wide berth. She walks on and spots the rows of vegetables. The crops are too small to interest her. She spies Rebel staring at her and ignores him, small fry. Ahead the hint of water is becoming stronger, she extends her trunk, fully opens the end to locate the source and breathes in. She has found the well. Sunahara Kaan looks again at the house and decides it isn't safe to go to the water. She's afraid to get close to humans again. She'll have to find another water hole. Annoyed, she moves along, her bad mood getting darker as she smashes her way deeper into the undergrowth. She's sure this is the right direction, nonetheless she has to be prepared to take detours as necessary to stay safe.

. . . . .

Faye hears the commotion of the crows, their noise nudges her from slumber. *What is it?* She feels across the mattress with her hand. Joseph is not in bed. *Where is he?* Remembering suddenly last night's row and watching his back as he stalked away in anger. *He hasn't returned, has he?*

Fully roused now.

*What's upsetting the crows? It's barely daylight. What's that noise? It sounds close to the house, a crunching, crackling sound! Oh my lord! Rebel!*

She bursts out of the house, warrior-like, wild red hair flying horizontally behind her. The first thing she grabbed as she rose from the mattress was the thin sarong that covers them at night, wrapping it loosely round her as she ran, gripping the top with one hand to stop it from sliding off. Her eyes frantically searched the tree tops for eagles as she thundered across to the banyan tree and Rebel. Equally frantically her eyes scoured the roots of the large tree. Thankfully she spots him but notes he's stood, stiff legged, unmoving, silent, intently staring into the same place in the undergrowth as when the wild pigs came to visit.

Attempting to comfort him Faye shouted above the crows cawing,

'Mum's here, Rebel,' and threw herself down beside him and scanned the direction of Rebel's gaze. Her eyes, screwing up, darted from one dark cavernous hole to the next. The loud cracking and rustling continued but further away and she cocked her head trying to locate the sound and wished the crows would shut up. The sun had not yet fully lit the air and the undergrowth was even darker. Faye unconsciously attempted to pinpoint, nasally, a scent known to her, but in the panic and confusion, she failed to grasp the same smell as at the sanctuary.

'What is it, Rebel?' she shouted to him. He didn't move, he was like a statue. She stayed with him, searching the dark he was staring into. Glancing over to the chicken coop she was relieved to see they were unaffected, already busy scratching the ground and looking for food.

Finally the crows calmed down. Rebel came out of his trance-like state. Nothing had invaded his territory. He looked Faye up and down expectantly. *She always comes with food,* he thinks, *and it's breakfast time.* Disappointed when she appeared to be empty handed, he turned his circles until he found the right spot and settled down for a nap.

Faye, concerned and puzzled, accepted that whatever had visited them, had left and patted Rebel on his back. He allowed her to give him some reassurance and in return lifted his head for long enough to give her a short stare and a slight sigh.

'I think we are safe now, Rebel. What on earth was it? Eagles? Pigs? Something else? What?' She patted him again, waiting for a reply. When none came, she told him,

'I'll get you some breakfast soon, sweetie,' and returned to the house to light the fire and make some tea.

Faye struck a match and carefully coaxed a flame to bite at the dried grass and twigs. Satisfied it had taken, she gently piled more thin twigs, pyramid style around the flames and then rushed around to the butt to fill the kettle. *I'm getting quite adept at lighting the fire.*

After placing the kettle on the tripod, she fed the fire with wood chips and prepared her cup for the tea. Sitting back she recounted the most recent row with Joseph.

.    .    .    .    .

Last night, after they had eaten their meal, she touched on the subject of her phone. Joseph, in his usual manner, became instantly defensive.

Bringing all her determination to the fore, Faye swallowed hard and knowing this moment wasn't going to be pleasant, jumped in with a no nonsense attitude.

'I want my phone back Joseph, it's my property, not yours. It's had more than enough time to charge. You have no excuse not to give it back. And I want my bank card. You have no business keeping it. I want it back now!'

He stared at Faye coldly. Before he could start his arrogant retort she quickly added,

'I want to phone Sally, Joseph and I think I need to go to Shamoga to do this. I also need to check my bank balance. Goodness knows how my bank account is by now. I could be bankrupt for all I know. Don't give me any more excuses, Joseph. I need my things back now!'

'You are right, Faye, I will bring them tomorrow. I have to go . . .'

'No, Joseph, that is not acceptable. I don't want them tomorrow, I want them now. Where are they? Have you sold my phone? Is that what it is? I noticed you have new shoes and trousers. Have you taken all my money from my account?' She could hear her voice getting louder and higher.

'How dare you speak to me like that?' he shouted, halting her diatribe. He jumped up from his cushion, his face a picture of pomposity.

'How dare you? You are the most ungrateful person I know, after all I have generously given you. My house, my land, provided you with a water well to make your life easy. I have given you a farm to keep you happy and now you are making more demands. What is the matter with you, woman?'

She countered,

'You cannot keep my bank card, Joseph is not yours to keep. And as for making my life easy? Are you joking? Apart from one or two days when you helped, I have toiled in the heat, on my own to make your miserable house a home and your land workable. Plus you use me like a skivvy for your meals and your sexual needs,' she paused for breath but could see him preparing to come back at her so quickly carried on,

'And another thing, Rebel and the chickens, the seeds, the water test, have I paid for them all, with money from my account? Is that why you can be so generous,' she motioned with her fingers putting inverted commas around 'generous', 'with all those? I am not happy at all, Joseph, so I will thank you to hand over my phone and bank card at once.' During this outburst she too stood from her cushion and faced him, staring fiercely in return. She held her hand out, palm up and continued,

'And while I'm at it, you expect me to stay here, on my own, while you are goodness knows where, getting up to goodness knows what, telling me not to speak to anyone in the village. I am not a nun, you know.'

'Oh no! I know you are not a nun! You soon proved that, the night on the stairs at the hotel!' He applied a disgusted look to his face, 'You couldn't get down the stairs quickly enough and open your legs! You needed a man, a home, you needed to run away from your job after you made such a mess of it and needed peace and a solitary lifestyle. Now you are biting the hand that feeds you. You are a crazy woman. I will give you your things when I feel the time's right and take you to Shamoga, but it's obvious by your tantrum the right time is not now!'

Shocked by how he could turn the argument around, Faye opened her mouth and gasped before continuing at a screech,

'Tantrum? Tantrum? You think I'm just having a tantrum? Well let me tell you. I don't deserve this kind of treatment. For your information I know I can get on a bus at the shop. Viren told me it comes and waits there so I can get a lift, I don't need you to *take me to Shamoga!*'

Joseph's tone expressed suspicion, 'How do you know Viren?'

'I met him when I went to the elephant sanctuary, he showed me around, he was very nice and very helpful. So I'm not leading the solitary life you think I am.'

'You are making a fool of me woman! I will not have you hobnobbing with that man or anyone else from the village.'

'Why not? They are good people.'

'They are not good people and will only make things difficult for you as they always have for me. I forbid you to go to the elephant sanctuary again!' he shouted.

'You forbid me?' she shouted back exasperated.

'And you are only allowed to go to the village when I tell you. I will do the shopping in future,' he paused, took in a breath and as if resigned continued, 'I cannot leave you to do anything. You astound me!'

'You cannot tell me where I can and cannot go!'

'I can and I will, you will see.' he said with an evil smirk, 'I am going to my friends now, do not try to block the door again or I will wrench it off its hinges! Be in bed when I get back!' he ordered, staring directly into her face. Faye forced herself to stare back and not be the first to break away. His fierceness frightened her but she would not admit that to him.

He sneered into her face,

'Watch yourself, madam!' he uttered menacingly and with that he stalked off, down the path into the darkness.

When he was out of earshot, furious to her core, Faye plonked herself down on her cushion and cried tears of anger and frustration until she couldn't cry anymore. Eventually, she mopped her face and wiped her nose. Full of conflicting emotions; defiance, despondency, despair, determination, she crawled onto the mattress. Amazingly she slept, the anxiety and tension must have exhausted her. That is until this morning's riotous melee woke her.

. . . . .

After drinking her tea, she fed Rebel and the chickens. She was miserable as she surveyed her rows of vegetables. Sighing, she turned and dragging her feet, returned to the house to get washed and dressed.

Crouching, she opened her suitcase to choose the days clothes. Incomprehensibly she stared, open mouthed at the insides of the case. A small amount of underwear and toiletries sat on top of her beach towels. Nothing else. *Where are all my clothes?* She gaped for seconds longer until it dawned on her. *Joseph has taken my clothes, he has taken them so I haven't anything to wear to go to the village or the sanctuary, let alone to Shamoga and home. I'm imprisoned here, I can't get away. Well, the sneaky lowlife! How did I sleep through him rummaging through my things? The furtive, thieving bastard!*

Faye rose out of her crouch and, still wrapped in the paper thin sarong from the mattress, the only item of clothing left to her, searched her fabric bag. It held her purse, containing very few rupees and her passport.

Weak at the knees, she staggered outside, stood in the sunshine and stared up at the blue sky. Tears coursed down her cheeks as helplessly she howled to the crows, Rebel and the chickens,

'What am I going to do?'

Moments later Faye's disbelief at Joseph's nastiness changed to rage and spurred her into action, with her eyebrows knitted together she scowled as she shouted,

'OK Rebel, he is not having it all his way. Watch this! If he thinks he can control me without repercussions he has another think coming!'

202

Running back into the house, she dragged Joseph's pile of clothes from the floor at the end of the mattress and pushed them out into the porch. Carefully with dried grass and thin sticks, she brought the dying fire back to life. When it had a strong blaze she fed on the chopped wood and watched as it took hold. Gently she placed each item of clothing one by one onto the fire, watching each item char and burn. Smiling to herself, it was strangely satisfying.

She sat on her cushion as the flames devoured all his clothing, delighting in her revenge, giggling. Two shirts, four tee-shirts, his black trousers he wore at the hotel, two other pairs of trousers, numerous underpants and socks, his favourite rag he wrapped around his hips, his flowery shirt from the hotel. A pair of canvas sneakers and a pair of black leather lace ups. His new shoes and trousers, she noted, were not there. Faye even considered burning the dirty old mattress but decided it was too heavy for her to pull through the door. The two pairs of flip-flops she saved until last as they were made of rubber.

Suddenly acrid smoke spiralled up from the fire and filled the porch. It collected in the roof space and quickly came down to Faye's level, black and thick. Faye slid off her cushion and crawled on her hands and knees out into the open air, coughing like an old man.

'Oh my God, Rebel, that'll teach me!' and she chuckled in between coughs, 'I'm no good at being bad!' The heat of the day and the heat from the fire made her sweat. She wiped the back of her hand across her forehead and brought off a blackened smear.

'What must I look like?' Slightly hysterical amid wheezing she stayed on her hands and knees enjoying the feeling of vindictive payback. So involved in revenge, it didn't occur to her she could have worn his clothes to get away!

Looking up at Rebel in between bouts of coughing, she laughed out loud as best she could, coughing all the while. Rebel was staring back at her and she would swear he had an amazed look on his face, as if to say,

'What on earth are you doing?' which made her laugh and cough even more!

When the coughing finally stopped she checked that the house wasn't burning down and  head held high, she headed round to the butt for a wash.

## 34

### Green earrings

She hopped from foot to foot, clapping her hands with excitement, as he slowly searched first one pocket then another. He was teasing her. Finally, he produced her latest gift, the green dangly earrings Faye had worn  at the Grand Evening Bazaar, to look pretty, with such hope in her heart. Joseph, pretending to be in love, generosity oozing from every pore, gave them to the Doe Eyed girl, to hang from her cute little lobes.

'Oooh! I love them, they're beautiful. Do you think they suit me Joseph? Do I look handsome Joseph?' She tilted her head back and forth swinging the earrings from side to side and peeped coquettishly to see Joseph's reaction.

'You are perfect, my little sweetmeat. Now, show me how grateful you can be.'

Joseph's intimate intentions were halted by a ringtone. He frowned as she jumped away from him to pick up her phone - Faye's phone! He had no option due to the secrecy of the relationship to wait until she ended her call.

'I love my new phone, Joseph. All my friends are jealous. Thank you so much.'

'You are worth it, my darling. Now can we go through to your bedroom and you can show me your earrings again. They look better when they're the only thing you are wearing. Come, my little peachnut.'

She giggled and he led her by the hand through her father's house to her room. He kissed her soft lips at the same time as unrobing her, leaving her earrings in place.

'By the way, Joseph, I have some good news for you,' she uttered nonchalantly.

'Oh yes?' he mumbled, distracted by the caramel coloured nipple between his lips.

'We are going to have a baby. We will have to get married. I am so excited, Joseph. We will be a family. I can come and live with you and we will be happy. I love you Joseph.' she rattled innocently and planted a light kiss on the top of his head.

Joseph heard only the first sentence of her speech. His ardour shrivelled. Eyes wide open, blinded by her words.

Stuttering he tried to fake delight, all the while his mind was working overtime,

'That's … that's … that's great news. Have you told anyone? Anyone at all?' What should he do? Where could he go? *Abortion?*

'Sweetheart,' he crooned, 'you are young, you have your whole life ahead. Why don't you have an abortion and we can think about having a family after we are married?'

'Get rid of it?' she exclaimed, alarm in her voice, 'No, I won't! It's our baby, Joseph. We will get married before I start to show. I haven't told anyone yet. I wanted to tell you first. It is good news, isn't it? You are happy, aren't you?'

'My darling, if you are happy, I am happy. Unfortunately I cannot stay today. I have to see a man about a job.'

'Yes, you need a job, the baby will need lots of things, a cot, a pram, lots of things. I would like a girl but if it's a boy I don't . . .'

He interrupted,

'I must go, we will talk later. Remember don't tell anyone, my darling. Rakel promise me, not until we are ready.'

'I won't.'

He turned and fled, making haste out of her father's house and headed towards the town. Entering a hotel he found the bar. It was early but he needed a drink and a little time to think and work out a plan. He had to get himself out of this mess.

A couple of hours later, the Doe Eyed girl's father came home from work for his lunch. He walked into the house and found his daughter happily cooking in the kitchen. His meal was ready.

'Go and wash then sit down Papa, it will be just a moment.'

He was so proud of her. She was beautiful, stunning in fact. Since her mother died three years ago when she was ten years old, she had looked after him and the house and all without complaint. She was his angel and he loved her beyond understanding.

Coming back from the bathroom he patted her arm as he passed her. She gave him a beaming smile in return.

'Papa, I have some wonderful news to tell you.' She placed his plate of food in front of him and sat down opposite.

'Oh yes, what is it?' He tore his chapati in half and looked across at her expectantly, smiling at his lovely little girl.

'I have found a boyfriend, Papa, a nice boy called Joseph.'

His smile slid from his face and the chapati stopped mid dip in his gravy.

'Oh yes?' He felt his stomach clench. He knew it would come but didn't expect it yet for a year or two.

She didn't recognise his facial reaction and prattled on,

'Yes and we are going to have a baby. He said not to tell you until we are ready, but you are my Papa and I want you to know. We will . . .' she stopped, eventually seeing the look on his face.

Her words sunk in. After a second of silence, the table, the crockery, the glasses and all the food on it, went up in the air as he screamed,

'Joseph who? Where is he? I'll kill him!'

## 35

## *The pregnancy*

Faye wandered around the house, she walked down to her rows of little vegetables, loving them for bringing new life into the world. She sat beside the chickens for a few minutes, affectionately observing their odd behaviour. She pushed her hand into the straw in the laying box and discovered an egg! Their first egg! It was still warm! Faye's sadness was coloured with a little pleasure. She kept it safe within her palm, treasuring the treasure.

A flash of colour caught her attention out of the corner of her eye. Glancing to her right she saw her lovely sarong hanging over the bamboo fence where she left it yesterday after rinsing it out. It fluttered in the gentle breeze.

*Ha! So he thought he would leave me without clothes. Well, I'll show him!* She nodded with a rye smile to the chickens, her despair lifting a little and went to retrieve the sarong.

Looking at Rebel, Faye knew she had to find a way to keep him safe. Biting her lip as she scratched his back, she wondered if anyone in the village kept pigs. Maybe if she peeped through all the fences she may see some and ask if they would take Rebel. But that would mean he would eventually be slaughtered and eaten. *There's no other choice. I could ask Viren. Yes, I'll go down, find Viren and see what he thinks. Now I have something to wear. I can go and sort my life out, one way or another.*

From day one, Faye had not known what time Joseph would come back to the house. Today was no different, she pondered, no amount of worrying will change things. *He would need to do something quite extraordinary to make me want to stay now and that is highly unlikely.*

'I'll go down to the village when I'm ready. I'm not neglecting my little family for that snake. What do you say, Rebel? Do you want some breakfast, little man?'

Faye went about her duties as normal wearing the tatty, thin sarong. After feeding, watering and weeding, she tidied the house and porch. Cleaning out the fireplace she smirked as she threw away the charred remnants of Joseph's belongings. She washed and changed into the colourful sarong and readied herself for the walk to the village and the sanctuary.

It was probably around two in the afternoon. Faye came out of the house with her fabric bag over her shoulder. She was determined to ask Viren for help, firstly for Rebel and the chickens and secondly to find out if he could assist her to get away from here and Joseph.

She didn't know the state of her bank account but if it was, as she suspected, empty, it was not so simple as to phone Sally and ask her to send money to her account. Joseph had access to the account until she could get into the bank to cancel her card. Besides, she didn't have her phone which held Sally's number. Also being a foreigner in this land, she needed Viren to interpret and vouch for her identity. She had her passport but Faye wasn't confident that would suffice.

With all this going on in her mind as she stepped out of the porch, she didn't notice the crows announcing visitors. Around the corner of the porch came a man. An angry man. He held, by the wrist, a young girl, appearing to be around thirteen or fourteen. The girl was crying, evidently very unhappy. The man threw the girl to the floor in front of the porch. She landed on her hands and knees in the red dust causing a small dust storm to billow up around her. From within her sarong fell a mobile phone. It was in a case decorated with London sightseeing attractions.

As soon as she saw it Faye knew it was hers. *I can phone Sally!* She dived forward attempting to catch the phone before it landed on the ground but wasn't quick enough. The case flew open as the phone fell. It hit one of the stones surrounding the fire shattering the screen. Faye gasped horrified. In the same second as she felt relieved to welcome her phone back, she watched the screen smash, ruining any hope of contacting her sister. All her contact numbers were hidden forever behind the splintered glass. The girl lifted her head and looked defiantly, first at Faye then at her father.

As the Doe Eyed girl turned her head, the sun glinted on something dangling from her ear. Faye's eyes widened as she spotted her green earrings swinging from the girl's ear lobes.

'My earrings!' Faye blurted as she watched the scene. She couldn't comprehend at that moment how the girl could have got her hands on her phone and her earrings. The girl lifted one hand to the earring. She'd heard her. Then in less than a second, she knew. *Joseph: The lech! The thief!*

Whilst Faye's eyes darted from one object to another, the girls father was bellowing,

'Joseph! Joseph, come out here and sort out your mess!'

Of course it was in his own language and Faye didn't understand the words but she understood the connotations.

'Do either of you speak English?' she cried above the noise of the girl's wailing, the father's shouting and the crows cawing.

'I do, a little I learned at school,' the girl snivelled. Thereby they managed to hold a conversation.

'OK, tell your father Joseph is not here. I don't know where he is. He hasn't been back here for two days.'

'My father says to tell you I'm carrying Joseph's baby!' the doe eyed girl muttered, facing down at the ground.

'What? No!' Did she hear right? 'You're pregnant?'

The girl nodded, crying quietly. Faye knew it was the truth, otherwise why would the girl have her phone and her earrings?

Discovering Joseph had been unfaithful, faintness took over, she needed to sit down and flopped onto her cushion. *Oh my God!* She rested her head in her hands for a minute. Although it didn't surprise her, it still hurt.

210

The father and daughter stared at her until Faye regained her composure.

'I don't know if Joseph will come back to this house,' she told the father. 'You should involve the police, he has broken the law, your daughter is only a child. Joseph is not a good man, as I have found out to my cost!'

The girl kept her earrings, they didn't matter. The smashed screen made the phone unusable but Faye kept it anyway.

The father stormed down the path to the village where he left his car. He muttered in Hindi to himself as he left, gripping his daughter's wrist tightly again. Faye could hear her unhappy cries for several minutes after they were out of sight.

'What more can happen today, Rebel?' she asked, sinking to the ground beside him. Her legs were like jelly. She closed her eyes, feeling a little sick. Taking deep breaths, she sat trying to analyse the most recent events, absentmindedly stroking Rebel.

'It's too late to go to the village now, let alone the sanctuary and I really don't think I can take anymore today! I'll go tomorrow. Joseph can return if he likes but nothing he can say can change anything between us. If it wasn't over before this, it definitely is now!!'

A feeling of sadness, strangely tinged with relief overcame her. After a few seconds she felt Rebel alongside her thigh. He was cosying up to her. She sneaked a peep at him. He lay there contentedly, stretched out full length, at ease. Finally he accepted her, now when she planned to leave him! She sighed, sniffed and wiped away a tear.

'How can I leave you, my precious baby?' No answer came.

## 36

## Saving the child

Faye was still shocked the following morning by the revelation of Joseph's unfaithfulness and the pregnancy. Quickly, as though on autopilot, she worked through her chores. Joseph hadn't returned to the house. She was glad and more than a little relieved. Throughout the morning the same feeling kept surfacing. Having known Joseph only a matter of weeks, how could he be faithless and feckless so early in their relationship? She couldn't understand it. She felt totally betrayed.

Sitting with Rebel, she nibbled at a rough bit of skin on her thumb as she analysed the situation. Was it her fault? Did she drive him to it? She never denied him anything. She tried to be fun and entertaining, worked hard and after the first couple of mistakes in her culinary skills, she thought she had done pretty well.

She looked at Rebel and remembered how unfeeling he was towards the little piglet and to her when she expressed her maternal emotions. Joseph is simply not a nice person. How did she ever become involved with such a swine?

'Who could threaten to eat you? You are so cute. I love you, Rebel, not him. I'll never let anything happen to you. Don't worry,' she smiled at him. Rebel made a contented snorting noise and stretched slightly to the right so she could reach the correct spot on his back to scratch.

Around noon Faye set off down to the village. She planned to find Viren and ask for help to get away. *Maybe he knows someone who could mend my screen then I can phone Sally. One step at a time.*

Faye felt more positive now she was taking action to get herself home, her head was full of alternative possibilities as she walked down funnel spider avenue.

Halfway there, Faye heard something to her right in the jungle. She stopped and listened. It sounded like the meow of a cat. Immediately after, voices could be heard far in the distance. Female voices. She carried on walking unperturbed. A minute later she could make out a group of women coming up the path towards her. They were too far away, she couldn't determine who they were or what they were doing but they didn't appear to be purely walking, more like stopping and starting. Faye stood still and put her hand across her forehead, shading the sun to help her see better.

At that moment, again from her right within the jungle, came a reedy cry. Faye whipped her head round to look in the direction of the noise. Of course she couldn't see anything, the jungle was thick, dense and dark. She stiffened and held her breath. Yes, there it was again, it could be a cat but she was sure it was a child.

Without hesitation Faye dropped her canvas bag on the path and pushed her way through the first few yards of almost impenetrable bush. She called,

'Hello, I'm coming. Where are you?' Unmoving and holding her breath again, she listened. Sounds came from dead ahead, sounds she didn't recognise, but nonetheless she moved forward striding over webs and knots of ropey growths. The fine silk of spider webs clung to her bare arms and hot, damp face. Thorns grabbed and ripped her lovely sarong but she forced her way forward nonetheless.

It became quite gloomy a few feet away from the path as the trees, bushes and creepers crowded in to exclude the sun. She could only see, clearly, the growth directly in front of her. Even though Faye was shaded by the tangled canopy above, the humidity was intense.

'Hello, where are you? Let me know where you are,' she called and she continued deeper into the jungle as the child's cry came back to her.

Something grabbed Faye's ankle, stopping her progress!

'Argh!' she gasped and shot a look down, fearful of seeing a snake. Relieved to see a creeper, she spent a few moments untangling her foot from the tenacious vine.

'I'm coming,' she called. At last she pulled her foot clear and moved through another layer of undergrowth. To get over a felled bough, green with moss, she had to straddle it. She felt the skin of her inner thighs prickle and smart as the rough bark scraped her delicate skin. Finally she found herself stepping into a small clearing. An immense tree stood in the centre, streamers of hairy creepers and roots hung from its branches. The spread of its boughs darkened the clearing even more except for a few shards of brightness where sunbeams fought their way through thin gaps in the canopy. There was a taste of decaying leaves and humidity. It was steamy, a place of lichen, toadstools and dampness, strangely wrapped in absolute silence.

Faye's pupils adapted to the scene as she searched the ground for the child. There!

'Thank the Lord! I'm here baby. How did you get out here all by yourself?' she called and prepared to stride over to it.

To the right of the large tree trunk, a tiny child sat in the dead leaves and branches, half covered by the detritus on the ground. Its eyes were wide and brimming with tears, the sun's rays sparkled in the teary puddles. As the baby saw Faye appear through the bushes, its watery eyes watched her for a few seconds then it looked to its right and turned its head fractionally as if to sneak a look behind but then changed its mind and concentrated on Faye. It expressed a picture of fear and unhappiness.

The baby's action hinted there was something behind and caused Faye to bring her gaze up above the baby's head and focus beyond it. Directly behind the baby, a sheet of sunlight fell as a glowing backdrop obscuring everything behind within the jungle. Faye took an excited

214

step forward to reach the baby but stopped short and sucked in an incredulous, 'Oh my God!' as an enormous elephant pushed its head through the curtain of sun. The elephant's body was hidden in the dark undergrowth but the head, lit by the sunbeams, appeared to hang unsupported above the tiny mite sitting on the ground.

It was staring right at Faye! Did her heart just stop? She was sure it had.

'Oh my God!' Faye whispered again, rooted to the spot. Her hand felt behind her and found a thin sapling to hold on to. She needed steadying and looked from the elephant to the baby and back again. 'Remember, they are still wild animals, don't be disrespectful.' Viren had said.

*What shall I do? Go to the sanctuary for help? It'll take too long. Shout? No-one will hear, the ladies are too far away! Run? No!* For the first time since she stepped off the path into the jungle a finger of fear crept up Faye's spine, real fear! Still she knew, albeit unconsciously, she would try to save the child. There wasn't a choice! She swallowed.

'Don't move, baby,' she whispered as she took a step forward. The elephant raised its trunk and let out an ear shattering roar. It was a 'Don't come any closer!' roar. Faye felt her chest vibrate and the ground tremble as the roar washed over her. *Shit!* She took a quick step back. The baby sobbed great gulps and the elephant dropped its trunk and with the tip touched the child once on its head.

The baby let out a fearful wail and looked at Faye. Its eyes said 'please help me!' A tear overflowed from each eye and ran down its cheeks.

'Oh God, don't move baby, don't move,' she whispered, and took a slow step forward again. The elephant roared at her again, louder, its trunk in the air and shook its head. As it did, the ray of sun streaked across its ears and Faye noticed the colours. Her hand came up to cover her mouth,

'Oh my God, no!' she recognised the colour of the flapping ears! Her hand reached back again for the sapling. Sinking to her knees became a real possibility. The baby screamed. Adrenaline pumped into Faye's stomach and sweat ran down her face and back.

*It's Sunahara Kaan, the missing elephant.* Rapidly the phrases Viren had used when he spoke about Sunahara Kaan at her last visit to the sanctuary shot through her mind:

'She has shown aggression . . . she may have pain or infection . . . on no account approach her . . . her state of mind is disturbed . . . she is very dangerous!'

'Hush baby, hush, it'll be alright. I'll get to you in a minute. Hush, baby, hush.' Faye promised in a sing-song calm voice she didn't feel.

This is not the same as being at the sanctuary or the village with the mahouts close by, Faye acknowledged.

'OK, OK. What shall we do? Stay calm baby, stay calm. We'll work this out, we'll work this out baby, stay still,' she rambled quietly, as much to herself as to the baby, and very slowly tried another step towards the baby and the beast. Her legs felt weak, she didn't know if they would support her and was loath to let go of the sapling. Assessing the space, she was probably ten steps away from the child and eleven from the dangerous beast. Trying not to breathe and make any alarming movements she stepped forward again. The baby had not moved an inch.

ROAR!! Vibrating again she gasped and stepped back and held up her hands. She noticed they were shaking. The baby let out a wail.

'Don't move, baby, keep quiet, we'll sort this out.' Trying to look braver than she felt for the baby's benefit, she tried to speak with authority. In reality her voice quivered and cracked. Taking a deep breath, she tried to control her breathing. She was in danger of hyperventilating!

'OK, I'm not going to hurt you,' and louder she said 'Sunahara Kaan, I am your friend, I won't hurt you.' Faye deliberated for a moment whether she should look the elephant in the eye or avoid eye contact. She didn't know! Did the elephant know her own name?

'Sunahara Kaan!' Faye called gently but louder and dared to take a small step towards the baby. Nothing happened.

'Sunahara Kaan!' she called again and sidled seamlessly forward another six inches.

The large beast raised her trunk. She was about to roar, the human was sneaking towards her, getting too close, she didn't trust her. She took a deep breath and prepared to give this human a piece of her mind when her palate took in a known taste.

*This human is known to me. She knows the name my mahout calls me. Who is she?* Sunahara Kaan recognised the taste of her from the day at the sanctuary and the village when Faye fed her.

*She is known to me, I know her scent, she's a friend, she knows my mahout.* Sunahara Kaan lowered her trunk.

*This human has come to take the baby human. The baby human belongs to my mahout and is part of my human family. I don't know why it's here alone but I won't allow it to come to harm. This human knows me and my mahout, she can take the baby.*

Sunahara Kaan stood thinking for a few moments. She made the decision  that she could leave her charge and with some relief, turned and disappeared into the darker reaches of the trees, bushes and creepers, crashing away.

Faye couldn't believe it. One minute the elephant was there, overpowering the backdrop, dominating the scene, then in the next minute, with a shake of leaves and a loud splintering sound of breaking foliage she had gone. Amazed, Faye stood a second getting her breath before dashing over to the baby and lifting it into her arms. She hugged it tightly. The baby clung to her, crying softly. Faye put a few speedy yards between them and the clearing before picking brown soggy leaves off the baby's clothes. She wiped its eyes and nose on the hem of her lovely sarong and reassured it that all would be well. Faye laughed out loud with relief as she clambered back through the creepers, webs and bushes with the child on her hip. The child's eyes never left her face.

'Come on, sweetie, let's go and find your mummy. She won't be far away. I know you. You are Jolindas baby aren't you? Come on, let's find her.' The large dark eyes Faye had seen on her first visit to the village stared up at her. The baby hiccupped occasionally, the after effects of its sobbing.

Struggling back to funnel spider avenue, Faye fell out of the jungle onto the relative safety of the path. The group of ladies she spotted before were much closer now. Faye waved her free arm at them and as they saw her on the path holding the baby, they started to run towards her. Faye recognised Jolinda running at the front of the group.

Her arms outstretched, tears streaming down her face, Jolinda screamed, 'Motes, Motes,' as she ran, closely followed by Nahla and five more women, two girls and a small boy.

Everyone seemed to be talking, no, shouting, at once as Faye passed the baby over to Jolinda. Jolinda continued to cry, the baby cried again and Faye cried. Jolinda put her spare arm round Faye and hugged her. The women crowded around them, patting Jolinda, patting the baby and patting Faye, all struggling to stay within the constraints of the path. Not an easy thing to do with the funnel spiders webs in close proximity, but that's how it was.

All in Hindi, Faye could only be gracious as they thanked her and thanked her. Quietening down the noisy chatter with her hands held up, palms forward, she acted out the scene - what she did, what the baby did, and most of all what the elephant did. The ladies watched her performance with wonder. When Faye said the name Sunahara Kaan, one lady turned to the small boy and sent him off with instructions. He went at top speed down the path, his flip-flops kicking up dust behind him with every step. Faye assumed he was going to fetch Rav for the elephant.

The ladies insisted Faye accompany them to the village and into Jolinda's house. Like a festival parade they marched down the path to Jolinda's. Everyone was happy and joyful.

'It's beautiful,' Faye uttered as she gazed around the house. It was clean and fresh. She could see more than one bedroom leading off the main room. There was furniture, polished and maintained, order and homeliness. Jolinda smiled back at Faye. Not a smug smile but an understanding smile. She knew the state of Joseph's house.

Outside around the back, a chicken coop took pride of place. Faye counted the birds. Jolinda had four. It was a large coop, Faye considered, there would be sufficient room for nine more.

The baby turned out to be a boy named Motes, who after a nappy change, a drink and a cuddle from his mummy, didn't appear to be any the worse for his ordeal. How he came to be in the jungle with the elephant in the first place, Faye couldn't discern. But all's well that ends well. He was passed around from one lady to another, having kisses and cuddles. His manner accepting of the adoration and his large dark eyes taking it all in.

The ladies chatted away. It appeared to Faye that they all spoke at the same time. Faye felt left out and alone as she was unable to join in with the conversations. However, the ladies showed their gratitude by bowing to her and putting their hands on her shoulders, laughing and smiling into her face. Someone put a glass of cold orange juice in her hand. Nahla inspected Faye's lovely sarong, now torn and soiled. She turned and brought Jolinda's attention to the rips. Faye didn't feel a hero but somehow bringing the baby back to his mother gave her a very pleasant sensation inside.

After an hour or so Faye intimated that she needed to return to the house. Her intention to seek out Viren and ask for his help had to be postponed today but it didn't matter. The safety of the baby was the most important issue. He would be more concerned with that and returning Sunahara Kaan to the sanctuary than some silly girl who had got herself into a bit of a pickle. *It's your own fault,* she told herself as she held Motes close and enjoyed the endearing baby smell and softness. She kissed his head and passed him back to mum and left the happy, celebrating ladies.

As she neared the end of the village street, three men and the little boy passed across it walking towards the sanctuary. Over their shoulders, like rifles, they carried thin branches topped with lush foliage. In their wake Sunahara Kaan plodded obediently along. Her eyes were on the foliage, she didn't look in Faye's direction. Behind her, two men followed. One of them was Viren. He spotted her and waved. He shouted something to her. It sounded like 'see you tomorrow', but she couldn't just catch it. Anyway it cheered her and to see Sunahara Kaan being calmly guided back to the sanctuary, where she would be cared for, rounded off the day. She hadn't needed darting or chaining. It all ended satisfactorily for all concerned.

No untoward events occurred on the way back to the house and she was strangely glad to be home. She went to the Banyan tree and sat and recounted the day's events to Rebel. She told him she had saved a baby. She had actually saved a baby's life. It felt good in her heart. She thought of Motes and she thought of Charles. Sitting in the warm sunshine scratching Rebels back, she acknowledged a little balance had been reintroduced into her life. Faye didn't know that Sunahara Kaan, in her own way, was simply protecting the baby, but it didn't matter, equilibrium had been restored in Faye's world.

## 37

## *The visit*

Faye fed Rebel and the chickens. Whilst the chicks were gobbling their corn she pushed her hand into the nesting box and found four eggs this afternoon.

'Well done, girls. I'll have an omelette for my tea, thank you!'

She lit the fire and prepared for an evening alone in the porch. She found she didn't mind. The events of the day kept her warm inside and happy. Joseph wasn't expected. Somehow Faye knew he had gone. She didn't know where and but she knew why. *He's a selfish coward, that's why.* But to be without the worry of his mood swings, his approval, his demands, it was a relief, she felt free, her independence and personality resumed.

Faye made a hasty naan and cooked the omelette. It was delicious and licking her lips, silently applauded her girls in the coop. As the night curtains drew across the sky, she removed her good sarong, not lovely any more, and sat on her cushion in the porch. She made plans for the following day:

Wash the lovely sarong - it will dry in no time in this heat.
Feed Rebel and the chicks.
Water the plants.
Wash and dress.
Go and find Viren and start the beginning of the end of her time here.

Contented, she sat and enjoyed the night sounds. The same night sounds that terrified her on her first night at the house. Then laid herself on the lumpy mattress, pulled the thin and tatty sarong over her and slept.

.   .   .   .   .

As she guessed, the sarong, stretched out on the bathroom wall, dried quickly and she wrapped it around her. Sadly she examined the several small tears in the fabric caused by her sojourn into the hostile jungle yesterday.

*I will have to try to mend these before I travel. I'll look in the sewing machine draw when I come back this afternoon and see what Joseph's mother would recommend.*

Luckily she had completed number four on her list when the crows announced an arrival.

Faye came out of the porch to greet Jolinda and Motes, Nahla and Viren. Jolinda carried Motes on her hip as usual. Nahla carried a bag with interesting angles poking through the fabric. Viren brought up the rear also loaded with a bulky looking bag.

'Hello Faye,' Viren called to her.

'Hi! Come in, come in,' Faye gestured towards the porch. They settled in the shade and Faye lit the fire to make chai. She presumed this was the custom. The visitors didn't appear startled so she guessed she was right. While the kettle boiled Viren explained their visit,

'Jolinda wants me to interpret for her. She would like to tell you how grateful she and her husband are for rescuing Motes yesterday.'

Jolinda smiled and nodded at Faye whilst Viren spoke.

'I don't need thanks, Viren, tell her. It is thanks enough that I was able to pick him up and give him back to his mother. I'm satisfied with that.'

'Ah, but I'm afraid you have to accept their thanks. It is the custom.'

He reached over for the bag he brought. Nahla passed hers to him at the same time. Out of the bags he pulled two boxes and some items wrapped in greaseproof paper.

'Here, by way of gratitude, they would like you to receive this food.'

In the boxes and the greaseproof paper were samosas, croquettes, cheese rissois, which had an appearance of mini cornish pasties, and slices of sweet mangos. Faye opened each box and package and laughed happily. It all smelled delicious and was very welcome after her own attempts of Goan cooking.

'Wow, this is lovely! Tell them I am extremely grateful. It smells wonderful. It's not necessary, as I said, but I will enjoy every morsel. I'm not the best cook,' she laughed deprecatingly and watched Jolinda's face as Viren translated.

Jolinda pointed to the other bag and said something to Viren.

'She says this is the real gift.' He lifted the other bag and drew out a bolt of fabric and held it towards Faye. It was a deep red sari with a pale green and cream embroidered pattern repeating along the edges. The fabric was fine and light. It was beautiful. Faye was speechless. She ran her fingers along the fabric and felt the slightly raised embroidery.

'Oh, I can't accept this, it's beautiful, it's too much, tell her, please.'

Viren spoke briefly to Jolinda. Jolinda answered and Nahla also had a say.

'They both agree you have to accept it. They say they will help you to wear it correctly and there is something else . . .'

Nahla passed a glass jar to Faye. The atmosphere in the porch stiffened. The three people from the village glanced at each other.

'What's this?' Inquisitively she unscrewed the jar and sniffed the contents.

'It's oil for your hair, coconut oil. The ladies say it will tame your hair and make it easier to plait and control.' Viren looked away embarrassed. 'They say they will also show you how to apply it,' he coughed.

'Well, I don't know! I have never been able to control my hair.' Faye laughed out loud and reached out her hands to Jolinda and Nahla. They took a hand each and held on. The atmosphere softened and it was smiles all round.

'They didn't want to offend, just to offer help.'

Laughing, Faye said, 'No offence taken at all. I am very pleased to try anything to tame this lot,' she mussed up her hair and waggled her head.

The kettle boiled and Faye made chai. It could have been an English afternoon tea except they were sitting on the floor on cushions, crossed legged in 40 degrees of heat.

'Tell me Viren, how did Motes get lost in the first place?'

'Jolinda put him down for a nap, she thinks he woke, climbed out of his cot and crawled away whilst she was doing her work. Her husband had taken the boys to search for Sunahara Kaan and she thinks one of them left the gate open. Motes can move very quickly now he is crawling.'

Viren ruffled the baby's soft dark hair affectionately and explained to Jolinda and Nahla what was being said.

Jolinda made exasperation signs and acted out the joy of getting her baby back. Nahla rolled her eyes and laughed.

All's well that ends well. Jolinda will check the gate in future, Faye was sure.

'Whilst you are here Viren, can I ask a great favour, please?'

'Of course. You saved my nephew from an angry wild elephant, you can ask for anything at all!' he laughed.

'This is difficult, I hate to admit it but I have been a fool. Joseph has disappeared, I think. He has my bank card and I suspect he has taken most of my money. My phone, which he gave to his 'girlfriend' is smashed and unusable,' she made quotation marks with her fingers around 'girlfriend' and said the word through gritted teeth as if to show disbelief. Viren nodded knowingly. She paused and drew in a large breath, then continued,

'A man came with his daughter. She's thirteen or fourteen and pregnant! Joseph is the guilty party. The father was furious. If Joseph had been here he would have killed him, I think! I told him to contact the police!'

'We've already heard about it. It's all over Karnaka and Shamoga. Joseph will be miles away by now if I know him!' Viren said.

'Oh my Lord! Now I'm really embarrassed! Everyone knows! What an idiot I've been! Most embarrassing of all though, he has taken all my clothes. You can tell Jolinda I am so happy to receive this sari. I have only this I am wearing to my name!' she indicated to the sarong she had on. The one she bought at the Grand Bazaar.

He encouraged, 'Go on.'

'I need to go home, Viren. But in order to do that I need to visit a bank where I can cancel my bank card. My phone needs repairing so I can contact my sister for funds, and then buy a rail ticket back up to Calangute where I can book a flight home,' she stopped and looked at him.

'Oh, is that all? Of course I'll help you. Will tomorrow be alright, I have to get back to the sanctuary now.'

'Tomorrow will be fine, thank you so much.'

'No thanks necessary. Call it payment for returning our Motes.'

'How is Sunahara Kaan, by the way?'

'She is in the pen. She's calm and resting, eating well and allowing Rav to attend to her. We don't know yet what has upset her, but in the next few days, I hope we will solve the puzzle.'

'I'm so glad she's safe. I wouldn't want her to be destroyed or hurt in any way. One more thing, please ask Jolinda if she will take my chickens. I have nine. They are laying!' She added the final sentence to prove the value of the chickens in case it was necessary.

Viren relayed Faye's request. Jolinda nodded to Faye and spoke to Viren.

'Yes she will be pleased to have them. She asks if it's possible for her to send someone up for them in the morning?'

'Thank you,' Faye smiled towards Jolinda as she spoke, 'that would be perfect. Tell her she can take the coop too if she needs it.' Faye paused, reluctant to broach the next subject because she knew she didn't want to hear the answer.

'I have a piglet too, I don't quite know what to do about him. I don't want him to be slaughtered, he's such a sweet little thing.'

'That's why we rear pigs, to eat them. Some-one in the village will be glad to take him. I'll ask around.'

'Thank you, let me think about it.'

Jolinda and Nahla were prompting Viren to leave.

'Come to the sanctuary at midday tomorrow, Faye and I'll take you to Shamoga and we'll sort your bank out. There is a phone shop in town so we can do both in one day. Now I must go but these impatient girls want to show you how to wear the sari and what to do with your hair.' He laughed at Jolinda and Nahla and waved as he left the porch and took off with long strides down the path.

Jolinda and Nahla stood and indicated to Faye to remove her sarong. Slightly embarrassed, Faye did as she was bid. Whilst Jolinda pointed and gestured, Nahla wound the sari around her. Faye was pushed and pulled and turned and twisted until finally the ladies were happy with their ministrations. The sari, perfectly applied, looked glorious. Faye looked down the length of her body, she craned her neck to look around her back, first one side and then the other. Putting her hands together as in prayer, a wide grin on her face, she bowed. Jolinda hugged her and Nahla clapped her hands. Language-free they all laughed.

Next Nahla removed the sari slowly, refolding it as it unwound from Faye's middle. Faye hastily rewrapped herself in the Grand Bazaar sarong.

Nahla made brushing hair motions and Faye ran inside and brought out her hair brush. Nahla brushed Faye's hair for a few minutes and then scooped a good amount of oil out of the jar. She rubbed it between her hands then slowly massaged it through Fayes length from her scalp down to the ends. When she was happy it had covered every strand she parted the hair at the crown into three and commenced plaiting. Very soon Faye's hair was in one long snake down her back. The house didn't possess a mirror so Faye had to trust the ladies to improve her hair style. She felt around her face and neck with her hands. At that moment there didn't feel to be a single errant curl anywhere. Jolinda and Nahla nodded their approval. Faye hoped she portrayed how pleased she was. Her hair had always been a nightmare. Faye kissed Motes and again there was more bowing and hugging before the ladies took their leave.

## 38

### The way home

Faye rose from the old mattress as the sun was lightening the sky, knowing that she was, at last, going to be making her way home to Sally, to her comfortable and familiar home, to Dad, and to her work. Or maybe not to her work?

In between the dramas she seemed to attract during her stay in Joseph's house, thoughts of her career as a social worker had popped in and out of her mind.

As sure as she knew coming here was a mistake, and going home was what she wanted, going back to her job made her feel uneasy. Her heart wasn't in it any longer. It hadn't exactly kept her awake at night but niggled in and out when other pressing matters subsided.

The one thing that had disturbed her sleep was Rebel. She couldn't see an acceptable outcome for him and as she didn't have a solution she sighed and attempted to put the thought to one side. She tried to make a mental list of tasks she had to do at the house before heading to Shamoga with Viren. She hoped not to come back here today.

First, she fed Rebel and took time to reassure him that all would be well.

'I'm really reassuring myself, Rebel. I can't bear the thought of you being fattened up for Sunday lunch. It breaks my heart.' As Faye scratched his back in the usual spot, Rebel noisily guzzled his breakfast and allowed Faye to stay close.

'I think we need a little miracle to solve this one, eh? Rebel? Do you have any miracles hiding behind those knowing eyes?' Rebel didn't produce a miracle or anything else so Faye sadly wandered off to feed the chickens.

She left the bag of corn by the coop, it would go with the chickens as they departed. *This is so hard. I love my baby piglet and my chicks.* Faye's throat thickened and tears filled her eyes as she stood, hands hanging by her side, shoulders stooped, as she watched for the last time the chickens feed and Rebel circling to find his comfy spot.

Allowing the emotions to go with her as she continued with her list, she bent over the well and halfheartedly dragged up the heavy bucket to fill the butt. Suddenly she stood up straight!

*Why am I doing this? It's Joseph, he really has me trained! Ha! Well that's the last time I'm straining and sweating over the level of water in his butt!*

Faye took only sufficient water for the crops and for her personal needs and let the bucket drop back down the hole.

Looking at her suitcase, she realised she didn't have enough possessions to warrant taking it home. She had her new sari and coconut oil from Jolinda, two beach towels, her straw hat, the wooden elephant she bought at the Grand Bazaar, her purse, phone and passport and an odd bit of underwear. The remnants of her toiletries could be thrown away. If she gave the beach towels to Jolinda, everything else could go in her canvas bag. It would make travelling easier. Decision made, she was soon packed and ready to go. Her suitcase was left where it stood from the day she arrived, but as an afterthought, unable to allow Joseph an inch, she took the sharp knife and slashed the suitcase's lid, making it useless.

As she surveyed the house for any more belongings, the crows commenced their racket announcing movement. Faye guessed it to be Jolinda and her friends arriving to pick up the chickens. She went outside to greet them but there was nobody there.

'Hello?' she called. Puzzled as there was no replying call, Faye looked around. The crows were swarming, protecting their territory. Faye recognised this behaviour so naturally her next thought was of Rebel.

And sure enough, Rebel was standing stiff legged, peering into the undergrowth. Faye ran over, skidding to a halt beside him, she fell to her knees and placed a protective arm around him, not knowing what the jungle hid this time. She squinted into the darkness searching for movement. Rebel stamped his front feet a couple of times and grunted.

From within the gloom, the distinctive shapes of the wild pigs became visible. As before, when they visited, they stood and looked at Rebel and Faye as if waiting. Faye glanced at Rebel. He stamped his feet again and made the grunting noise. The noise was echoed by the largest wild pig. Faye realised with awe that they were speaking to each other in their own language. Rebel looked at Faye and back to the wild pigs. Faye knew! She knew then she had to let him go. The rope around his neck was thick and hadn't moved since Joseph put it on him. Faye didn't know if she would be able to untie it.

'Wait there, baby, I'll be right back.' she said quietly to Rebel and louder, directed toward the wild pigs, 'Wait for him, he is coming with you.'

She ran across to the house, grabbed the sharp knife and ran back. She had to do this before the wild pigs disappeared again, leaving Rebel behind.

Hacking at the rope, just above the knot, which was behind his right ear, Rebel squirmed and let his discomfort or impatience be known. As he let out a scream the wild pigs took a few steps back.

'No, don't go, please don't go! How can I keep them here? I know . . .' Faye jumped up again and ran back to the house. She returned within seconds carrying all the remaining naan bread and croquettes. Tearing the naan into small portions and the croquettes in half, she threw them at the wild pigs hoping to keep them there until she could free Rebel.

It worked, the wild pigs concentrated on finding the food on the jungle floor while Faye sawed at the rope. After desperately sawing, strand by strand, the rope finally gave up its purchase and fell from Rebel's neck.

Rebel, used to being tethered, didn't understand he was free. He continued to look from Faye to the wild pigs.

'OK, there you are, off you go,' she gave him a gentle push on his little rounded bottom to encourage him to go towards the herd. Rebel looked at Faye as if for confirmation,

'Go on Rebel, go to them.' He took a few steps. The large wild pig grunted in support. Rebel turned his head and looked again at Faye.

'Go on my love, you are free, you may go,' and with that he ran. The herd waited until he was in their midst, turned as one and in a second disappeared into the shadows. Faye sat back on her heels, unable to take her eyes from the place where Rebel had vanished. She was astonished at what had just occurred. Again her throat was closing but this time she didn't fight it, she allowed her love for the little piglet to flow out in tears. The miracle she had wished for had happened.

It was some time before she could move, she felt a mixture of grief and relief. Her baby had gone but he was safe. She took his water bowl, washed it out and put it in the cupboard in the house. The rope from around his neck, she put in her canvas bag.

.   .   .   .   .

As the crows started up again, Faye brushed the red soil from her sarong and ran her hands down it in an effort to smooth out the creases, lifted her chin and went to meet Jolinda and Nahla and help take the chickens to their new home.

They walked down the path, each carrying a sack containing three chickens, Faye did not look back, neither did the funnel spiders worry her. It was over, she was going home.

At the end of the village street, Faye passed her bag of chickens to Jolinda. In return Jolinda gave Faye a piece of paper on which were several words in Hindi.

## शांति से जाओ
### आपके यहाँ हमेशा एक घर होता है

'Shaanti se jao. Aapaka yahaan hamesha ghar hai.' Jolinda read.

Faye raised her eyebrows and shoulders as if to say 'what does it mean?'

Jolinda simply said 'Viren.' That was all. They kissed each other and hugged and Faye left them, tucking the piece of paper into her bag.

Viren was waiting for her at the sanctuary as promised. Faye explained she had received the piece of paper from Jolinda and asked Viren what it said.

'Go in peace. You always have a home here, ' he read.

'Oh! How lovely,' Faye smiled, remembering how intimidated she was by Jolinda and Nahla the first time she went to fill the water bottles at the pump. She tucked the paper safely away again.

Soon they were in his car driving to Shamoga. Faye found herself overawed when they arrived in the town. After her extended time of isolation at the house where the only interaction with people was at the village, the town appeared frantic and bustling. However, Viren was an excellent guide and saviour. Very soon he had the bank manager sorting out Faye's account. It was apparent Viren was well known and respected in town by the manager's attitude towards him.

'You have very little money in your account,' he told Faye, translating what the manager said. 'You were right, Joseph has taken most of it. However, don't worry. What you did for my nephew is worth more than a fare to Calangute. Let's go and get your phone repaired then I'll buy you a train ticket. I would take you myself, all the way, but I'm afraid my responsibilities won't allow it.'

'Oh, please! Viren! You are doing too much for me already. As soon as my phone is repaired I'll phone my sister and I'll be fine from then on. She'll sort it all out. She always does!'

Whilst they waited for her phone to be mended, Viren took Faye into a bakery and bought her pasties and

232

cake to eat on her journey. Faye protested but to no avail. Viren insisted she should be comfortable.

With a new shiny, clear screen, Faye delightedly brought up Sally's contact details and pressed the button. It rang until an unknown voice said 'The number you are calling is unavailable, please try later or leave a message.'

'Ah! No!' Faye, frustrated, after all this time waiting to contact Sally, was pipped at the final post. She hastily texted. 'Sally I'm on my way home. Please put £500 in my current account. Tell you all when I get home. Pls text me when you get this msg'.

Confident Sally would text her back within a short time, Faye and Viren headed to the railway station.

## 39

### Two long journeys

Sally and Gabby settled down on the plane for the long flight.

'Do you know when George and Sunny are arriving at the hotel?' Gabby asked.

'No, not yet. George knows we are setting off today. He said he'd be there within a day or two.' The plane's engines revved up a notch ready for take-off.

'I'd better turn my phone off,' Sally said and reached into her bag for her mobile. She held her finger on the button until the screen went black.

At the same time, as Sallys phone switched off, almost 5000 miles away, Faye stood in the phone repair shop beside Viren and pressed the button to phone Sally. The sisters had anxiously waited to speak to each other all this time but at the critical moment missed each other by seconds!

The girls settled back to enjoy the flight to Goa, the start of their mission to find Faye. Sally finally felt better now that she was doing something practical to locate her sister.

. . . . .

Meanwhile Faye said a grateful thank you and goodbye to Viren and boarded the train to Udupi. He had purchased a ticket that would take her all the way to Calangute. She could have felt sad to leave Viren but the aspect of getting home overshadowed any other feelings. Instead she thanked him profusely and swore she would be

234

back to repay his kindness. Viren graciously accepted her vows, doubting she would return but did not disagree and helped her board the carriage.

The train wasn't as congested as when Joseph brought her down so she soon found a seat. Plus it was daylight so she could watch the world go by. Dressed in the Grand Bazaar sarong and with her newly tidy plaited hair. no-one appeared to stare at her; she felt at ease with herself. She settled into the window seat to enjoy the journey.

At Udupi Faye managed to find an English speaking porter to show her to the platform where the train to Calangute would depart. She acknowledged to herself there wasn't time to explore the town and vowed to return to savour the place at leisure. It seemed so much easier, calmer and pleasurable. She thought the country, as it whipped past the window, was stunningly beautiful.

The people, with the exception of Joseph, Faye found to be genuine and charming. What a shame she became tangled up with him. She couldn't believe how foolish she was and how easily she was taken in by him. Well, she had learnt her lesson. Never again!

It was a long journey, Faye remembered how it had seemed endless on the way to the house. As night fell she managed to sleep this time, even sitting upright on the hard, moulded plastic seat. In the morning when the man came along with his tureen of chai, Faye had her money out and easily ordered, albeit in sign language, a cup of the sweet tea which she enjoyed with a pastry from Viren. After a while, Faye went to the toilet compartment and freshened up. She changed from her once lovely, now tatty sarong, into the red sari, the beautiful gift from Jolinda. Her hair, dark and shiny from the coconut oil, as the girls had promised, had kept its place and remained obediently plaited.

. . . . .

Meanwhile, Sally and Gabby endured the mayhem at the airport with its queues and masses of people. They arrived at The Royal Hotel, tired and dusty and ready for a rest. Both girls were reminded again of how tiring travelling is. This time they shared a room. It was agreed they would have a nap then come down for an evening meal in the hotel. Neither had the energy to dress up and go out into Calangute itself.

Later, at 6.30 in the evening, they selected a table by the side of the pool, as they did on their first night during the previous visit. Sitting facing each other, Gabby looked over the pool area and Sally viewed the long drive down to the tall pillars at the entrance of the hotel grounds.

'As soon as the receptionist arrives in the morning, I'm going to talk to her and obtain Joseph's address and any other detail about him that they have. Will you come in with me, Gab, please?'

'Of course I will. Come on Sally, cheer up a bit. You are doing everything you can. Soon we will be on our way to find her and you will be reunited.'

'Yes, I'm sorry Gab, you're right. Let's enjoy our time here at the hotel. We don't know what's in front of us. At least we'll have the two fellows with us to fend off any difficulties,' Sally laughed. 'Just think, if you hadn't sat next to George on the plane, we may not have him and Sunny as our protectors now.'

'I know, and if we hadn't met in the queue for the loo, I wouldn't have been here today with you,' she chuckled.

'I'm sorry, I'm dragging you all over the world searching for my errant sister.'

'No, I don't mean it that way. I'm so glad we met. I don't know what I'd have done without you guys. I couldn't have survived without you. I'm really happy to be here. Thinking about you and Faye saves me from thinking about myself and my troubles, so I'm grateful to Faye, in a strange way, for getting me out of myself,' Gabby chortled and touched Sally's hand on the table, 'Oh that sounds awful and so selfish.'

'No it doesn't. I'm glad we can be of assistance to you,' she smirked to show she was kidding. 'But you are right. Let's enjoy what we have for now,' Sally grinned and raised her hand. A waiter approached.

'Now what shall we have to drink?' They scanned the drinks menu.

. . . . .

It was that time, between daylight and darkness, where things are not always clear but remain visible. The fairy lights around the trees had just come on and the spotlights around the grounds were popping on, one after the other.

Sally was taking a sip of her gin and tonic. Over the rim of her glass she was watching, without a great amount of interest, a young woman walking up the hotel drive. In the half light she appeared slim with fairly dark skin, an Indian woman, Sally assumed. The young lady wore a striking red sari, she had a large brimmed straw hat on her head and strolled confidently up towards the registration building.

As she came level with the dining tables she paused and looked around. Her gaze passed over Sally and Gabby's table and she seemed to do a double take and stare intently at Sally.

Gabby spoke, she said something about a vegetarian curry but Sally didn't take it in. Sally watched as the woman in the red sari abruptly changed course and headed directly for their table at speed.

'Sally!' the woman in the red sari called, 'Sally, you are here! I can't believe you are here. Why are you here?' She drew nearer to their table and under the brighter light of the dining area, Sally at last realised who it was.

'Oh my God! Faye! Oh, Faye! I didn't recognise you!' Sally was out of her chair and her arms went around Faye in a big squeeze.

'Oh my Lord, you are so thin. I wouldn't have known you! How come you're here? We were going south to look for you. Gabby is here,' she half turned and noted Gabby's astounded face. 'She's here, Gab, we've found her already!'

Sally started to cry, tears of joy and relief. Faye cried tears of happiness, she was back where she belonged with her precious big sister. Gabby, not to be outdone, jumped up and ran around the table to be included in the huddle and cried too.

'Didn't you get my text?' Faye blubbered.

'My phone! I've forgotten to turn it on after I switched it off on the plane. What did it say?'

'Never mind, it'll wait. I can't tell you how glad I am to see you, and you Gabby, how are you?' She wailed loudly and tears poured down her cheeks. She took a few moments to get her breathing in order, 'I've a lot to tell you but first of all I must say, I'm so sorry for leaving with Joseph like I did. I felt so bad afterwards and still do. I can't apologise enough Sally,' she lifted Sallys hand to her lips and kissed it, 'I wouldn't hurt you for the world. I don't know what came over me. Will you forgive me?'

'Of course I will. I know what came over you, it was that rat, Joseph!' she spat out his name, 'Where is he anyway?'

'Long gone and good riddance! You won't believe half of what I've been through. You were going to find me? What? To Joseph's house? Oh, Sally, oh! It's so good to see you. I couldn't phone you, I tried, I did, but I couldn't get a signal, then I had no charge! Then Joseph took the phone! It was a nightmare. But you're here! I can't believe it! I didn't think for one minute that when I got here you would be sitting in the dining area with a drink in your hand!'

She started to laugh. It was a belly laugh which soon turned to hysteria. Screeching with laughter, tears streaming down her face, Sally and Gabby joined in and within seconds the dining area was in uproar. The boys behind the bar, alarmed at first, recognised the girls from only a few weeks ago. They looked at each other, smiling and laughing and came across to their table to welcome the girls back, especially Faye. They'd watched with concern as Faye became entangled with Joseph. The other guests smiled and laughed in sympathy even though they didn't know what on earth was going on.

After some form of order had resumed, Gabby described their plans to drive south with George and Sunny to find her. Faye was astonished, especially at the kindness of George and Sunny.

'They're coming as well?' Faye exclaimed.

'Yeah, they're on their way. They'll be pleased to see you, Faye, and what's more they'll be pleased to see each other! So although the mission to find Faye is no longer going to happen, I don't think they will be too worried about it being a wasted trip,' she smiled kindly.

'Our return flights are booked for two weeks today. I'll try to get you booked onto the same flight as us, Faye. Did you book a room here?' Sally asked

'No, I just wanted to get here. I felt if I was here, I was half way home, somewhere familiar, I suppose. It must be some kind of psychic phenomena that we both arrived here today. Sisterly love I suppose.'

'Yeah. I'll pop in the reception and see if there's someone there who can let us have another room. Meanwhile we have two weeks in Goa. Now we don't have to search for you, what will we do?' Sally looked at the two girls questioningly.

'Simple, we'll top up our tans, eat and drink well and after such an extraordinary time, we'll relax and get over it!' Gabby declared.

'And one more thing. You,' Sally pointed at Faye, 'are not leaving my sight!'

'You don't need to worry about that!' Faye grinned, 'I've learnt my lesson.'

Over the course of the evening, the girls sat together and Faye described her experiences. Sally and Gabby were spellbound by her account. She didn't go into detail about the love making side of it but she described the state of the house. She told them about the chickens, the rows of vegetables, the well and, of course, her darling Rebel. She spoke at length about him. By the end of the evening the girls felt as much love for Rebel as did Faye.

Faye told them about how Joseph's behaviour changed. She said about her bank card which led seamlessly to the phone and the Doe Eyed girl. When she talked of the father dragging the Doe Eyed girl up to the house and his revelation, both Sally and Gabby grasped Faye's hands in horrified support.

As she described the elephant sanctuary and Viren and then finding Motes in the jungle, Sally and Gabby, listened open mouthed. She expressed several times how the sanctuary impressed her, the dedication, the kindness and  the atmosphere.

Gazing across the pool Faye said thoughtfully, more to herself than the others,

'I wish I could recreate it.'

'Wow! What a time you have had. How did you get through it?' Sally asked, putting her arm around Faye's shoulders and drawing her in tight.

'Well, I had no choice. At one point I couldn't see a way out. And of course I had Rebel to consider.'

Sally slipped into the reception and managed to book another room. Gabby agreed to move to enable the sisters to stay in the twin room together.

Two days later George arrived. He was amazed to find Faye already there. He didn't consider it a wild goose chase, but rather looked at it as a bonus. Sunny arrived in the evening and they spent unexpected precious time together.

One day, during the second week, as the girls lay on their sunbeds around the pool, Faye reached across and took Sally's hand saying,

'Sally, I don't want to go back to social work. I feel I have learnt such a lot during my short stay at Joseph's house. I can't explain, Sal, but the feeling I had whilst I was caring for Rebel, the chickens and growing the vegetables, well, I just felt so calm, so happy. I didn't realise how stressful my job was until I lived this different life.'

Sally turned on her side to look at Faye and pushed her sunglasses onto the top of her head.

'What do you want to do then? You'll still have to earn a living.'

'I've given this a lot of thought over the last few days. Sally, I want a plot of land, probably with living accommodation of some description, where I can develop my idea. I want an ice cream parlour.'

'An ice cream parlour?' Sally cried incredulously. 'Never in a hundred years did I expect you to say that!'

Understanding Sally's surprise, Faye laughed, nodded and continued,

'Not just an ice cream parlour. I want a leisure destination where families can come and enjoy themselves. I want it to include a play area but not just a set of swings and a slide, I want an adventure playground like you've never seen before. It will have zip wires, nets, climbing frames up to the treetops, stepping stones, tunnels, hidey holes. Robust apparatus that can stand children at unrestrained play. It will all be made of natural wood and be in a little forest and be full of safety aspects, but unseen safety aspects, so they can play without fear. For example, rubber floors, nets under the climbing apparatus and cameras so the children are safe in all parts of the play area.

I want chickens, proper free range chickens, probably rescued battery hens, who can enjoy their lives but will supply eggs I can sell in the ice cream parlour.'

'What about pigs?' Sally enquired.

'No, no pigs. I don't want any animals on the site that may, at some point, have to go into the food chain. I know you could argue about the chickens and the eggs, but eggs are a byproduct of our interfering with their breeding, so I would get the big brown hens and give them a good life. Space to roam by day and safe, roomy coops by night. Maybe pop in a few of those different breeds of hens for interest, you know, the ones with the feathery feet. The sale of the eggs would pay for their keep.

Don't get me wrong, I would love to have some piglets but the outcome for them as they grow is not what I would wish for them. However, from what I saw at the elephant sanctuary, I have an idea. The kindness shown to the elephants was amazing. They came in from the jungle on their own accord to accept the help and medications from the mahouts. It was a special place and funded by foreign visitors going to the sanctuary a couple of times a week. This made me think about opening my own sanctuary!'

'What? You are going to have elephants?' Sal screeched. Laughing, Faye told her,

'No, not elephants, you nut! Donkeys! More in keeping with the British countryside, don't you think? There are lots of donkeys requiring homes. I remember reading an article about it a while ago, before we came on holiday. Some have lived such sad lives and simply need a touch of kindness to enable them to live out their lives in comfort. Some need help from a vet. I want to have a herd of no less than six, maybe more, as they need to live with their own kind. They are such characters, they can become features of the ice cream parlour and they will draw people in. I don't mean for children to ride on, no, the donkeys will be retired. But the children can learn about them, learn about kindness, feeding, cleaning, etc.

I also want enough land for polytunnels and have a designated area to grow vegetables and fruit. I'm thinking about a plot of land, four or five acres would possibly be large enough, maybe larger.

There will be a cafe with seating for forty customers or more and outside a terrace with more tables. I also thought about putting some picnic tables amongst the trees in the play area.

I want to sell ice cream, obviously, but also snacks; salad, sandwiches, pasties, cake, scones, tea, juice, that sort of stuff. But I want to be vegetarian, so veggie burgers, veggie hot dogs, veggie meals, you know, that kind of thing.' Faye raised her eyebrows at Sally and waited for her response.

'You will need a chef!' Sal said laughing. 'You have given it some thought, I'll give you that, Faye. I will support you if it's what you want.'

'Thanks, Sal, it is what I want. I can picture every square inch of it. I can't wait to get home now and get started!'

## 40

*Twelve months later*

## Joseph

The very same day that the Doe Eyed girl announced her pregnancy, Joseph sat in a bar in Shamoga and planned his future.

With a drink in his hand he planned his next move. He knew he wouldn't be popular in Shamoga or the village. It didn't worry him. He visited the bank with Faye's debit card one more time and headed to the railway station where he purchased a ticket to Kerala, South Goa.

Faye didn't enter Joseph's mind again after he left the bank. She was a thing of the past. He had taken all he could from her. Neither did he consider the Doe Eyed girl or their unborn baby. He acknowledged his time at his mother's house was over for the foreseeable future.

Looking ahead, he knew there was little time to get himself established in Kerala before the end of the season and the start of the monsoon. He smiled to himself. He trusted his well practised charm to achieve what he wanted.

One year on he is settled into a large five star hotel, 200 metres from the beach. Unknown to the management and staff, his reputation did not come ahead of him. Dozens of staff are employed to cater for the hundreds of happy, rich holidaymakers. It's better for Joseph at this hotel. He's one of many so his cunning, sly ways are less obvious. He's enjoyed a lucrative year focusing on the older ladies. His own bank balance is looking healthy and the gifts he receives from the ladies please him. Luckily, he hasn't had any complaints this year, so far.

The hotel allows the staff to remain at the hotel during the closed season. They undertake painting and repairs necessary for the year ahead. Joseph is content to remain there, not interested in going back to his mothers house. He feels no guilt with regard to Faye. She is from his past, he has moved on without a thought.

## Gabby

Although she appears happy, her smile often doesn't reach her eyes. Gabby suffers from sleepless nights. During the long lonely darkness, she ruminates over her marriage. She plays different scenes over and over in her head - what she could have done - what she should have done- what she could have said - what she should have said.

Sometimes, at night, she considers asking her husband to come back to her. He and the young girl split up soon after they were discovered. She goes over and over various avenues of getting back together. Sometimes she explores excuses to contact him, to ask him to come over to the house, to meet for a drink, to talk about the children. Then as dawn breaks she backs off and realises she couldn't trust him again. As low and lonely she becomes during the long night hours, her pride remains in place and halts any moves she may think of making. The hurt she felt at the time remains the same. Her heart is broken and irreparable.

Gabby is still in the family home with Pip and Daisy. At the divorce she was awarded half of everything including the business. At first, full of anger and feelings of revenge she wanted to destroy and humiliate Graham. Now, twelve months later, she finds revenge is not the answer and tries hard to fill the void her husband has left. She knows it will take time.

Pip left his father's firm immediately the affair was known to him. He is a salesman with a major competitor of his father's company and is enjoying himself. Every sale he makes is one in the eye for his father. He takes his job very seriously. It's his way of dealing with it.

Daisy came out of university with honours in business. Both Gabby and Graham attended the ceremony. They were in the same room, in the same space, but could have been days apart for all the connection they showed. Pip and Daisy both refused to speak to Graham. Gabby, for a second, felt sorry for him. It wasn't the family event Gabby had always imagined when Daisy first set off to university.

Her working days are at the office as usual. Her job remains the same, comfortable and secure. Alternate weekends she spends with Faye, helping out. She puts on a happy front and lends a hand in whichever department Faye needs her. Sally joins them on Sundays, most weeks and the girls continue to enjoy each other's company as they did on holiday in Goa.

Gabby appreciates the friendship of these two girls and acknowledges she possibly wouldn't have survived without them.

## George and Sunny

After the unexpected holiday the men shared when they agreed to help Sally find Faye, they have not met since.

Sunny received some bad news. His wife has been diagnosed with cancer. It's very sad, for although Sunny loves George, he loves his wife and family and will always put them first. George knows and understands. He may not like it, but he loves Sunny sufficiently to support his decisions and be a shoulder to cry on, albeit, with many thousands of miles between them. When possible Sunny calls George but it's not very often. George is unable to phone Sunny as he spends much of the time at home with his wife.

Sally's call for help, and their unexpected two week stay at The Royal Hotel therefore, in hindsight, has become very precious to the men. They may not see each other again for a long time. Both of them have fond memories of being at the hotel, meeting the girls, and simply spending unfiltered time together, each with the love of his life. Reminiscing can bring a tear to George's eye or a smile to his face. He patiently waits for Sunny to be available again. The secret of life is that one never knows the secret which waits around the corner.

George is pleased to be involved with Faye's plans and pops up to the ice cream parlour whenever he can. He too is happy to lend a hand in any department where he is able.

He continues to travel to purchase fabulous items for his shop. In the last twelve months he has forayed to Vietnam and Cambodia, searching for something different and has been reasonably successful. He believes, if he doesn't travel to Goa, he won't miss Sunny quite as much.


## Sally

As the girls came home and all returned to near normal, Sally spent time initially at the salon, picking up the pace, repaying her marvellous staff, and getting back on top of things. A well run business in the first place, it didn't take her long to be happy with its condition. Her staff could see in her attitude and demeanour that she was happy with how things had turned out.

Their father, in his dementia, survived their travels unaffected and Sally was pleased to be able to visit him with a clear conscience, not having to hold anything back from him.

Helping Faye to obtain her dream gave Sally a good deal of pleasure as she could see how much Faye believed in what she was aiming for.

Sally will always be her big sister. However, now she feels that Faye has finally found the correct role in life. She doesn't need to mow the lawn for her, she doesn't need to ensure she is shopping and consequently eating well. When Sally sees Faye now she sees a woman in her element, fearless, organised and sometimes surprisingly well dressed!

A woman in the prime of her life. Sally's chest is full of pride, she is fit to burst.


## Faye

Twelve months on and Faye's dream is reality.

On their return from Goa they put the family house up for sale and started looking around for the perfect piece of land. The house sold quickly. With her idea incorporating different aspects, the land didn't need to be completely flat. Very soon an ideal plot of nine acres came up for sale and Faye's excited bid was accepted. She met with the architect and he used the various levels and dimensions of the site to enhance the different themes she had described. Faye proudly found herself in charge of her own destiny.

The family home was owned by both sisters, Faye owes half of the proceeds to Sally. Presently, Sally doesn't need the funds so Faye used the whole amount to set up the business. However, Faye insisted they sign an agreement for her to repay Sally back over the next ten years.

Sally gave Faye a quick course in accountancy so Faye could keep on top of her finances during the development and when the entrance fees and cafe sales started to come in.

George offered to design the cafe's decor. He listened to how Faye imagined it and came back several days later with his version of Faye's idea. The walls of the cafe look like the edge of a forest. Decorated with foliage, large leaves, grasses, tree bark and hanging creepers, interspersed with brightly coloured flowers. Peeping through are several comical caricatures of donkeys. And of course, donkeys feature quite regularly around the cafe as coat stands, tray rests etc. It's a work of art. Faye loves it and can't thank George enough for his vision.

Faye designed the advertisements herself and in addition batches of leaflets were distributed far and wide. Gabby volunteered for this job. Daisy helped and worked tirelessly promoting the new venture for her friend.

With regard to living accommodation, in order not to be homeless, initially Faye bought an old caravan and put it on the land. Finally, as the site developed, she purchased a chalet style wooden house with an outside decking area. Erected at the rear of the site and insulated against the chilly British winter weather, it's cosy and homely, with two bedrooms, bathroom and lounge with a small kitchenette. On the wall opposite the front door, in pride of place hangs a framed, embroidered piece of fabric. The wording says,

शांति से जाओ
आपके यहाँ हमेशा एक घर होता है

Go in peace.
You always have a home here.

Faye embroidered it herself during the long evenings over winter. She was surprised and pleased at the brilliant job she made and thanked Joseph's mother for leaving the little draws of the sewing machine full of colourful cotton thread which inspired her.

It seemed to be slow progress leading to the day she was ready to open to the public, but it finally arrived, all items in place, all tested and working and waiting for customers.

Early in the morning of the Grand Opening Day, Faye examined the whole site. The sun was up and a pale golden hue lay lightly over the park. It was a crisp morning with the promise of warmth.

She saw her vegetable plots and polytunnels. The beginnings of life peeping up out of the soil, showing commitment for the future. Buds and blossoms covered the fruit trees. The fruit and vegetables would be on sale as they came in season. Faye had approached some of the local restaurant owners who will also purchase the fresh, quality produce.

The stable doors were open, indicating the staff were busy working with the donkeys, preparing them to look their best on the first day open to the public.

The donkeys - Lily, Elsie, Jack, Chico, Matey, Bob, Bertha, Eeaw, Dick, Lotte, Ruby and Jenny. Faye knew them all by sight and had connected with each one, mostly due to many hours of giving love and care in their first weeks at the sanctuary. She feeds them treats and they know she always comes with pockets full of tasty morsels. Already she feels maternal love for them.

The paddock, in front of the stables, was swept and tidy. It had a large sturdy pergola for shade from the sun or rain.

Faye had adopted twelve donkeys, more than she expected, but they all needed her, so they came, in twos, alone or in a group.

Lily, Elsie, Jack and Bob were rehomed because their owner, an old farmer, had become unable to care for them through his deteriorating health. The foursome had been together for years. They were solid friends, slow ambling oldies, happy to stand in the sun and they enjoyed the staff giving them a good brush over their old bones.

Chico and Matey came a long way in a horse box from Spain. They had been maltreated. Working donkeys, they carried building supplies for their owner. He built water canals, from the mountains to the plains, the donkeys traversed distances impassable by vehicles in intense heat or bitter cold. The International Donkey Rescue heard about Faye and offered her these two. They are recovering from their hard life and can be suspicious of people. They are uncommunicative with the staff but with time, love and care, Faye hopes they will settle and be happy.

Eeaw and Dick are two young fellows purchased as a present for two small boys. However they turned out to be quite naughty and a lot more work than was expected so had to be found a new home. Eeaw, named after his extremely loud bray, is the bossy one. Dick is quieter but mischievous and sneaky. They need an eye keeping on them. It's obvious to all that the older donkeys watch them with mirth or sometimes irritation. The boys love to be a nuisance. Faye adores them, she finds their antics hilarious.

Bertha, Lotte and Ruby were rescued from a rundown property. They had been neglected and were in a poor, dirty and unhealthy state. The RSPCA cleaned them up and brought them to Faye to continue improving their health. They are gentle beasts and grateful for every kindness.

Jenny. Faye first noticed Jenny when she was driving over to Sally's one Sunday morning. She was standing in the corner of a field, all alone, looking sad and lonely. The following week, it was raining, and sure enough there was Jenny standing, wet through, alone again, looking depressed. When Faye saw her the third week, she detoured to the nearby farmhouse and enquired about her to the owner. From there Faye made an offer to take the lonely donkey. Jenny was the first donkey to join Faye's sanctuary and so has a special place in Faye's heart. Jenny has palled up with Ruby although she quite likes running with Eeaw and Dick if it's sunny and windy. Wherever she is, if she sees Faye approaching she shrieks and bolts to the fence to enjoy a rub and a carrot or an apple. Jenny is now a happy donkey.

Behind the stables is another paddock, this one is grassed and it leads to a large expanse of wooded meadow where the donkeys are free to roam, run, chase and just be themselves. The visitors are able to observe the donkeys enjoying their freedom from a distance. They can enjoy their antics without disturbing them. No more than six donkeys will be in the front paddock at any one time to reduce overcrowding, arguing and fighting. Furthermore changing the donkeys over will ensure they don't become over tired by the visitors and give each one equal time in the meadow. Faye is happy with it. A board at the side of the paddock, for the visitors to read, has photographs of each donkey and describes how it came to be at the sanctuary. The local vet, Rosalind, is Faye's new best friend and she has given the sanctuary her blessing.

Before she left Shamoga, Faye said she would return to the elephant sanctuary to visit Viren. She knew, as did he, when she said it, that it would probably not happen. Now, more than ever, is it doubtful she will ever travel that way again. So accepting that her life is going to be different - in a good way - Faye wrote to Viren describing the donkey sanctuary and explaining it is the inspiration she took from Viren and the elephant sanctuary that made the donkey sanctuary happen. She invited Viren to visit her instead. She hasn't had a reply yet but is hopeful.

Faye walked towards the chicken coop. She could hear them before she could see them. They were whooping and clucking. Twenty-five brown hens scratched the ground, doing the same repetitive dance as her Goan hens. Faye laughs at them, they are so funny. These girls were rescued from a battery farm. They were 18 months old. If Faye hadn't taken them they were due to be transported to the butchers. Most of their feathers had recently grown back, their red combs were now bright and upright. They looked well and happy with so much space, fresh air and tasty tidbits to eat beside the mixed corn and pellets. What's more, they were laying brilliantly. The chickens may live another year or another ten years, Faye didn't know but they would live out their lives free and content. Several full egg boxes were piled up on the ice cream parlour counter ready to sell on today's opening day. Faye also had contracts to supply three hotels in the nearby town and they appeared very happy with the eggs.

The adventure playground glistened under the morning dew, waiting eagerly for the first children to enjoy the experience. Sturdy wooden stepping stones, winding tunnels, parallel bars, tall climbing nets reaching up to the trees, a sandpit filled one corner, a wooden castle with a climbing wall, a drawbridge and a slide, toadstools, zip wires, ropewalk bridges. It was a large space and the staff, already at work, waved at her as she examined the area. Faye had tried to fill it with everything she could. She wanted happy children. Next year, if the finances allowed, she hoped to put in a swimming pool.

Outside the ice cream parlour and cafe, tables and chairs were regimentally placed expecting families to fill them. Steam rose from the cafe's silver chimney, suggesting staff were preparing for a busy day ahead. The windows gleamed in the morning sun reflecting the playground and the shiny tables.

Having cast a critical eye over each domain, Faye felt proud and excited that it was ready for opening. She strolled the length of the drive past the car park to the entrance gate. A feeling of fulfilment, completion and happiness suffused her being. Emotionally she placed her hand over her heart. With a gentle smile and a sigh, she looked up and read the sign above the gate. The sanctuary was named after a very important little person.

# 'Rebels Retreat'
## Ice Cream Parlour, Cafe
## Adventure Playground and Donkey Sanctuary

### Rebel

Twelve months after Faye cut the rope from around his neck, Rebel is reaching maturity. He weighs approximately 100 kilos. He looks slightly different from the others in the herd. He has pink spots on his white face as opposed to the black and brown colour of the wild pigs. Nor does he sport tusks and he never will. He may be considered good looking in the pig world but perhaps that's only our opinion.

Rebel has had to relearn some things, for example, humans are a threat and should be avoided at all costs.

He struggled to understand the hierarchy of the herd, having been an only child, so to speak. The head sow has put him in his place on more than one occasion. The large male pig doesn't accept cheek either. Some of the lessons he learned were harsh and painful. There are numerous scars on his body. But he has survived. He knows who eats when, who walks where, who goes first, who cuddles on the inside and who on the outside. Nevertheless he is happier than ever before.

In his herd there are three large females and two small females. Five small piglets showing their immaturity, only now losing the stripes on their backs, these little ones are three months old at present. Then come the babies of the family, seven tiny piglets only six weeks old. They are constantly dashing and playing and getting under foot. Rebel loves them. They look up to him as their big brother. In addition there is a two year old male who is Rebel's arch enemy. He resented Rebel from the start but, in fairness, has taught Rebel more than any other of the herd. The two year old will be leaving the herd shortly to go on his own.

The large male comes and goes at intervals to visit with the large females. He mostly ignores Rebel unless he happens to get in the way.

Roaming for miles through the dense jungle, they skirt the human villages as much as possible. Foraging for food as they go, their diet consists of nuts and berries, roots and tubers, insects and reptiles, carrion and occasionally a young deer. When the quantity of food is poor, they wander towards a village. The scent of orderly rows of crops becomes too tempting to deny and they make organised rushes at the crops, grabbing as much as possible in their mouths before dashing back to the safety of the jungle.

At times like these Rebel's memory gives him a little nudge and Faye enters his mind . . . invariably she comes across to his Banyan tree carrying sweet tasty treats for him . . . in the next second he is dashing off with the herd, Faye forgotten.

Sequel to The Indian Love Apple by
Christine Reeve

# Rebels Retreat Ice Cream Parlour Adventure Playground and Donkey Sanctuary

On the rough ground of a cold windy turnip field in northern
England, a tiny donkey foal is born. Her mother dies within the
hour.
Rebels Retreat Donkey Sanctuary takes in the foal. They name her
Mona.
Faye, the sanctuary owner and her team of stable hands
immediately fall in love with the little foal. Jenny, a lonely hinny,
adopts her as her own and they all enjoy watching the start of
Mona's development.

One night Mona disappears! Faye and her team are distraught.
Jenny is inconsolable.
Who's taken her and why?
Faye looks at the people around her.

Chantelle, a stable hand, is fighting her own battles.
Nikki, head stable hand and Faye's friend, appears distracted.
Michael, a volunteer and always reliable, is not answering his
phone.
Dean, a local bad boy, visited the sanctuary only days before the
disappearance.
Adrian, spurned, could he want to hurt Faye by taking Mona?
And what about Oscar Winterbottom and Mr Hardcastle?

Where is Mona?
PC Mann arrives to investigate.

Printed in Great Britain
by Amazon